Taken By Force

I0692814

Erotic Stories
of Abduction and Captivity

Edited by
Christopher Pierce

STARbooks PRESS

Herndon, VA

Published in the United States STARbooks Press PO Box 711612 Herndon VA 20171 Printed in the United States

Many thanks to graphic artist Emma Aldous for the cover design. Ms. Aldous may be reached at emma@starbookspress.com.

Herndon, VA

ACKNOWLEDGMENTS

Thanks to STARbooks Press for the opportunity
to edit this anthology.

Thanks to Milton Stern and Emma Aldous
for their invaluable contributions.

Special thanks to Master Matt,
who has had me kidnapped several times.

CONTENTS

INTRODUCTION:
Waiting for the Man
in the Black Ski Mask

Kidnapping, in an erotic context, is one of my ultimate fantasies.

There's something incredibly hot about someone wanting me so badly that they take criminal action, risking prosecution and imprisonment, in order to have me. To be ambushed, captured, bound, gagged and carried off to be ravaged by a stranger (or even someone I know) is a scenario that has been part of my erotic makeup since I was very young. When my movie and television heroes were captured and spirited off to the villain's lair, my imagination went into overtime, fantasizing about what really went on behind those closed doors. And, in my fantasies, I wasn't always the abducted hero – sometimes I was the diabolical kidnapper who had them in my power at last, and they were helpless to resist anything I would force upon them.

Anyone who's read my fiction knows that abduction, from the point-of-view of the victim or the abductor or both, plays a large part in my work. Actual kidnapping, though possible with meticulous planning, is largely impractical in our modern world. How do you explain to the police that you want to be tied up in the trunk of a car? So, I have had to make do with a rich tapestry of fantasy abductions.

When I was given the opportunity to edit this book, I wanted to explore other people's kidnapping fantasies as well as my own. From the large pool of submissions I received, I believe I have assembled a fascinating, surprising, perhaps shocking collection of stories – not to mention fucking hot!

I found myself intrigued, aroused and captivated by these tales. I think you will, too.

Enjoy TAKEN BY FORCE.

Christopher Pierce

June 21, 2008

FRAT-NAPPED
Logan Zachary

It truly wasn't my fault. I'll admit I had two beers at the Frat party, but I'm twenty. I know, but I started kindergarten late due to a Halloween birthday. For the last two years after graduation, I've bounced from job to job. This weekend, my brother Greg invited me to check out his university and see if I could meet some of the professors – maybe get a jump on my application.

My parents wanted me to choose a major.

I wasn't even sure I wanted to go to college.

The party started out fun enough. I nursed a beer for over an hour. The last few swallows were as warm as … well, what it looked like.

The second beer went down faster with all the chips and pretzels I ate, but once I started eating the fruit, the alcohol hit me. Little did I know, the fruit was spiked, and I became really tired, so I decided to go lie down on Greg's bed.

I staggered up the wooden stairway to the third floor and found his room. I flopped down on his bed and was asleep before the dust settled.

The next thing I knew, I felt hands all over me. Something was placed over my head, like a pillowcase, and a roll of duct tape screeched in protest. I was groggy; otherwise I would have said something sooner or put up more of a fight.

Something was thrown over me, and I felt my body being rolled up in it. I was lifted and carried away. I tried to escape, but my arms were pinned to my sides, and my legs were held together securely.

Wake up, wake up, I told myself. Being the center for the varsity football team, I was strong, but rolled up like an enchilada, I was helpless.

Male laughter surrounded me. Maybe Greg's frat brothers were playing a prank on me. Was I supposed to be in his room? Then the thought struck me. Even though Greg was my big bro, I was the same size. Did they think I was him?

Down several flights of stairs, the cool night air enveloped me. I heard a car door open, and then I was dropped inside. The engine revved, and I was in motion. I could feel a few bodies next to me, but I couldn't speak. Whoever taped the pillowcase to my head covered my mouth too well.

We drove around for a while, and then, we stopped. Doors opened and hands grabbed and carried me again. The next thing I knew, my arms were tied above my head, and I was dangling from something. Whatever had been wrapped around my body was gone, and I was free. Well, not quite.

The pillowcase still covered my head. A hand gently pushed me, and I swung in the air. My body spun around and around. I felt the weight of my body, pulling hard on my wrists.

Then a hand caressed my ass. It stroked one cheek and then the other. Two fingers ran down the seam of my jeans that hugged my butt. A small hole at the corner of one of my back pockets exposed my underwear. I felt a finger explore that opening and rub my briefs. The finger moved them, and then touched my bare flesh.

Excitement washed over my body. I felt a stirring in my loins. *Don't sprout a woody now*, I thought.

The finger came out of the rip, and my body spun free again. Half way around, hands stopped me. They both touched my knees and worked their way up. The thumbs trailed along my inseam and came together at the crotch. Each thumb ran over a ball, and I could feel them lift up against my body. Semi-wood was quickly hardening. My jeans were tight, and there wasn't a lot of extra room in them. If my hands were free, I would have adjusted myself, discreetly.

As if reading my mind, a hand moved my package. I sprang to instant hard-on. The fingers outlined my cock, and worked their way up. The button on my jeans tightened, but the hands opened it without a hesitation. The zipper slowly clicked down, and then my body started to buck. My legs kicked back and forth, I pulled hard on my arms and tried to raise my lower body.

But rising up only made it easier for the jeans to be slipped down in the back, exposing my underwear-clad ass. The hands pulled my jeans down, and I felt the denim slipping away. Once they were off, a pair of hands grabbed my right leg and another pair grabbed my left. They pulled in opposite directions, holding me spread-eagled in the air.

Another set of hands pulled up my T-shirt and traced the waistband of my Hanes.

I kicked hard with my legs, but I was held firm and fast. I felt a face press against my erection, and the hands pulled my butt forward. The hands massaged each cheek, as a tongue licked my balls through the fabric. I could feel a wet spot growing on the thin white material. How many people were watching? It felt great, but I didn't want everyone watching me get stripped.

The hands pulled the Hanes down in the back, and my smooth, bare ass was exposed. Fingers explored all over it. Pinching and caressing, digging into the cleft, and wiggling around.

The hands that pulled them down touched me, and it seemed as if they walked around behind me. A face was pressed into my ass. I could feel a nose and chin in my crease. The hands spread my cheeks. A wet thing explored next. It licked up and down the groove and dove in deeper.

My whole body went rigid. *Not there, not there, not …*

And then the mouth found it and kissed my hole. It seemed to suck on it, trying to open me up. It pulled hard on me, and my body refused to move. Then the tongue stuck out and explored the hole, and my body went wild. I thrashed and jerked and floundered around.

The hands held me in place, as the tongue drove in deeper and deeper. I could feel my underwear slipped down in front, as my hard-on strained to escape. *How many people were watching? All guys? All girls? Was I being videotaped?*

The pleasure from having my butthole licked was amazing. Was this what they meant by being rimmed?

A cold metallic feeling started at my hip and worked its way up. Snip, snip, snip, and my shirt was off in pieces. Only my underwear barely covered part of me, and the waistband was slipping.

More hands appeared, two caressed up my sides and combed through the hair in my armpits. Sweat poured out of my pits as I hung helpless. The touch tickled, but stimulated more than that annoying tease.

Another pair played across my shoulders. The fingers combed through the patch of hair that grew out of the center of my chest and gently pulled on it. They then spread out to the side and caressed my nipples. Both rose to sharp peaks under their touch. *How many places in the human body caused you to feel this way?*

A new face took over licking my ass. I knew it was new, because bristly hair of a moustache and beard tickled my tender hole. A closely buzzed head scrubbed my ass cheeks.

The extra movement finally dislodged my underwear. My cock sprang free, fully erect and hard. It was the only thing holding my briefs in place, and now they slid down my legs. A hand pulled them off one leg, and before I could resist, they were gone. Now I was buck-ass naked.

Free of clothes, my cock became fair game. One hand touched it lightly and ran down the underside. The nails teased my fuzzy balls and made them jump.

My cock rose up higher, as a tongue played along the underside. Flicking side to side, it worked its way slowly to the swollen tip. The mouth opened and pulled the tip inside. It closed around the end, and the tongue ran circles around it. The mouth pulled it in deeper, and a sucking pressure made my head fall back in pure pleasure. The mouth engulfed all eight inches and tickled my balls as they rested on his chin. Slowly, my cock withdrew.

"His hair tickles," a man's voice said, at my waist.

"Shave him," another man answered.

"Shave him, shave him," was chanted in the room.

I tried to cross my legs, but they were held firmly.

All was quiet for a few moments, and then I heard the sound of shaving cream coming out of the can. A foamy cream blob landed on my groin, and a hand smoothed it around my erection and down and across my balls.

"Hold very still," a husky voice commanded. "You wouldn't want me to slip."

A cold sharp edge of a razor blade touched my pelvis, right above my cock. The metal scraped down to my cock's base, removing a strip of hair along the way. Another smooth strip followed, along side the first one. Cold metal quickly removed the hair above my penis.

The hand massaged my dangling balls and pulled one down gently. The razor shaved along one. The fingers rolled my ball as the razor did its deed. The hands moved to the other testicle and repeated the process.

A warm washcloth wiped along the inside of my leg and moved to one smooth ball. It pulled it down and moved to the other. It cleaned above my erection and moved to clean along my thick shaft. Once washed, something waved in front of me, drying me. As the water evaporated, the sensitive skin cooled by the breeze.

Someone said, "Bong him."

I heard a few beer cans crack open, and a cold spray crossed my bare leg.

How was I going to get the bong, when my mouth was duct-taped closed?

I didn't have long to wait. A rubber tube was placed between my ass cheeks. All the saliva still remained and had loosened my virgin butt. The tube slipped in easily.

"Bong him, bong him," a chant started.

Suddenly, ice-cold beer filled my ass. Pressure rose as I filled up. *A beer enema? How embarrassing.* I couldn't just let it all go in front of everyone. More beer poured into me, and I squeezed my butt cheeks together, tighter, but the tube was still inside. I was going to burst.

"He's going to blow," someone called.

The tube was removed, and a plastic bucket was jammed against my butt just as the pressure became unbearable. Beer flowed out of me, and my body went limp. I was so glad my face was covered.

"Bong him, bong him," the crowd started again.

A small trickle of beer ran down my legs, and I felt the tube reinserted. This time it hurt. The cold beer must have tightened my hole. Fingers found my hole and plunged in, the tube followed.

Another wave of cold beer entered me, and a few more cans were opened. My butt filled up, but this time a hand held the tube in.

"Who wants to drink first?"

The tube was adjusted, and I felt the pressure lessen.

"I'm next," someone said, and my body shifted.

7

"He's empty."

"Fill him up again."

Another cold wave entered me.

This time as the pressure rose, a mouth engulfed my penis. Lips slid down my length as a hot, wet tongue worked the underside. My balls bounced off his chin and swung back for more.

The pressure inside my ass pushed against my prostate.

A hand stroked my shaft as the other one played with my balls. My cock slipped in and out of his mouth, beating the back of his throat.

The orgasm hit, and I filled the willing mouth. My balls drained, my butt drained, and I was drained.

My body was overwhelmed. I couldn't focus on anything. I must have passed out, for the next thing I knew I was being lifted down. I was gently placed on a soft pad.

My limp body was gently rolled over. I felt my ass being raised up, and a pad was placed underneath my belly. Hands grabbed my ankles and spread my legs apart. My butt cheeks opened, and I heard a collective gasp.

Drops of oil fell on my bottom and trickled down my crack. It hung onto my body, being so thick. My smooth balls were quickly covered with it. Small drops fell as the amount increased. A finger ran down the crease and circled my hole. It explored as the oil continued and followed the tip's trail. I could feel my opening fill with oil, and it pooled there. As the finger inserted itself, the oil flowed inside me. Another finger followed from someone else, and I could feel myself open up. More oil poured in, as the two fingers played and teased me.

Despite my spent cock, it rose from the semi-hard state to full erection. An applause greeted it.

I felt my cock jerk up and down as if taking a bow.

Hands massaged my bubble-butt and spread my cheeks. The fingers that were exploring were removed, and the thumbs of the massaging hands took their place.

I felt someone move closer behind me. The hands worked my butt, and a thick cock slipped along my butt crack. The fat fleshy cock sandwiched between my cheeks like a brat. As the hands worked, his hips matched their rhythm.

The cock slid along me, and the tip pressed the tender spot. It teased the hole, trying to get in, but slipped across it, rubbing the meaty shaft the entire length. Heavy balls bounced against my ass and slowly rocked back and forth.

My ass begged for his entry. The penis teased and tormented me, until the hands grabbed my hip bones and posed the rigid member on target. With one swift thrust, he was inside me, to the hilt. The furry balls pressed against me, seeking entry also.

Slowly, the hard-on slid out to the mushroom head and popped out. It pressed forward and entered me again. It felt as if it had swollen, double in size. The thick veined shaft filled my virgin ass. He drove into me, burying himself in, all the way to the base. His balls mashed against my butt.

I could feel how low they hung down my cheeks. I swore they dangled and banged against my own nutsack, furry against my newly shaved scrotum.

The pelvis drilled in and out. It drove in and out the full length. With each stroke, the speed and intensity increased. His balls slapped against my cheeks.

The pleasure was amazing, and I adjusted my position to enjoy it more. As I moved, my ass clamped down on the hard cock as it drove inside. His balls pulled up along my ass cheeks. He pulled back and frantically entered me again, shooting a hot load inside of me.

My ass spasmed around the thick cock, sucking all the hot cum out and milking it for all it was worth. My greedy ass wanted more and tried to pull him in again.

A low moan sounded behind me as the shaft was removed.

I felt the man collapse to his knees behind me. His mouth landed on my hole and his mouth sucked on it. His tongue entered, trying to retrieve what his cock and just deposited.

I pushed my ass into his face and rode his tongue. Thick, hot fluid passed from my ass to his mouth and back. Suck and blow, suck and blow, fill and empty, fill and empty.

I wanted my arms and legs to be free, so I could touch and handle all that was around me. Never had I realized my body could feel such pleasure.

As the hungry mouth finished eating, my body was moved again. This time, I found myself flat on my back. My cock sprang free and slapped against my belly.

Lying there, I waited, not sure what to expect next. A hairy leg brushed alongside my leg. I felt someone climb across my narrow hips, and a tight butt sat on my cock. The ass hung in mid-air for a moment, swallowed my dick, and slid down, along my shaft.

It didn't take long. The explosion that arose in my balls tore out of my shaft and filled his ass. The tight ass continued to ride it. My pelvis pounded into him, as wave after wave of come spewed out of me. My body tingled and shivered with the overload of sensation. As the last drop left my cock, my body became heavy, all energy left, and I lay exhausted on the floor. Everything spent from my body. I couldn't move.

Several minutes passed and gentle hands worked the tape from the pillowcase. The pressure holding my mouth closed released, and I rocked my jaw from side to side to loosen it again. The tape ripped off, and the pillowcase rose.

The bright light blinded me at first, but a smiling face greeted me. "Are you ready to apply now?" my brother Greg asked. "The brothers at the Frat house would love a younger brother."

I looked around the room.

All the heads nodded in agreement.

My head joined them; it was all I could do.

When the weekend was over, I returned home, Mom and Dad waiting for me.

"So? How did it go? Did Greg show you a good time?"

"He did," I smiled, at the memories.

"So?" Mom asked.

"I start spring term."

Dad clasped my hand and shook it hard.

"I'm proud of you son."

"Have you decided what you'll study?" Mom asked.

I smiled.

"Anatomy," I answered proudly, and I couldn't wait to start my lessons.

TAKING BRIAN
Shane Allison

It was now or never. Do or damn die. I had 45 minutes and counting before Brian's shift was up. Searched for a rock or a fake plastic plant. A place I figured he would stash a key beneath. I thought of the welcome mat, but in a place that obvious? Lifted it, and there it was. He always was a presumptuous fuck. Couldn't believe he was still living in this same dump – an apartment complex subject to flooding, gangs, hookers, and crackhead hustlers. He treated me to Hamburger Helper and old episodes of *Sex and the City* back when we were on speaking terms. Took the key and pressed it into the slit of the door's knob. I walked in with my gym bag of goodies. His pad smelled lived in, faintly of hoagie sandwiches. Place was a wreck. How could he find anything in that mess? Works forty-hour weeks, and he's still dumpster diving for hand-me-downs, salvaging sofas from the treasures of other people's trash.

It was time to put my plan into action. One wrong move, and I was fucked. Made my way to Brian's bedroom, which was a war zone of dirty clothes strewn. I sifted through his closet, piles of dirty unmentionables. Looked to my watch to check the time. 2:00 am on the dot. Wasn't long now. I fished out a nasty pair of underwear from the laundry basket. Planned to use it to gag his sweet mouth. Brought the duct tape I borrowed from the toolbox on Daddy's truck. Stuff can take off a layer of skin if you're not careful. Scarred for life. I took my place and waited for him. I was ready. This shit was going to be good. He was not going to be like the others, for I had something special planned for his ass. Within minutes, I heard the door, the screaming of hinges. I cracked the closet just slightly to watch his moves. Brian threw his bag on the couch, flicked on the TV, the light in the kitchen. He talked to himself thinking he was alone. He looked tired, but I didn't give a shit. Dick-tease wasn't deserving of my empathy. Not the way he reached in and fingered around in my heart. He made his way to the bedroom, sipping a soda, kicking his shoes out on the floor. I steadied myself, ready with the hanky laced with chloroform. Watched Brian get undressed, undoing an ugly shirt, fingers making their way down a ladder of buttons. There he was half-naked and bare-chested, stretch marks across love handles. He sat on the edge of the unmade bed to peel khakis off one ashy leg then the other. White briefs hugged his ass beautifully. Cotton stretching across two dark chocolate cheeks. Own dick started to stiffen in my jeans. My palms were mitts of perspiration. Gums were salty and itchy with anticipation. He bent over to take them off. One foot and then the other showing his x-rated parts. My heart was a racehorse, sweat dripped from my pits inside my Polo pullover. He walked naked to the bathroom and flicked on the light. Brian stood at the toilet to take a piss. A tongue of pee-pee rained. He flushed and exited. I dreamt of tweaking his nipples, smearing my face in his big-belliedness. His dick was soft, peanut size. Brian fished out a pair of boxers from one of the open drawers. This was it. With his back turned to me, I ran toward him with the chloroformed cloth and held it hard over his face. Brian stammered and struggled, clawing at my arms and hands, yet had no nails to break any skin. The drug was instant, knocking him out like a prizefighter. He was a fat, heavy slab in my arms. I dragged him to the bed and threw his naked self upon the tussled sheets that smelled of ass and sweat. Brian was done for, unconscious. I took the duct tape and rolled tongues of the heavy duty adhesive around his mouth, careful not to get his eyes or nose. Did the same to his wrists and ankles. He wasn't going anyplace. I locked the front door and turned the Venetians closed. I killed the living room lights and those in the kitchen. I made my way back to Brian's naked brawn and stared at him. I was about out of breath, and my glasses were smudged. Started thinking of that day we met. Two lowly English majors. We were enrolled in a playwriting class. He was different than the gold-chained obsessed brothas I was used to seeing, who bullied me in high school, called me a sissy, a faggot in woodshop and Consumer Math. Brian was nerdy and spoke like a white boy. He had gained weight since our undergrad days. Pleasantly plump in all the right places. Thighs, gut, and a firm bubble-butt I've always wanted to sink my dick in. I always picked him to be in my play up until the roles turned gay. Didn't want those in class to think he was a homo. So stupid. It was only a play. I had to scramble fast for someone new. Some cute punk boy named Sam, a Korn fan with a piercing through his bottom lip. We all passed the class with Bs 'cause we had the kind of instructor that said none of our work was worthy enough for excellence. Thought about Brian everyday. Hardly made it through the semester. If he was gay, we would have made the perfect couple. I channeled my love and lust for Brian in balled up Kleenex and the creases of gay porno mags. Composed erotic poems in tattered notebooks about sucking his dick, fucking his ass. When I thought to share a few verses with him and those in the thousands by publishing it online, it broke my heart when he said he didn't want to talk to me anymore, didn't want to hang out over cans of cherry soda and the good episodes of *Sex and the City*. I burned the journals of scarlet-red glitter hearts and swore there would be no more poems written about him, but he said the damage was done. Tried to call only to be sent to the phantom zone of his voicemail. That was it. The shit was over, but not for me. I had to have him.

Sat the duct tape on the dresser close by as well as the bottle of chloroform. Gave him a swift whack across his ass. Dirty pup. Was the type of thing I liked using my hands for. It was time to take it out on his flesh, to do with what I wanted. I started to massage his hips, knead brown-skinned fat. Brian was coming to. I quickly started to reach for the chloroform, but decided against it. He started to struggle, attempting to pull his wrists free from the tape.

"Be still," I told him, "or you're going to pull the skin off." He whimpered, breathing heavy, soiling the tape with snot and tears. His cries were useless on me. My dick was harder than a pipe as I rubbed it through the denim. Didn't want Brian to see my face, so I ripped a tuft of the bedspread and used it to blindfold him.

I mounted him and whispered, "Shhh, stop all this mess now. It'll be over soon." I applied more tape to his mouth, wrists and ankles.

I dismissed myself to the bathroom. The lights were bright and burned my eyes. I searched the medicine cabinet for something to rub on my dick, some stuff to slather up his asshole, but the only thing that came close was rubbing alcohol and citrus-flavored cough medicine. So I checked in the kitchen knowing good and well I would find something kinky. Brian lay there still and tied with his butt in the air to me ready for whatever. Searched the cabinets first, which had all the usual condiments: mustard, herbs, and spices. And then there was the fridge: relish, chocolate syrup, grape jelly, fat-free salad dressing. I've used it all 'cept jelly. I took the jar and returned to Brian's bedroom. I sat the jar on the bedside table and undid the lid. Pulled my jeans down around my ankles. Underwear stained with shit streaks pulled tight across my legs. The stench of crotch musk permeated throughout the room. I left on my shirt. My dick-ring around my balls kept my stuff erect. Because they don't have a store in Tallahassee that sells them, I had to special order my piece. I dipped three fingers into the jar of artificially-flavored jelly and slathered it between Brian's half-moons. He winced to my cold touch. He objected, but with the tape double-layered, his screams were but a muffle behind the tough adhesive.

"Hush now," I whispered.

He only got himself to blame. A little of the jelly dripped on the floor in dark, purple clumps. The smell of the sweet stuff mixed with the ripeness of Brian's ass, cold cut meat and pubic stink. I reached over and shoveled out more jelly and applied some on my dick. Stuff was cold as shit going on. Clumps more fell to the bedroom floor. I slipped slowly a finger into Brian's ass. He bucked slightly to it. The jelly matted my pubic hairs, pulling with my fingers as I stroked my hard-on. My hairs hurt as I veered up, down.

Brian's bent legs were between my own as I maneuvered my dick directly at the crack of his ass. I stretched my shirt over my head, around my neck away from obstruction. With his arms bound behind him, I took hold of his shoulder with a free hand and slowly began to work my dick in with the other, past his sticky cheeks. His face was slippery with sweat. Slid in easily due to the gelatinous lubricant. My tender muscles started to ache as I began to fuck Brian. I reached around to feel for his dick. It was harder than my own. I would take pleasure in blowing it later. His ass was a dream. I wasn't worried about him telling anybody. Men who get raped never report it. Besides, I knew where he could be found. Felt myself getting close to coming, which was odd considering it takes me a while to pop. I chalked it up to being too excited, too randy to taste Brian for the first time. I pulled out slowly, dick sloshing out of his butt. Held my dick above his ass and shot thick streams of white fire across the supple, dark skin of his back. I plunged a single finger in again. Brought it to my face, to my lips, and sucked shit and jelly from the digit. I wasn't done with him just yet. I wanted to know what a nerdy boy's dick tasted like. I checked the security of my flower-printed blindfold. Still, it was holding. I rolled him over on his back stained with my spunk. Wrists still bound, mouth sullen and ankles slapped together with gray tape. Brian's dick was slightly curved pointing to the ceiling fan above us. Its blades caked with dust. His stuff was a sticky, circumcised piece. A dew of sweat damped his face and throat. I reached over into the jelly jar again. Two fingers this time. I dappled it on the delicate head, ran my fingertips along the hotness of his shaft. The roof of my mouth was dry. Held his dick and began to tickle the head with my tongue. He was so sweet tasting. As I sucked him clean, I turned his nipples. Brian was such a nasty mess. Felt his dick tense in my mouth, past tenacious lips. I played with his balls, jelly matted the sac hairs. Other than the blowjob that was issued to him from that Asian girl from Korea he told me about, I knew he was safe, clean cum surging in his black body. I pressed harder upon his nipples when his dick jerked, gorging me with semen. I swallowed. I left Brian lying there stained with his own cum, spit and jelly as I hauled off to the bathroom to clean up. Made sure I didn't leave as much as a hair behind. I tried to scrub the jelly out of the carpet with a damp washcloth, but only made the stain worse. I wiped the rim of the jelly jar clean from stray crotch hairs, and put the lid back on. I sat it back between the salad dressing and the mayonnaise. I packed all what I had brought with me leaving Brian taped up and dirty. I unlocked the door and opened it to a sliver to check if it was clear of drunken college students. I threw the spare key under the mat. As I walked frantically to my car, I pulled off the latex gloves and threw them in a sewer drain. It was done. I got away with it. Brian wasn't going to say anything if he knew what was good for his ass.

BLOODLESS COUP
Mark Apoapsis

My four litter bearers were shirtless despite the cool weather, and the muscular upper backs of the two men in front of me, both the swarthy one on the left and the ruddy freckled one on the right, were already slick with sweat. Glancing behind me, I saw that the chest hair of the peasant bringing up the rear on the left was matted down against his pale skin. You would think that these mongrels would be used to the higher gravity here, having lived on this moon all their adult lives. I made a mental note to travel this way more often, to keep my subjects from getting soft.

We were flanked by two of my elite palace guards. I had chosen Corporal McYang and Major Chanson for the honor of serving as my personal bodyguards this morning for several reasons: for their confident, upright bearing, for the underlying physical strength that made that possible even under this higher gravity, and for their purebred, attractive noble faces. They looked cool and competent striding alongside the litter in their blue and yellow uniforms, their clear green eyes scanning the crowd alertly. But then, they came from superior bloodlines, not like the four motley peasants beneath me.

Obviously, being from a superior bloodline myself, I could have easily walked the distance if I'd cared to, but after a grueling sixty minutes on the exercise treadmill back at the palace, I deserved to relax for a while. Fresh from a long hot shower and dressed formally for the inspection tour in the aquamarine vest, my House color, over my royal purple shirt with its stiff collar, I was in no mood to exert myself.

The interim governor had done a good job of building my mining outpost until I was of age. There was outdoor plumbing throughout much of the village, more than enough to serve the basic sanitary needs of the thousand or so residents. The streets were lined with prefab cottages assembled with local labor, each housing six to eight men in six bunks with enough space in between to serve as either a common area or floor space for the seventh and eighth man. The gray shirts and pants of the men we passed looked ragged but clean, and many of them even had shoes. There was an expansive cemetery outside town, and any accidental fatalities were removed on a daily basis. Few men died of disease here, since we vaccinated them against every known disease before shipping them here. In nearly every way, my subjects had a much better life than peasants had ever had two thousand years ago on Earth.

The men walking down the street, who stopped to bow down to me as I passed, all looked strong and healthy, due to the salutary effects of physical labor under moderately high gravity. They seemed to all be in their early twenties to late thirties. I knew that in fact they were shipped here at the age of 18 to 19 and that the average life expectancy was 33, with accidents claiming the average man's life before the toxic dust of the mines could do enough damage to cause symptoms.

The peasants seemed well trained in the matter of the courtesy due to their prince. Corporal McYang only had to use his electric prod on one oaf who was too lazy to put down the sack he'd been carrying. Probably a miller's apprentice, since the sack contained the native plant they grind to make that disgusting gruel they like to subsist on. The electricity shocked, even through the man's coarse homespun shirt, caused his limbs to spasm, and the sack fell to the unpaved street and burst open. The man recovered and belatedly sank to his knees, but Corporal McYang was not satisfied. He picked the poor fool up by his shirtfront and stuck the end of his electric prod into the pit of his exposed stomach. Finger hesitating over the trigger, Corporal McYang looked questioningly at me. The peasant's watery blue eyes widened, and he stared at me pleadingly.

Knowing that a shock against bare skin so near the solar plexus would be excruciating, I shook my head. Then I loudly called out, "No, let him go," to make sure all my subjects nearby would witness my beneficence. They'd been conditioned all their lives to hold my family in awe, but I'd been taught that it was a good idea to reinforce their reverence occasionally.

That was the one slip that any of the peasants made. All of the beast-drawn wagons and the occasional hovercraft pulled over to let us past in the narrow street. All the pedestrians stopped to bow. I was impressed when we passed a line of men waiting for the central shower in the town square, their naked bodies the usual haphazard range of too-pale to too-swarthy, and they all faced me and made a self-conscious bow. Even the man who was actually under the shower bowed, his hairy legs shivering visibly as he allowed the water to course over his broad shoulders for several minutes as my litter bearers carried me slowly past.

When we arrived at the entrance to the mine, the chief engineer rushed up to greet me as soon as the sweat-drenched bearers knelt down to let me alight with help from my other guardsman, Major Chanson.

"Welcome, Your Highness," he said effusively. As a skilled professional, he was dressed in a crisp gray uniform, but his muddy brown eyes, pale skin, and straw-colored hair marked him as a peasant. He seemed to be in his early thirties and was probably nearing the end of his life, even if he continued to avoid accidents. "We're so honored that you would choose to inspect your holdings in person!"

He led us into a large control room just inside the entrance. It was staffed by a mixture of peasants and noblemen, the latter distinguished as much by their green eyes and smooth olive complexions as by their rich clothing.

"Would you care for some refreshments after your journey from the palace?" the chief engineer asked. "I'm afraid all we have to offer is ..."

"No, thank you," I interrupted. "You may begin the tour."

"Of course! If Your Highness would follow me ..."

I let Corporal McYang lead the way, confidently holding his energy rifle at the ready as he remained on alert. Major Chanson brought up the rear. I wondered if bringing both of them into this secure area had been overkill, since the unarmed peasants, even if they were inclined to disobedience, would be foolish to attack the well-trained and genetically superior elite royal guard.

* * * * *

The mine was primitive, I observed during the tour, depending more on the plentiful supply of unskilled labor than on technology. It did have an air filtration system to keep the toxic dust and gases under control; my host assured me that it was effective enough that short-term exposure would pose no risk to my health. "It's similar to the life support system used in the royal navy ship that brought you here," he explained, "only a generation or two out of date."

"I noticed that the hatches look airtight, like the ones on my ship," I said.

"A most astute observation, Your Highness. That technology is almost identical, having not changed in a century. In case of a gas leak, we seal off the affected chamber in order to limit the number of casualties. We can also douse fires quickly by sealing a chamber and flooding it with nitrogen." As he spoke, the hatch we had come in through closed. On cue, he explained, "The hatch behind us is closing as a safety precaution."

"Then why didn't the others close?" I asked curiously.

The engineer took a deep breath. That isn't unusual, in my experience, when someone is carefully considering his words, and since I'm accustomed to being addressed by men who know I could have them stripped and flogged with a single gesture if their answer displeased me, it didn't occur to me that anything was amiss. A few seconds passed before I realized that he had been holding his breath for a long time and showed no signs of intending to speak. Just as this occurred to me, the engineer smiled and carefully sat down against the wall, finally exhaling. A second later, I saw Corporal McYang sink to his knees and heard Major Chanson's rifle clatter to the floor behind me, followed by the meaty thud of a big body hitting the floor. I never felt myself fall.

* * * * *

When I awoke, my guards were gone, and I found myself dressed in a miner's gray coveralls and cap.

"What is the meaning of this?" I snarled.

"Get on your feet, you arrogant inbred bastard," the chief engineer ordered. He was flanked by two particularly strong-looking miners.

"If you think you can attack your prince and keep it a secret, even ten meters underground ..."

"On the contrary," he said. "Get him on his feet."

The miners hauled me to my feet and held onto my arms.

"Where are my own clothes? Whoever ..."

The engineer interrupted me. "You will walk out of here quietly and not speak again until we get to the street." He took a small tool out of his pocket. "This is a laser chisel. It can slice through solid rock at fifty millimeters per second. It can sever a man's foot in far less time than that, from halfway across a room. I'll be right behind you with this in my pocket. If you say one word, or look up from the ground, or stop walking, you'll never walk unassisted again. Do you understand me?"

This wasn't the time to boast about how quickly our advanced medical facilities back home could regrow a foot. The facilities here were barely up to healing a broken leg. I allowed myself to be herded back the way we had come. When we finally passed through the control room, I was confident that I'd be recognized immediately by my regal bearing, even dressed as a miner and with my green eyes half hidden under the cap. But no one met my eyes even when I dared to glance up. The noblemen all ignored me as if I were just another peasant beneath their notice, and the common workers seemed very intent on their work.

We exited to the street, and my three captors led me around a corner. "There's our ride."

It wasn't the litter we had come in, or even a hovercraft, but a common wagon, the kind that would normally be drawn by a beast. Instead, two dejected-looking men were harnessed to the pole. They weren't my litter bearers; their bare chests were a golden brown, not the mix of pale and swarthy skin tones of the men who had carried me here. As we approached, I looked at their faces and was shocked to recognize Corporal McYang and Major Chanson. I had assumed they'd been killed when I was taken, but this debasement was almost worse: stripped to the waist on a public street and forced into a role normally filled by beasts, or occasionally by peasants.

Corporal McYang had a surprisingly hairy chest, suggesting that he was not as pure-bred as his facial features suggested. One of his distant ancestors may have been no more noble than the man he'd used his electric prod on. He saw me staring at his chest and slumped even further in his harness. Major Chanson, in contrast, had a pattern of chest hair not to different from my own – a light sprinkling across his pectoral muscles, with a denser matt nestled between them, continuing straight down his chest and fanning out slightly on his belly. A noble pattern, meant to be hidden beneath rich garments or flashy uniforms, not laid bare on a public street!

The engineer reached into the passenger compartment and drew out a bundle of richly colored clothes. "Put these on," he ordered.

"What, here on the street?" I looked around and noticed that a crowd of men had gathered, grinning at Corporal McYang and Major Chanson. Maybe they recognized the royal guardsmen, even stripped of their uniforms, or maybe they just saw two noblemen hitched shirtless to a wagon.

"You wanted your own clothes back."

"I'll put them on in ..."

"Strip him!"

The two big miners seized my arms and quickly stripped me of the boots and coveralls someone had dressed me in, leaving me wearing nothing but my own black silk briefs.

"Now, if His Highness would care to get dressed?" the engineer suggested mockingly, thrusting out my clothes again.

Under the watchful eyes of the crowd, I pulled the trousers on. "The shirt is missing," I complained.

"The shirt represented the position we're kicking you out of. Be glad we left you the vest, only because we wanted you to be recognized."

They made me sit up front like that, with my shoulders, chest, and feet bare, right next to the swarthy, gray-eyed driver. The driver gleefully snapped his whip above the bare shoulders of my former guardsmen, who struggled forward, the muscles in their broad backs standing out.

They paraded us this way through the streets, back the way we had come. Men gathered along the street to cheer.

Corporal McYang and Major Chanson were exhausted by the time we reached the town square, and the driver was ruthlessly using his whip, leaving red welts across both men's backs. Fortunately for them, no further progress was possible, since the streets were thronged with foot traffic, mostly heading away from us.

"They're going to storm the palace," the driver informed me cheerfully. "We've all been trained from birth to hold you in awe, like you were some kind of god, and most of us had trouble overcoming that training. Until now."

"The palace guards can easily handle a rebellion by unarmed men," I boasted, wondering if rescue would reach me before they could do anything further to me.

"Not if they ate the lunch your servants cooked for them."

That answer chilled me, but I forgot all about the palace when I saw that a crude scaffold had been erected in the middle of the town square since we'd last passed this way. Ropes were draped over it. I wondered if they intended to execute me. Instead, they strung me up by my wrists, with my toes barely grazing the dirt. Meanwhile, the crowd unhitched my men, who resisted weakly. Some of them forced Major Chanson to his knees and made him watch my humiliation, while others surrounded Corporal McYang and took turns poking at his unprotected skin with his own electric prod. They laughed every time he cried out in pain.

Most of the crowd, though, was gathering around me. A piece of overripe fruit struck me square in middle of my bare chest. Another quickly followed, knocking the wind out of me when it struck my belly. Soon every exposed bit of skin was covered with the stuff. It was even sticking to my armpit hair. I had my eyes closed against the fruit dripping down from my forehead. Then I felt hands tugging hard at my soiled vest until the seams split. The expensive garment was ripped from my body, exposing fresh targets.

At one point, a hoarse scream made me involuntarily open my eyes. Near the spot where Corporal McYang was being tormented, a man was waving the guard's trousers triumphantly overhead like a flag as he cheered on his companions, who were kneeling around the position the guard presumably lay. "Get him stretched out again!" the man with the trousers yelled.

Loud, hoarse begging was cut short by another scream.

* * * * *

The overcast sky gave no hint of the time, but it seemed like hours before they finally cut me down and forced me under the freezing spray of water from the outdoor public shower. Every scrap of clothing was long gone. Hands scrubbed my shivering body roughly and intimately. They wrapped me in a coarse homespun blanket and threw me in the back of the wagon. I landed beside the nude, unconscious body of Corporal McYang. He was still quivering from the aftereffects of so many shocks, or possibly because the weather had turned chilly. I wrapped the scratchy blanket more tightly around my own naked body and wept silently as Major Chanson, grunting with the effort, struggled to get the wagon moving.

* * * * *

From the window of my prison cell in the tower of the palace, whenever the sky was clear and dark, I could see all the inner moons as they crossed in front of the violet-and-maroon-banded disk of our system's primary gas giant, surrounded by the green and blue pinpoints of the outer moons. It would be beautiful if I didn't know who lived on each one of them. Every inhabited moon that had not fallen over the centuries into the hands of rabble, as this one had, was ruled by one of my older brothers or by an uncle or cousin. If they could stop arguing with each other long enough to pool their military might, they should be able to overcome this moon's defenses and rescue me, if not for love then at least for the sake of our family's dignity. Failing that, at least they should be able to afford to ransom me.

They gave me homespun clothes to wear. For the first several weeks of my imprisonment, I made a point of sleeping fully clothed and was careful to always change clothes in the tiny washroom, the only spot that had no obvious cameras. Eventually, though, holding onto the last scraps of my dignity began to seem pointless and wearisome. They kept the room unbearably warm, especially for exercising. And if I refused to exercise, they stopped feeding me my daily gruel. Before long I resigned myself to the degradation of stripping in front of the cameras. I knew that I was constantly observed, not only by the prison guards, but also – whenever there wasn't a ball game on – by the patrons of some of the more prosperous taverns, which had started installing view screens. Recently, I had stopped bothering to get dressed at all, and spent every morning sitting in my underwear in front of the newsreader, trying not to think about the camera pointed down at me. Lately, I'd read that even some of the larger private residences could now afford view screens: certainly the fraternity houses that had sprung up, and there were a few four-man households that got screens installed even before indoor plumbing.

It amazed me that the population had skyrocketed despite the mass exodus after the government offered a free ticket to anyone wanting to emigrate. And a zero birth rate, of course. Of all the laws I had imposed, the one I thought the peasants would be in the biggest hurry to repeal was almost the only one they had kept. They had decided there were plenty of established worlds were a man could move to if he wanted to start a family, or that he could visit to satisfy his temporary needs. Instead, they'd decided to leverage the moon's status as the only all-male world in the system. From the new sports arena outside town to the gentleman's club in the new settlement to the south, from the monastery in the hills to the homosexual resorts springing up along the coast, the economy was booming, and there were plans for a new spaceport. There was an entire resort village that called itself "Boys' Week Out." Hordes of tourists from the mob-rule moons were flocking in – all men – and they didn't seem to mind that the closest thing to women on the entire moon were the holographic performers in the center stage of the new Circle Jerk Theater.

I knew that the initial influx of capital that enabled this boom had come from selling off the surviving palace guards. Slavery was legal on one of the many mob-rule moons the rebels now traded with. I'd done business with that moon myself, much as I disliked dealing with democracies; I'd sold them a few hundred men per year, which had brought in a modest sum, but apparently there was an extremely lucrative and hitherto untapped market for green-eyed, olive-skinned slaves. An appalling number of my guardsmen had been sold off. Appalling, because they should have gone down fighting, not allowed themselves to be taken alive. I was still fuming about that, three years later to the day.

Someone opened my door – not bothering to knock, of course. Without preliminary, he said, "Get dressed. Unless you want us to drag you out in your shorts."

"What? Is it Independence Day already?"

"You know it is. And you know the drill. Same as the first and second ones."

I put on my old trousers and my aquamarine vest, similar to the one that had been ripped from me three years ago today, and allowed myself to be led down the hall – past closed doors that used to lead to my private rooms but were now numbered in gold in a manner that looked suspiciously like a luxury hotel – and down the carpeted stairs. The first floor of the palace had been turned into a museum, housing such attractions as a line of mannequins displaying the uniforms the palace guards had worn at the time of the revolution. One wall was painted with a mural showing the guards kneeling in submission as they surrendered the palace, while another was filled with a life-sized photograph of a line of naked men in chains meekly filing into a freighter at the captured spaceport.

Parked outside the front of the former palace was the traditional wagon. I was almost glad to see Corporal McYang and Major Chanson waiting there, already in harness. They were the last familiar faces from better times, and since the last of their comrades had been sold off almost a year ago, I'd been afraid I would never see them again. They looked more muscular than ever. Maybe it was true what I'd heard, that they were rented out throughout the year to carry wagons full of beer-swilling jocks, too drunk to drive a hovercraft, to the stadium for all the major games.

"You again?" I asked the driver as I took my place.

"I come back every year for tradition's sake," he told me cheerfully. "And to spend a few weeks with my old buddies. And root for the football team. They joined the major leagues this year, you know. That makes our stadium the highest-gravity stadium in the major leagues. Hell of a home field advantage."

The streets, now widened and paved, were more crowded than I'd ever seen them, and full of leering men, most of them getting ready to watch the big game for which my public degradation was the pre-game entertainment. The whole street smelled of beer. It was more built up than last year, and to the extent that I could think about anything beyond the personal humiliation of being paraded through the streets again, it hurt to see a productive mining output turned into a tawdry tourist town filled with sports bars, video arcades, breweries, wrestling rings, hovercraft race tracks, and souvenir shops.

The reenactment grew a little further removed from the original rebellion every year. This year's addition was a marching band, just ahead of us. I've never cared to watch a recording to find out what the rest of the parade looked like. After I was strung up on the scaffold in the festively lit town square, there was a speech by the newly-elected president, a veteran of the rebellion who looked about thirty but would probably live to finish his four-year term, now that robots had been imported to do the more dangerous jobs at the mine. Cameramen took his picture with me hanging there as the backdrop, then moved closer to me and took more pictures to be sold as postcards.

The honor of ripping my clothes off this year went to the leader of an expedition that was setting out to explore the interior of the continent. To save him from being pelted himself by the excited crowd, they had him strip me completely naked before the barrage began, historical accuracy notwithstanding, and then paused for more postcard pictures.

Then the ceremonial two pieces of rotten fruit were thrown by the captains of the home and visiting football teams in place of the usual coin-toss to determine which team would receive the first kickoff. My armpits were worth 50 points, anywhere on my chest 10 points, my belly 20 points, my crotch 100 points, and so on. The Council had decided after the first year to ban fruit-throwing by the general public, due to the expense of cleaning it up; instead, onlookers were allowed to purchase globs of brightly-colored synthetic glop. This year my genitals wound up being painted bright red and my chest mostly blue and green with a splotch of yellow, and my face purple and green, making a distinctive collectable postcard for this year. I was so thickly coated I could feel the increased weight on my arms. In contrast, last year's postcard showed clean untouched flesh below my left nipple and right hip, with the edge of my pubic hair still clearly visible. Attendance was clearly picking up.

"I jerked off into this one, Your Helplessness!" taunted a rascal who looked barely old enough to get a visa. It smacked into my right shoulder, adding a final splash of red, and spraying goop into my armpit. Was it my imagination, or did it feel warmer and stickier than the other missiles?

Finally the horn sounded, marking the end of the bombardment and the beginning of the precession to the stadium. As the photographers took their final pictures for the official postcard, everyone climbed into vehicles – hovercraft far outnumbered beast-drawn wagons this year, I noticed – and the crowd dispersed, leaving me alone except for my harnessed former guardsmen waiting to take me back after the game, four policemen assigned to protect me from any permanent injury, and a few stragglers.

A man walked up to me, and for some reason the police allowed him to approach to within an arm's length. I looked up, and although his face was unfamiliar, I noticed that he had green eyes and was formally dressed in a dazzlingly white suit that set off his olive-green complexion.

"My sincerest apologies, Your Highness," he said without apparent sarcasm, "for approaching you under these less than dignified circumstances." He looked steadfastly up at face, pointedly not even glancing at my naked, goop-encrusted body hanging before him, allowing me to pretend that he hadn't witnessed every step of my degradation from the back of the crowd. "I wanted to present myself to you in person rather than letting you read the announcement in the news tomorrow, and since they wouldn't permit me visit you in your prison cell ..."

"How the hell did you get here, and why are you here?" I blurted. I wanted to add, walking around unbound and fully clothed in a place where every other man of noble blood is being publicly humiliated or sold into slavery, but could not bring myself to say it.

"Well, you see, I'm the new ambassador from His Majesty's government."

I was stunned. "My brother sent you here to negotiate a ransom for me?"

That didn't make sense. The king had even less love for me than my other three older brothers and had pledged only a token amount during the negotiations that had stalled years ago. Why send someone to negotiate in person now?

"Well, that, and also to establish an embassy."

"Wait ... My brother has established diplomatic relations with the rebels?"

He hesitated, as though trying to think of a properly diplomatic term for "diplomatic relations," but he must have failed since he didn't correct me. "I arrived and presented my credentials two weeks ago, but the government decided to hold off on the official announcement until today."

Independence Day. Of course.

"My brothers aren't going to ransom me, are they?" I asked miserably. "Or rescue me?"

"Well, to be perfectly frank, an invasion would cost even more than the ransom would. That was true from the moment your technicians rebelled and took over your spaceport and your orbital defenses. And, apparently, the new government feels that your brothers' ransom offer is far outstr... is far exceeded by your value to the local economy."

As a tourist attraction.

"I'm never getting out of here, am I?" I asked tonelessly. "This is what it's going to be like for the rest of my life."

"Well, your best hope, Your Highness, is that your cousin recently made a very generous ransom offer."

I had a lot of cousins, but only one was rich enough to make such an offer: the powerful tyrant who ruled the innermost moon and had his peasants convinced that he controlled its many volcanoes. We were doubly related, since he was also the brother-in-law of one of my brothers. We despised each other. If I fell into that sadistic bastard's hands, he would soon have me begging him to send me back here.

"I doubt they'll accept his generous price either," he continued, "but it is by far the highest bid. Excuse me, the highest offer."

That was one slip too many for a trained diplomat.

"You're enjoying this, aren't you, you bastard?"

The ambassador bowed deeply. This time he made no attempt to keep his eyes fixed on my face, but allowed his gaze to rake down the length of my body.

"Your royal brother sends his regards, Your Highness," he said, "and bids me to inform you that he craves to hear from you." He smiled up at me, showing his teeth. "Perhaps you could send him a postcard."

Excerpt from FOG
Jeff Mann

January is the month of mists. The cove's full of white this morning, making fuzzy shapes of the spruce trees surrounding the house. If I didn't know better, I'd say that someone had plastered the windowpanes with translucent paper, that we were moored inside a pearl. The glass of the pane is frigid beneath my touch. Winter's dedicated to invasions, insisting on its right to enter whom it will.

The fog's pallor continues inside. The pale body on the bed is silent yet, and still, as if carved from cloudy quartz. The only movement this sleeping sculpture makes is the almost imperceptible rise and fall of breath. White, white, wrapped, here and there, in strips of silver-gray.

He's been out for many hours, a chemically induced unconsciousness that's held over two days and several state lines. My fingers still chilled by the windowpane, I bend down and caress his bare belly. Smooth, solid, warm. Skin satiny with youth. I drop to my knees by the bed, kiss his forehead, and suck gently on his hard little nipples.

"Rob," I whisper. "Rob Drake."

No response. I sigh, rise, and settle into a rocking chair to wait. The air is very cold. I'm thankful for my rag wool sweater, the heat of the coffee cup in my hand.

Soon my partner Jay will be home for lunch. Soon Rob will wake. Until then, I want simply to sit here in this silent, fog-swathed house and watch our captive sleep.

Jay drops the Sonic bag on the kitchen table and unpeels his army jacket. His real name's Jeff, but I've learned to call him Jay. Jay and Al – we've been coaching ourselves for a year now, ever since this plan began in earnest, to call one another by pseudonyms. We don't want to give Rob any auditory evidence, in case we decide one day to let him loose, which is a big *If.* A pit in the forest floor is a more preferable denouement, as far as Jay is concerned.

"Drake still out?" asks Jay.

I nod, dumping out the bag's contents: five containers of tater tots, five foot-longs.

"That extra's for him. Feed him when he comes to."

I nod again. I do a lot of nodding around Jay. Have ever since we met in my office. Something about his brawny frame, deep-set eyes, bushy black eyebrows, and deep voice always seems to make him convincing and make me obedient. From ex-con's parole officer to ex-con's lover to ex-con's accomplice in a kidnapping. Not the smartest series of moves I've made. Nevertheless, here I am sharing a house with not one but two men I feel passionately about.

Jay and I sit in silence for a good while, chewing on our dogs, before I say, "You know, it's really chilly in here, and I ..."

Jay interrupts. He does that a lot, as if trying to spare me from articulating yet another stupid thought. "I want it chilly. I want him to suffer. If you're cold, put on another layer. I want that little shit shaking and whining. No blankets. Don't coddle him, Al. He isn't a guest, he's a captive. You know what his father did. Just 'cause you think he's pretty ... okay, I think he's pretty, too ... but he isn't your sweet boy, he's my tool. Okay?"

"Yes, Jay," I sigh. I need to toughen myself, I know. Jay has reminded me time and time again that Rob deserves what he gets. Sins of the father, and all that.

That's when the noise begins upstairs, behind the thick door of the back bedroom, the ragged cries that Jay's handiwork has so effectively muffled.

Jay grins and takes another bite of his second dog. "Sounds like our boy's up." When I rise, Jay grabs my forearm. "Sit down and finish your lunch. Let him roll around a little and wonder where the hell he is. No one can hear him out here."

As usual, I obey. I sit down and dip a tater tot in ketchup. The noises continue, shouts for help dammed up by rubber and tape. We move to the living room to share one of Jay's hand-rolled cigarettes. "You're right, Al. Sure is cold in here," Jay says. He pulls an afghan over our laps and leans back into the couch's plump pillows. The noises continue, dull thump of a body hitting the floor, bare heels drumming hardwood. Jay puffs out a series of smoke rings and smiles. The noises pause, mists swirl like curdled silence beneath the spruce, then continue: hapless pounding, stifled cries, glass shattering. "Don't have to be back to work till two today," says Jay, snuffing the cigarette. Stretching out on the couch, his head nestled in my lap, he slips into a nap. I stroke his worn, stubbly, beloved face and listen to Rob's fear. Distant, muted. Sharp edges wrapped in gauze.

Masks, just in case Rob ever manages to dislodge his blindfold: black Spandex, with eye- and mouth-holes. We look pretty frightening in them, and, as Jay likes to point out, fright is what this foray into abduction is all about. Our prisoner's yelled and thrashed on and off through Jay's lengthy nap, but the silence prevailing now behind the padlocked back bedroom door indicates that he's worn himself out.

Jay unlocks the door and eases it open. Rob's no longer on the bare mattress where we left him. He's lying on the floor on his side; blindfolded and gagged, bound hand and foot, back against the far wall. His chest's heaving, his head's raised and cocked toward the sound of our entrance. Signs of his struggle scatter the room: mussed throw rugs, a tipped-over chair, a shattered lamp.

"Here's our boy," Jay says sweetly. "Active little shit, aren't you? Broke a lamp, too." He rights the furniture, then strides over and, without a word of warning, kicks Rob in the gut with his steel-toed work boot.

Rob gasps, rolls away, and curses.

"Shut up, boy," Jay snarls, kicking him a second time. Rob curls up into a ball like a sow bug, groaning.

"Jay, don't ..." I begin, but as usual Jay cuts in, this time with "I'll treat him any goddamn way I want." He presses his boot sole into the side of Rob's face, then growls, "Get over here and help me get this little fucker back on the bed."

As soon as we touch Rob, he starts thrashing. He's six feet tall and pretty much all muscle, so he's a load, but Jay and I are both bigger and broader, and soon enough, despite our prisoner's vigorous struggles, we've dumped him onto the bed on his back. He's screaming again, but the sound doesn't seem to please Jay any longer. Rob's disobeying an express order to shut up, and Jay gets very angry when folks don't do what they're told. Pulling out his army dagger, Jay straddles Rob's chest and holds the blade to the straining chords of his throat.

"Okay, kid, that's enough," Jay hisses through gritted teeth. "I've had enough of your noise now. Fun's over. Shut up and keep still, or I'll cut you bad. I've gotten this blade mighty sharp just for you."

Rob's young – early twenties – but he's not stupid. Suddenly he's as unmoving as he was while unconscious, once again that fog-pale statue.

"Good boy," Jay grunts, patting Rob's cheek with the flat of the blade then climbing off him. "Watch him, Al. I'll be right back. Gotta fetch something from the basement."

I wait till I can no longer hear the tromp of Jay's boot soles before I touch Rob. When I grasp his shoulder, he jumps with fright.

"I'm not going to hurt you," I say softly. "I'm going to roll you over onto your side so your hands won't go numb. Okay?"

Rob lies there panting. He's obviously suspicious of my concern after the brutal treatment he just got. But then he nods, and I ease him over.

He doesn't resist as I squeeze his fingers to check his circulation. They're warm, not cold; pink, not purplish. All good signs. Jay's an expert.

"I'll bet you're hungry, right?"

Rob nods.

"I'll feed you once he leaves. You need to use the bathroom, I suspect."

Another wordless affirmative, this one more urgent.

"Okay, once he leaves."

There's a heavy tread on the stairs and the clinking of metal. Jay appears in the door, grim-faced, with an armful of chain.

Afternoon rain's replaced the morning fog. The wind's hard, blowing sheets of it against the glass. We thought about boarding up the windows in this room, but Jay decided that we were too far up the cove for anyone to hear anything as long as we kept Rob gagged. I sit in my chair, masked in black, rocking, sipping more coffee, studying our prisoner's pale body. Jay's ordered me to watch him, and that's a job I'm more than willing to take. I need to feed him in a minute, but first I want to take his youth and loveliness in, this boy I've come to care for despite my better judgment.

34

Rob lies where Jay left him, on the broad bed. His hands are duct-taped behind his back. Several lengths of tape are wrapped around his bare torso and upper arms; another strip of tape secures his elbows together. More tape binds his ankles. The big rubber ball filling his mouth is held in place with another few feet of tape we've wrapped around his head. To make sure he never sees our faces, there's a good bit of tape plastered over his eyes. The latest addition to these safeguards is the short, heavy chain Jay just padlocked around both Rob's neck and the headboard, to insure that he doesn't range off the bed and rearrange the furniture again. In other words, our captive's going nowhere. Jay's seen to that. He has no intention of seeing his revenge short-circuited after waiting so long for it.

The strips of silver-gray tape are wrapped around a physique of remarkable beauty. Rob's nearly naked. He's got nothing on but white briefs, his sweatshirt, running shorts, and tennis shoes having been removed once we had him drugged in the back of the van. This exposure serves several functions. He suffers from the cold, his sense of vulnerability and humiliation is intensified. Best of all, we can see the fine lines of his body, an athletic build shaped by years of gymnastics, as well as weightlifting and jogging the boy's been dedicated to lately in preparation for the police academy. I know all this about him and more, having spied on Rob for a long while now in preparation for his abduction.

His shoulders are very broad, his hips narrow and lean. His chest's hard and curved, like a Roman breastplate, and smooth, save for the brown hairs rimming his small cold-stiff nipples. The upper arms taped to his torso are lined with well-defined muscles that bulge and relax as he flexes them, silently and futilely, against the tape. His belly is flat, ridged, and hairless; a light line of fur begins below his navel and disappears into his underwear. His legs are as muscular as his torso, but, in contrast to his upper body, very, very hairy.

Right now he's lying on his side facing me, but I know – having cut clothes off him, having studied his bound and sleeping form over the hundreds of miles we've driven, having helped Jay lug him up here to this cold room in this remote cove – that the forearms bound behind his back are coated with golden-brown hair, his buttocks are firm, white, smooth, and dimpled with regular athletic exertion, the cleft between is fuzzy with brown fur, and there's an extensive tattoo on his back, deep black dramatic against his skin's white, a ladder of

35

tribal spikes and swirls that begins at his waist, climbs his spine, and covers his upper back like black fire, flickering over his hard lats and curling to an end over his shoulders and the nape of his neck.

His face? Well, that's pretty much concealed by the tape that gags and blindfolds him. But I know his handsome features regardless. I've come to dote on his friendly, trusting blue eyes, his long, straight nose, his thin lips occasionally pursed with thought but more often smiling, his chin occasionally shaved smooth but more often stubbly with a goatee that never quite gets there before he shaves it off again. Right now his chin and jaw are covered with a two-day growth of beard – we took him on Tuesday and today is Thursday – and I rub the roughness of it now before unlocking the chain around his neck, sitting him up on the edge of the bed, and peeling the tape off his mouth.

The ball is very big and his jaw must be very sore: he can't spit it out by himself, though he tries. I curve a finger into the side of his mouth and around the ball, then gently dislodge it. Rob gasps, and a little pool of built-up saliva dribbles over his lips and onto his chin. He works his jaw around a little, and I massage his face till he begins to speak.

The voice I recognize from my careful stalkings. I've sat near him in restaurants and coffee shops for months now, listening to his conversations both face to face and via cell phone. It's youthful and deep, but the usual jovial, macho, hearty tone – boy doing his best to be a man – has been entirely banished by his situation. Now his voice is trembling, a wet quiver. The change both disturbs and delights me. It's thrilling and saddening to see manliness so shaken, so broken down.

"Where am I?" Rob says, licking his lips. Stupidly, abruptly, he tries to stand, but his ankles are taped very tightly together and he almost falls. Wrapping an arm around his shoulders, I force him back down onto the bed.

"Careful, or you'll hurt yourself. If you promise to keep still and quiet, I'll tell you what's up," I say, trying to sound as determined and ruthless as Jay actually is. What I've got to fight back right now is the strong urge to take this scared boy in my arms and comfort him. "I took the gag out to feed you lunch, but you start making noise, the ball gets taped back in, all right?"

Rob nods. I hold him against me, steadying him. Goose-pimpled alabaster. Michelangelo's David wrapped in the tight anachronism of duct tape. He's shaking violently. I reach up and ruffle his short brown buzz-cut as if I were his gymnastics coach encouraging him back onto the rings.

What can I tell him? Nothing solid, for any of those facts would reveal our identities and motives and thus doom him. Ignorant, he has a good chance, after we use him, of being found by authorities in a roadside ditch, bound, gagged, but still alive. Aware of Jay's reasons for revenge, he's guaranteed a shallow grave. So I tell him he'll be kept here for a while yet, I pretend that we're waiting for a ransom, I assure him he won't be hurt if he keeps quiet and does what he's told.

He takes it all pretty well. Small-town athlete, working on a degree in criminal investigations, hoping to follow in his father's law-enforcement footsteps, he's deeply invested in traditional American concepts of manhood, and that means being brave, strong, and stoic in the face of danger. He takes what answers I give without pleading for more information, his voice steadies, his trembling subsides, he chomps on the hot dog and tater tots I hold to his mouth, gulps two glasses of water. When I cut his feet loose and walk him to the bathroom, he thanks me. He doesn't protest when I pull his briefs down – small, fright-limp penis in a fluff of brown hair, muscles of his lean loins shaped like Apollo's lyre – and when I gently push him onto the toilet seat to do some long-delayed business. He doesn't even complain when I wipe his ass, though a deep red flush spreads over his pale features.

This stoicism breaks down at once when I explain what I must do next, now that I have him bare-assed in the bathroom. Jay's ordered me to clean our hostage out in preparation for tonight. It's called an anal spike: a rubber sphere filled with warm water that's squirted up a man's ass to ready him for a good plowing. That's when Rob starts begging – when he realizes that his body is not only going to be kept immobile but also used.

"Please, oh man, please, no ..." His pleas break my heart and stiffen my dick. Panicked, he starts to struggle, staggering blindly against me, fighting my grip. When he begins shouting for help and won't stop, I ball up a washrag, stuff it in his mouth, and promise to fetch Jay's knife if he doesn't submit. When he falls silent, I force him onto his knees, bending him over till his face is pressed against the floor and his ass is angled up. I fill the sphere, lube up the plastic tip, spread his buttocks, and, as gently as possible, push the thin tube up Rob's asshole. He winces and shakes his head; his pleading soaks the washrag. Three times I squirt him full, order him to hold it in, sit him on the toilet, order him to release, before finally cleaning him up with another washrag, lifting him to his feet, and pulling his briefs back on.

I'm about to lead him back to the bedroom when I see the streaks gleaming on his pallid cheeks. Tears are trickling from beneath his tape blindfold. When I pull the washrag out of his mouth, he starts to sob.

"Ah, kid ..." I groan, gripping his shoulder, steadying his blindness. Having something pushed up his ass has made what's to come tonight far too real.

"Please don't!" Rob bawls. "Jesus, man, I have a girlfriend. Don't rape me! Please!"

Pity feels like a jagged rock caught in my windpipe. I can't help but hug him. I wrap my arms around him and let him sob. Standing there in the bright light of the bathroom, anal spike in the sink, lube on the back of the toilet, the nigh-nude young man I've helped to kidnap presses against me, weeping wildly. His face nestles against my shoulder, wetting the wool with his frightened boy's tears. He's still crying as I lead him back to the bedroom, tape his ankles together, and help him onto the mattress. He rolls into a fetal position, sides shaking.

"Kid, stop, please." Now it's my turn to beg. I stroke his shoulder, pat his head awkwardly, say stupid things like "Jay's determined to do this, I can't tell you why, I can't stop him," and, "I'll be here tonight, I'll try to get him to go slow, so it doesn't hurt too bad." If only Jay weren't so strong, if only I weren't so weak, if only Rob's father hadn't answered that APB so long ago. The boy's so handsome and pitiable with tape over his eyes, tears sliding down his stubbled cheeks. My attempts at being ruthless haven't worked too well, and now I give entirely into the tender ache his beauty and helplessness ignite in me. I climb onto the bed, wrap an arm around Rob's waist, snuggle up against him, his heaving back against my chest, and hold him until his tears are done.

As soon as Rob stops crying, he starts to shiver, a full-body quake. The fear I can't do much about. The cold I can, despite what I promised Jay. What he doesn't know.... I rise, cross the room, open the closet, and soon enough, I'm soothing Rob beneath a flannel sheet and a heavy comforter, our heads resting on the same pillow.

"Better?" I ask, hugging him close, warming him up, and Rob whispers, "Yes." I wipe the wet off his cheeks, and Rob whispers, "Thanks." He curls uncomplaining against my chest, acquiescent, accepting my affection, thankful, I suppose, for any kindness he can get.

"I'm going to have to gag you again before he comes home, and I'm going to have to put these blankets away. Understand?"

Rob nods.

"Don't tell him I let you get warm, all right?"

"I get it," Rob says. He's still shivering, so I pull him closer. He feels very, very sweet. Holding him feels like honey tastes. Our bodies fit together as nicely as I've always thought they would, ever since I started following him on Jay's instructions. I'd love to fondle his nipples and cock right now, but that might frighten him, so I refrain. Now that I'm holding him this close, I want inside him as badly as Jay does. I only hope he can't feel my hard-on beneath my pants.

"I'll do my best tonight, but you've got to face facts. Jay's going to do what he wants with you, and neither of us can do anything about it. He's my partner. He's older, stronger, wiser. I owe him a lot. I do what he says. He's been planning your abduction for a long time."

Rob swallows hard but says nothing.

"Try not to cry tonight. Weakness only makes him meaner. Just lie still as best you can and try to keep quiet."

Rob nods. We lie there together listening to rain drip off the eaves and patter the windows. Exhausted from terror and struggle, knowing instinctively that he's safe with me, Rob falls asleep in my arms. I stroke his face, kiss his tattooed shoulders, the fine hairs on the nape of his neck. He's young enough to be my son.

I watch the clock on the wall. Two hours pass. Half an hour before Jay's due home, I wake Rob, push the ball back into his mouth, tape it in, chain his neck to the bed frame, and return the bedclothes and pillow to the closet. I head downstairs to wait for Jay, leaving Rob alone to quake in the cold and the dark.

Jay gets home at dusk from the sawmill. He has lots of buddies around here, and, thanks to them, makes a decent living through odd jobs paid under the table. We have a few bottles of beer with the pizza he picked up. We watch the news. By now, Rob's been reported missing, but we're barely worried. We're states away now, we've left no clues.

It's rain-gusty dark when Jay decides it's time. He turns up the thermostat. He puts out his cigarette, grabs another beer, takes a long swig, and heads up the stairs. I follow. When we pass the bathroom, I stop Jay long enough to point to the anal spike in the sink as proof of my obedience and to grab the tube of lube.

Jay brushes a lock of hair out of his eyes, takes another gulp of beer, and grins at me. I love him so much. I understand why he's doing what he's doing. Rob's father was the cop who wounded Jay, who shot Jay's first lover to death, during that armed robbery attempt. Officer Drake's testimony sent Jay to prison for nearly a decade. He's lost so much, suffered so much. Things need righted. If only Rob weren't so young, so tender, so innocent. Why does suffering have to be a black wind-borne seed sprouting more of the same?

"What's that goo for?" says Jay with a crooked grin, gazing blankly at the lube.

"You know, when you … you know he's got to be a virgin. You'll need lots of … you'll need to …"

Jay's grin broadens with the glee he only displays when someone he hates is soon to be in pain. He's been waiting for this evening for nine years. Rob was thirteen when Jay went to prison and this hate began. "I don't need lube. I've got this," he says, hawking a glob of spittle into his hand. "And if he's too tight, I got this," he says, taking one last swig and holding up the empty beer bottle. Guffawing, he strokes the long neck of brown glass. Handing me the bottle, he reaches into a back pants pocket, pulls out his mask, pulls it over his face, from a front pocket pulls out his key ring, and unlocks the padlock on the bedroom door.

"You still don't get it, baby. I want him to hurt. For his father's sake. Now get your party mask on. I'm ready to celebrate. Fuuuuck, this is gonna be fun!"

I hand the beer bottle back to Jay and pull black Spandex over my face. The door swings open. The hallway light falls across the figure curled up on the bed. Rob's lying on his side, fetal, frightened, facing us. Beneath the tape blindfold, his blue eyes, I know, are full of animal panic, wet and wild.

"Light some candles, Al. I want this to be romantic," Jay says. He sets the beer bottle on the floor by the bed, then sits in the rocking chair long enough to unlace his work boots and tug them off. Standing, he peels off his jeans and boxers, pulls his sweatshirt and undershirt over his head, then from the pile of clothing retrieves his army knife from its sheath on his belt. He stands before me smiling in candlelight, naked save for boot socks and hood, thick erection bobbing and swaying eagerly before him, knife in his right hand. With his muscle-bound build, the thick dark pelt carpeting his chest and belly, the sharp blade, and the black hood, he looks like a magnificent and entirely fearsome executioner. I'm glad that Rob's blindfolded, because if he saw the man about to take him, he'd probably piss the bed. My response to Jay's sinister nakedness is one entirely different from what Rob's might have been; however, my cock grows stiff in my jeans.

"Take it easy on him," I say, gripping Jay's arm, my eyes roaming over his brawny body. Jay's hotter than anyone I've ever known. Every time I see him naked, any doubts I have about him dissolve like this morning's fog, every crazy thing I've done to please him makes sudden sense.

Jay laughs, shakes off my hand, and sits beside Rob on the bed. "Sure is chilly in here, Al, but here's a little man who can warm us up." He strokes the strips of tape over our captive's face and tugs at the chain anchoring his neck to the headboard. "You're a pretty sexy little guy, aren't you? Built like a brick shithouse, that's for sure." Shaking his head admiringly, he runs his hand over Rob's bare pecs, flicking a nipple. "I got something for you, pretty boy. It's been a long time coming." He grips the flesh of Rob's ass and squeezes roughly.

Rob shakes his head and starts begging. Despite the tape and the rubber ball, the intonation makes it clear that what he's murmuring over and over again is "Please." He's still begging and shaking his head as Jay warns, "I won't tolerate any fight, kid. Remember I have a knife. And if you thrash around too much, you'll choke yourself on that chain." He's still begging and shaking his head as Jay rolls him onto his belly and with the tip of the dagger traces the tattooed flames in the small of Rob's back.

"Shut up and keep still. I need to get you naked," says Jay. Rob obeys, save for a fine panting and shivering obviously beyond his control. Slipping the knife between Rob's left thigh and his briefs, Jay slides steel through cloth, severing the waistband, then does the same with the right side. Together, we tug the tatters of cloth off Rob's loins, baring his buttocks.

Our sigh is simultaneous. There's something ritualistic, faintly religious about this. Funny phrases from my church-going childhood run through my mind. *Penetralia*, tabernacle, holy of holies, the rending of the veil.

"Holy shit, you're fine," Jay hisses, stroking Rob's exposed ass with the flat of the blade. "This is going to be even sweeter than I thought."

Jay rests the bare knife on Rob's back, between his taped triceps, in the shallow valley between his shoulder blades, sharp silvery glitter nested in swirls of tattooed black flame. "That's razor sharp, kid, so lie real still now," Jay warns. Straddling Rob's thighs, with a fingertip Jay brushes the cleft between his buttocks, curls of brown fur between smooth curves of white. Bending, he brushes his stubble-rough chin over each trembling cheek. He wets a forefinger in his mouth, slides it between Rob's buttocks, and ranges enthusiastically, as if trying to uncover a buried jewel.

Rob gasps into his gag. Jay grins ... "Ah, here we are!" – and probes for a while. "Ummmmmm, sweet! So sweet and tight!" He smiles at me, licking his lips. I've never seen him happier.

"You need to open up, boy. If you don't, I got a longneck with your butt-hole's name on it."

Rob yelps and jerks as Jay burrows deeper. His shoulders stiffen, the muscles of his arms tense and flex, fighting the tight grip of the duct tape that binds them. I fall to my knees by the bed and fondle Rob's face. "Poor boy," I murmur. His unshaven cheeks are moist again, but he's taking my advice, for this time his weeping is not violent but silent.

"Easy, easy," I whisper, smoothing temples wet with fear-sweat. "Keep quiet. Try to relax." As if relaxation in the face of rape would ever be possible. Rob nods beneath my hand. He gulps, breathes deeply, and falls limp. The mattress beneath his face is darkening with tears.

"Yeah, comfort him, Al. We're like a pair of angels, huh? You be the comforter, I'll be the avenger," Jay growls. He pulls his finger out, spits between Rob's buttocks, and recommences his exploration.

Jay's probing, I'm caressing, Rob's wincing and quietly panting for a good while before Jay's had enough of this reconnoitering. "Got a finger in," Jay announces triumphantly. "A good start." Lifting the dagger off Rob's back, he climbs off the bed, slices the tape off our prisoner's ankles, and nudges his hairy thighs apart. He runs the dull edge of the blade along the fuzzy thicket of Rob's ass-crack, eliciting goose pimples and suppressed sobs.

Smiling, Jay looks up from his knife-play long enough to lob a few orders my way. "Al, baby, fetch a pillow from the closet. I want to prop his butt up at a nice angle. Then grab an old sheet and some towels to roll out beneath him. If he bleeds, I don't want this mattress stained. And get that rope in the bureau's bottom drawer. We'll need to rope his ankles to the bedposts. I want his legs spread nice and wide."

I know what Rob will be feeling. At least some of it. I know that hairy, heavy weight on top of me, Jay's rough chin chafing the back of my neck, his hand clamped over my mouth, his thick cock shoving in and out of me. I'm addicted to that feeling. It's one of the reasons I've done what I've done to stay with Jay. I spread my legs willingly. I open my well-lubed hole and rear back against him. I moan against the sweaty pressure of his palm, begging him to spear me harder. I love Jay's cock up my ass, his hips heaving into me, his growls filling my ears.

Now Rob's pillow-propped, spread and tied, just the way Jay wants him. But Jay's cock is too big and eager, Rob's hole's too tight and terrified. After a few unsuccessful attempts to push his thick dick inside, Jay smears the neck of the beer bottle with spit, just as he'd threatened. Again, I beg him to use lube; again, he refuses.

"Open up, goddamn you," he snarls, sliding the makeshift dildo between Rob's ass cheeks. The bottleneck jabs against resistance. Rob whimpers. Jay lifts the bottle to his mouth and deep-throats it, coating it with more saliva, then tries again. Rob's thighs strain – attempt to thrash his legs, cut short by the ropes binding his feet – his taped hands fumble air, and the bottle slides halfway in. Rob throws his head back, then slumps against the mattress. Jay grins, pushes, and the bottleneck disappears inside. Rob jerks violently, the chain around his neck rattles. Jay pulls the bottle completely out, then slowly pushes in again. Rob's buttocks clench, he emits a long, low groan. Jay begins a rhythm, slow at first, then quickening. Still on my knees by the bed, I stroke Rob's slick forehead. My hands are trembling, my dick is stiff. Rain slams the windowpane in torrents, makes drumming music on the tin roof.

What I have known, groaning beneath Jay during our years together, is consensuality, not fear and pain. My face contorts with ecstasy, not agony, when Jay enters me. This long-awaited night, as the bottle slides in and out, Rob's face, what parts of it the tape isn't concealing, twists with something I've never felt. He's beyond my touch now, my attempts to comfort. His brow is furrowed, his jaw set. Beneath my futile fingers, sweat rolls off his scalp. Each time the bottle's driven home, his fists clench, his head tosses like a storm-swallowed treetop.

"Good boy. All opened up for Daddy," sighs Jay. "And no blood either. So far."

Pulling out the bottle, he lays it on the floor on its side, where it rolls noisily across the wood till a carpet stops its progress. "Hold him down, Al," Jay orders.

A sheet of rain rattles the window. I climb onto the bed, stretch out on my side beside Rob, and drape an arm over his shoulders, my face close to his. "You'll be all right, kid," I say, caressing his wet brow and the tape over his mouth. "Just try to open up, so it won't hurt so much."

"Hmmm mmm," Rob manages, nodding beneath my touch.

"Jay, please be easy on him. I'm begging you. You know we can't take him to the hospital if ..."

"We'll see how it goes," Jay says, winking at me. "Depends on whether he acts like a man or a cry-baby." He kisses our prisoner's right buttock, then his left. He moistens his meat and Rob's hole with another palmful of spit, then rolls on top of him. Rob breathes hard through his nose as his abductor's furry heft crushes him into the bed. Jay nuzzles Rob's neck and cheek, just as he does mine when he's about to ride me, just as tenderly.

"Here we go, kid," he whispers, reaching beneath to position the head of his cock just right. "You gonna keep quiet for me?"

Rob hesitates, then nods. Jay wipes the wet off Rob's cheek, licks tear-salt from his fingers, and whispers, "You gonna take it like a big boy? Gonna stop crying?"

Rob hesitates, then nods. This time it's a firm, determined gesture, suddenly nothing of the quaking adolescent left in his demeanor. "Good boy!" Jay says, all triumph, proud as a doting parent, wrapping his arms tightly around Rob's torso and kissing his buzz-cut.

Rob does what he's been told – no sobs, no screams – as Jay's cock head slowly slides up his ass. Why Jay's taking him so slow, I don't know. I figured he'd shove the whole thing in with one thrust to insure the greatest pain possible. But now, weirdly, Jay seems to have caught some of my compassion. Or maybe he's just rewarding Rob's obedience or show of strength. Whatever it is, I'm relieved. I was expecting screams and blood all evening. Instead, Rob lies there, panting quietly, as Jay's thick dick fills him up. Jay even waits a minute or two to let our captive's hole grow somewhat accustomed to its fleshy invader before he starts a regular thrusting.

Rob hisses, falls silent, grunts, falls silent, gulps, falls silent. The storm outside continues its siege. I kiss Rob's forehead, hugging him to me. Jay sighs and gasps, "Jesus, oh Jesus." The candle flames shiver and leap. Jay rides Rob's pale ass, in and out, in and out. Jay grins over at me, pecks my cheek, grunts, "God damn, Al, you gotta get some of this." The bed creaks like sailboats in a windy harbor. The men upon the bed rock like sailboats on a rough sea, up and down, forward and back, forward and back, and I am a dingy in their wake.

This goes on a long time, a length I gauge by the tightness in my heart, the hard lump in my jeans, and the dwindling height of the candles. Then Rob's pleas start up again. He shakes his head and starts to struggle, twisting his torso within Jay's embrace. Now he's really starting to hurt, his bravery's quickly eroding.

Jay's response to this feeble protest is in character. "Shut up," he mutters, cocking an arm firmly around Rob's neck. "Shut the fuck up." The taped-tight pleading turns to whimpers. The whimpers grade into small choking sounds, soft snorts, as Jay slowly cuts off Rob's breath.

"Jesus, don't kill him," I say.

"Hand me the knife," Jay says. Without thought, I fetch the dagger from the floor where Jay had tossed it. Jay claps one hand over Rob's mouth and presses the blade to his throat.

"By God, you be quiet now, or I'll cut you bad."

One touch of the steel, and Rob's pleading and straining instantly stop. His fight wilts. He goes limp, utterly silent, lean hips bouncing beneath his rapist's thrusts.

Jay's angry now. His speed and rhythm are savage now, all mercy abandoned. Rougher and rougher seas. The headboard starts slamming the wall, the chain links clink.

"You like this, right? Tell me you like it, boy," Jay pants, sliding the knife over Rob's throat.

The tears have started again. I can see their sheen in the candlelight.

"Tell me, boy."

Rob gulps and nods, a very small nod, almost imperceptible, the knowledge of steel cold and sharp against his skin.

"Tell me you want more, boy," Jay pants. He flicks his wrist. Rob yelps. I don't have to see blood to know Jay's cut him.

"Jay!" I'm ready at last to push him off, to wrestle the knife away, to stop this cruelty.

"Just a nick, lover." He gazes up at me, winks again, then returns his attention to the bound and naked body pitching helplessly beneath him.

"Tell me you need more of this. Tell me you can't get enough of being plowed. Tell me you've waited all your life for this. Beg me to fuck you harder." Jay pounds into him, faster and deeper, knife still held to his throat, hand still clamped over his taped mouth.

The headboard clatters, the slave-chain rattles, the bound boy hums. "Mmmm mm MMM. Mmmm mmm MMMM. Mmm mmm MMMM." The musical accents of Rob's gagged moans match my lover's cock-thrusts. A slave's stifled acquiescence – it makes my dick leak. I squeeze Rob's shoulder and tug on my crotch simultaneously. Suddenly I know, as much as I love being Jay's bottom, I've been wanting a beautiful slave like Rob all my life.

"Say, 'Please give me more, Sir.'" Jay's voice is shaky. I can tell he's on the edge. "Say, 'Please come up my hole, Sir.'"

"Mmm mm MMM, mmm mm MMM, mmm mm MMM, mmm mm MMM." It rocks like a melodic phrase, like a baby's cradle.

"Tighten your ass around my dick, boy," Jay growls. "Squeeze my dick dry, boy, or I'll cut you again."

Rob bows his head, lifts his ass, and bucks back against Jay's thrusts. Jay shouts, "Oh, fuck, yeah! Oh, fuck, yeah, that's sweet! Yeah, that's right! Yeah ..." buries his cock to the hilt, stiffens, shudders, and collapses.

* * * * *

They're both asleep. Rob's in his customary fetal position, still bound and gagged, still chained to the bed, passed out from pain, terror, and exhaustion. Jay's curled up beside him, worn out with consummated hatred and delight, smiling in his sleep. One thick arm's sprawled over Rob, his face pressed against Rob's tattooed back. I bend down to kiss Jay's unshaven cheek, to kiss Rob's unshaven chin. I touch the dried blood on his neck, softly, reverently, and on the sheet beneath him, as if the red-brown smears were saints' relics. For a moment, I listen to the continuing batter of rain on the roof. Then I strip, blow out the candles, and fetch blankets from the closet. I cover the sleepers, then slip in beside them, nestling Rob between us. I wrap my arms around Rob, reach over him to stroke Jay's face. I fight off slumber for a good while, lying here, listening to the storm's turmoil, listening to my lovers' soft snores.

Yes, somehow I love them both. Somehow I will save them both. Somehow, through some miracle not yet comprehended or conceived, I will save us all.

THE COLONY
Logan Zachary

Driving down one of the back roads of South Dakota, my car decided to stop. Rich farm lands surrounded me. The fields were full of corn and soy beans, dark green for mid-July.

No traffic passed by. I flipped open my cell phone. No reception. Where was I? Images of *Children of the Corn* came to mind and I quickly brushed them aside.

I knew I passed a farmhouse a few miles back, but this was where "the colony" lived. I wasn't familiar with how they differed from the Amish or the Mennonites, but their German ancestry and respect for the Bible and living in a simpler time was their trademark.

The women sewed all their clothes, and they wore dresses right out of *Little House on the Prairie*, but these dresses seemed more severe. Black and dark blue with their hair pulled back into a tight bun with hair pins underneath a small black cap.

I stood in the center of the road and listened.

Nothing.

No cars, no traffic, no farm equipment.

I was alone.

I decided to wait because of the heat. Someone would be along in a while, and then I'd get help.

A half hour passed and the prairie winds blew. The Dakotas were famous for their wind.

Something rustled behind me in the corn, but it was probably only the wind. The feeling of being watching prickled at my neck, and I turned to look over my shoulder. A flash of blue caught my eye, but then it was gone.

The wind was playing tricks on me, or so I thought because a young man walked out of the corn and approached me.

"Your vehicle. Not working?" a thick German accent colored his words. His speech pattern was slow and deliberate.

"I'm not sure what's wrong."

"My father, he's a good mechanic. He can fix anything."

"These new cars have computer chips in them; no one can fix them anymore, except the dealership."

The boy tilted his head from side to side, trying to understand my words. Finally, he said, "Come with me." He motioned through the corn.

"I can wait here. I don't want to bother you."

"No trouble, it's almost lunch time. Come. Eat." I stood my ground. "It is not far. Come. I show you." He motioned for me to follow.

I was hungry, and he was being polite to offer food. How could I refuse? I walked over to him and entered the rows of corn. They were shoulder height and slapped at my face. Being five-foot-seven wasn't a bonus here.

The boy turned and hurried through the field. I tried to keep up, but his feet knew the land, while mine fumbled along.

The corn opened up unto what could only be considered a compound. Buildings nestled together. Large ones like community spaces, while smaller ones outlined the area, appearing to be private family homes.

"We all eat together. Come." He motioned toward a long building with many windows.

Long tables were filled with young and old alike. All the men wore the same thing, black slacks and a blue shirt. The older men had beards, but no moustaches, while the younger men were clean shaven.

Suspenders held up their pants along with a brown leather belt. No one wore sneakers or tennis shoes. All wore black boots that shined.

The women served the men. They all wore aprons over their clothes. It looked like a plain black dress underneath and a blue printed sackcloth dress over that. All their hair was neatly combed, pulled up under the small black cap.

"My name is Joshua Yoder, come sit over with my family."

I followed him to the long table and joined them.

Joshua spoke rapidly in German and motioned to me. His father nodded and motioned for me to sit.

Simple food filled the metal plate in front of me. A thick slice of bread with real butter rested next to a rich soup, which steamed from the bowl. A glass of lemonade was poured for me.

Everything smelled so good. I cleaned my plate in no time. After a second glass of lemonade, I felt sleepy. I could hardly keep my eyes open, slowly they closed and my head rested on the table.

When I awoke, I found my arms and legs were tied to the bed. A woolen blanket covered me in the darkened room. The bed was soft and a faint noise came from the side of the bed. A handsome round faced man rose and came to stand over me. He looked into my eyes and combed my hair back from my face.

"What do you want?" I asked. My head hurt, and I was still groggy, and then I understood, I had been drugged. But why?

"Help yourself to my wallet, I don't have much money, but you can have what's there."

The man smiled and shook his head. "We don't need your money."

I blinked a few times to clear my vision. He had a finely chiseled face and a warm smile.

"So, what do you want?"

"You'll see," he said, and left.

He returned a while later with three other men; the older one, who sat at the table, and two more.

The old man said, "Well, let's see what we got this time."

The other men moved to the bed and started to remove my shoes. They slipped them off and placed them on a chair. My socks came off next, and then my feet started to fight back. "Hey, stop that."

But the men ignored me. One moved to my polo shirt and unbuttoned the one button. His warm hand slid underneath and pulled it up to my neck. His hand trailed across my hairy chest. I could feel my penis start to stir, and I panicked. I bucked my hips and then saw the old man with a large pair of scissors.

"Hold still or I may cut you," he warned. With two cuts at my sleeves, the polo shirt was gone.

The other two men unbuckled my belt and unbuttoned my shorts. One unzipped the zipper and my cock grew to full erection. *This can't be happening to me*, I thought.

Two more cuts and my pants were gone, too. Clad only in a pair of briefs, the coolness of the room descended on me.

The old man nodded to the others. "You may leave. Levi will stay with me."

After the men left, the older man approached the bed with the large shears. He slid the blade along my hip and opened them. The cold metal scratched along my hip and slipped under the waistband. With one snip the side of my underwear pulled back.

One ball was exposed, but most of my erection was still barely covered.

The old man handed the shears to the younger man on the other side of the bed.

He took them and did the same thing to the other side of my briefs. The elastic gave way and my hard-on burst from the underwear. The man slipped them underneath my butt, and I was naked.

He came close with the scissors again and I almost screamed.

Instead, he handed them to the older man. He took them and said, "Inspect him."

The young man's hands grabbed my erection and pulled it down, making it stand straight up. His other hand cupped my balls and rolled them between his fingers. He had a gentle touch, but pleasure was the furthest thing from my mind. He stroked my cock a few times and pinched the tip.

The old man leaned over to get a closer look. He nodded and smiled, and then he pointed down.

Levi knew what he meant. He released my cock, and carefully slipped one finger underneath my balls and along my crease. He found the tight opening and touched it with his thick finger. It pressed at the hole.

I clenched down hard.

He removed his finger, placed it in his mouth, wet it with spit and reached down between my legs again. This time he applied more pressure and slipped inside. He dug in deep, exploring as he went. It found my prostate and he fingered it, letting it roll under his touch. My cock grew harder as a few drops of precum oozed out of the tip.

"Perfect," the old man said.

He pulled his finger out and wiped it on his pants.

"Let's see what we can get from him." The old man left and returned with a small glass bottle.

The younger man took the wide mouthed bottle, opened it, and set it next to my hip. Then he grabbed my cock and started jerking me off.

"Stop that," I said, but the younger man ignored me. He continued his stroking as if milking a cow.

I tossed and turned side to side on the bed, trying to free myself, but the restraints that held my arms and legs refused to budge. Then my body started to betray me. It started to respond to his stroking. My hips humped his hand, and a feeling rose deep inside my balls. My balls drew up along side of my shaft, and the man grabbed the glass jar.

He quickened his pace and soon an eruption burst out of me. He placed the bottle at the tip of my cock and caught my load. He milked my cock, even after it stopped spurting, draining every single drop. He wiped the lip of the bottle on my tip, taking all he could and handed the bottle to the older man.

The old man held the bottle up to the light and smiled. "He'll do nicely."

Levi took out a blanket from a cupboard and covered my naked form. He touched my head, gently, like he was petting a dog, and then both men left.

The night came, and Joshua entered with a candle and a sandwich. "I brought you food."

"I don't need food; I need to get out of here." I pulled on the restraints, but they didn't budge.

"You can't." Joshua set the candle down on the bedside table. He picked up half the sandwich and placed it against my lips.

"I'm not eating. I just want to go home."

"They have plans for you." He pressed the bread into my mouth.

A chunk of meat and bread broke off in my mouth, and I spit it out. "What plans?"

"I heard them talking, but they just told me to make sure you ate." He pushed the sandwich back into my mouth.

I clenched my teeth together and turned my head away from him.

"Suit yourself." He set the sandwich on the table and left.

Levi returned with a young blindfolded woman.

I started to yell.

Levi picked up a rag and stuffed it into my mouth. He took a strip of cloth and tied it around my head.

"Elizabeth, come here." Levi guided her to the bed. He pulled back the blanket, exposing me. He whispered to Elizabeth and she lifted her dress.

Levi helped her up, so she could straddle me.

I felt her naked skin. I felt her sex on my flaccid penis, and my body reacted. I tried to buck her off.

"That's it," Levi said.

Then I screamed in utter frustration.

Levi adjusted her dress and saw that I wasn't inside her. He grabbed my cock and rubbed it. He pushed it toward her vagina, but it refused to rise.

I continued to scream. I chewed on the rag.

Elizabeth understood and slid off me.

I continued to toss and turn and pull against the restraints.

"Sorry, Elizabeth," Levi said and helped her leave the room. At the door, he removed her blindfold and closed the door.

He stood at the door and waited for me to calm down.

I struggled to breathe and started to choke on the gag.

Levi came to the bed and removed it.

"Please let me go," I gasped, trying to catch my breath.

Levi picked up the blanket from the floor and gently covered me. He looked down at me and shook his head.

The candle burned down to a stub and flickered, threatening to go out. The door opened, and Levi returned. He locked the door and approached the bed. "The council met and decided what to do with you."

"I don't understand. What do you want?"

"There aren't enough men in our colony, and we have too many women."

"So," I said.

"We need more children, and too many of us are family."

The words he said chilled me.

'We need you to help us grow."

"I can't," I said.

Levi shook his head. "I saw. The world has changed, and we don't understand your ways."

"So what? You're going to let me go?"

"No," he said.

Fear shot through my body. "You're going to kill me?"

Levi swallowed hard. "Several of the elders suggested that."

My mind raced. Who knew where I was? My car was on the road. But they could move that. My cell phone was gone. My clothes were gone. I was gone.

I closed my eyes.

"I told them that I could help." Levi pulled the blanket down and revealed my naked form. He looked down at my body and knelt by the bed. He reached under the bed, and I tensed.

His hands reached across my body, and he touched my penis. His fingers ran up the length of it.

I shivered at his touch. But my body reacted to his touch, unlike when Elizabeth had been on top of me. Blood filled my cock, and it grew hard and firm. I willed it to stop, but nothing could stop it. His fingers wrapped around my shaft and rubbed up and down the length. His other hand massaged my balls and gently pulled on them, warming them up with his touch.

I held my body rigid and stiff, refusing to comply. I closed my eyes and bit the inside of my cheeks.

Levi continued his work. His hand worked my erection. His hand must have tired, for he stopped for a minute. Then I heard him spit into his hand.

I peeked out from under my eyelids, and then I felt a warm, wet feeling on my cock. His hand worked up and down, up and down. The warmth and the wet made Levi's work easier.

My cock slipped easier through his fingers. The sensation increased, and a moan escaped from my mouth.

Levi heard my response and spit into his hand again. This time he increased his stroke, and it didn't take long. My hips started to buck his hand, and he clamped down hard on my cock. He readied the glass jar and then released my penis.

Pleasure and spasms escaped from me. An orgasm like I've never had exploded out of my body and continued to pulsate again and again.

Levi carefully caught all my fluid in the glass jar and carefully closed the lid. He wiped his hand on a rag, the one that had been in my mouth. He looked down at my cock and wiped it carefully, almost lovingly. He placed the blanket back over me and blew out the candle.

This process repeated four to five times a day for the next week. Joshua fed me, and Levi jacked me off. I pleaded with both of them to release me. "Untie me, let me go. My family misses me." Nothing worked.

One day, Levi was working my cock, and the process was talking more time than usual. He looked down at me and chewed his bottom lip.

I didn't like the expression that came over his face.

He left and returned a little later with a small bowl. He set it on the bed and reached inside. He picked up a handful of pale yellow cream – hand-churned butter.

His hand glistened as he reached between my legs. My cock rose like Pavlov's dog, but his finger brushed my ass. Its tip explored and probed. He wiggled and jiggled it between my clenched cheeks, and found the sensitive spot. His finger teased my hole. He ran rings around the opening and slipped the tip in every time around. Each time, he pressed harder and harder, seeking entrance. The tip of his finger entered me, and he pushed it in to the hilt.

I almost shot then, but Levi was quick. He jacked my cock as he entered my ass with one finger. He tickled my prostate and tapped the gland. His hand jacked my cock, and the scent of hot butter filled the air.

Levi pulled out of me and inserted two fingers this time. That was all it took, and another wave after wave of cum shot out of my cock. I swore I filled the whole glass jar with my load.

Levi smiled. He was enjoying this. He was happy when he could extract a big load from my balls. When he recapped the jar, he gently rubbed my cock and balls with his butter covered hands. He spread some around the tender hole and gentle smoothed it all over.

I lay back with my eyes closed. How long was this going to continue?

And then, I felt Levi's tongue trace the length of my shaft. He started at the base, flicking from one testicle to the other. Then he ran his tongue up. It played on the sensitive area just below the ridge. He then moved up to the head and worked the opening.

His fleshy lips covered the tip as his tongue entered the hole and explored. His mouth opened up and then he swallowed my cock. His mouth ran down my shaft and deep-throated my cock. The scent of hot butter rose in the air.

He worked over my cock and my balls pulled up tight. I shot another load into his mouth. He hungrily sucked the cream and butter down. He sucked harder, draining me of all I had. Then I remembered the glass jar, but I was happy. He took this load all for himself.

"If you kiss me, I can cum faster," I told Levi the next morning.

Levi looked into my eyes and knelt at my side. His hand slipped under the covers as his mouth found mine. His mouth was closed and puckered as he kissed me, but my tongue slipped into his mouth.

He pulled back so suddenly, he fell back on his butt. He looked surprised.

"I love to kiss, but I use my tongue and an open mouth."

Levi slowly approached me and his hand worked over my cock. He held his head back, away from me.

I opened my mouth and licked my lips. "Kiss me," I hissed, "kiss me."

His hand worked my flesh, but his curiosity returned. His mouth came down on mine and my tongue found his.

I tasted him and taught him to kiss.

My tongue worked his, and my cock throbbed, ready to explode. I shot across my stomach and up onto my chest.

Just at that moment, the door opened and Old Man Yoder entered. He saw Levi and what was happening and quickly closed the door and left.

Levi picked up the glass jar and scraped the cum off my chest and belly. He quickly capped the bottle and followed Old Man Yoder.

Joshua returned with a mad expression on his face. He shoved the food into my mouth and left as fast as he could.

I waited an hour, and the door opened, but Levi didn't return. A new man entered with a glass jar. He set it on the bed and pulled down the blanket. He looked at my cock and closed his eyes. He took several deep breaths and reached over. His hand grabbed my cock roughly and pulled on it. Pain shot through me as his hand tried to get me off.

Disgust shown on his face as he worked my penis.

"If you let me, I can do that for you." It felt like some of my skin was being torn from my cock.

The man stopped jacking me off and considered my offer. He took the empty jar with him when he left.

A hand covered my mouth, awakening me from my sleep. I could feel the restraints loosen and one of my arms was free, for the first time in weeks. My other hand was free, and then the hand left my mouth. They went down to my ankles and soon they were free, also.

Shoes were thrust onto my feet and the blanket was wrapped around me. "Get to the road and lay low until a car drives by. Someone will bring you home." Levi was letting me go.

I tried to stand, but after weeks of no use, my legs refused to work. "I can't walk."

"Yes, you can," he said, but by the time we got to the door, he knew my legs wouldn't carry me. He ushered me down out of the building and up the stairs.

I smelled the night breeze and inhaled deeply.

Levi picked me up and carried me through the corn field. The humidity of the night felt good on my body, but the blanket was pulled tightly around me.

The corn disappeared and the open road stood in front of us. We sat at the road side for over an hour, when a truck came into sight.

Levi ran out into the road and flagged him down. He spoke with him and then returned to get me. He gently picked me up over his shoulder and carried me to the truck. He set me inside and turned to leave.

I grabbed his arm. "Please don't leave me."

"I have to go back." He stepped back from the truck, but I refused to let go.

"To what? Take care of me and I'll help you."

He looked into the cornfield and saw a figure step back. He looked at me and jumped into the truck.

A month later, Levi was tied to the bed. Both arms and legs were securely restrained. The blanket was pulled back to reveal his naked body.

"Now, it's my turn to repay you," I said. My hand gently ran down his chest, over his belly, along his treasure trail. "What have we here?" I asked.

"Let me loose," he said struggling against the ropes.

"Not on your life," I said. "It's my turn now." I picked up the butter container and showed him. "Trust me, you'll love this." I licked my lips and moved to his open mouth, and then slowly started down to his erection.

"Welcome home," I said.

THE DIPLOMAT'S SON
Hank Edwards

I. Abduction

Kyle Lassiter opened his eyes to an unsettling darkness. His wrists were tied behind his back with what felt like duct tape and some kind of clothing had been stuffed in his throat before tape had been slapped over his mouth. He tried to move his legs only to find his ankles had also been bound. On the verge of hyperventilating, he worked to slow his breathing and concentrated on staying calm. This was only beginning and as the son of an American diplomat in a highly volatile Latin American country, Kyle had been through enough training to be able to gather his thoughts. He had to stay calm.

He let his senses roam his confines and deduced he was in the trunk of a car traveling at a high rate of speed, undoubtedly the only highway heading in or out of the city. But in which direction was he being taken?

Kyle's breathing accelerated again as he considered the options, and he forced his mind to relax. He needed to stay calm. His father would find him, he would stop at nothing to save him, but what might be done to him in the meantime was anyone's guess.

Completely unbidden, his cock started to harden as thoughts drifted through his mind. He had been living in this country with his family for almost seven years now, since 1974 when he was twenty-one, and he had found there was a painful price to pay if men were discovered to be homosexual. But that didn't mean there weren't some hot-blooded, dark-skinned, uncut men gathering in dark, out of the way bars just waiting to meet a blond, fair-skinned American boy like himself. Kyle had had his share of dick in this country, and he had found he preferred these men to the men he had encountered in America before leaving it behind. These men were passionate and dark with hairy bodies and uncircumcised cocks, their manners were rough and their hands strong as they groped him in dark alleys and dank basement clubs.

The engine slowed, and Kyle shifted position to allow his erection more room. He needed to pay attention to his surroundings, look for a way out, and a hard-on would not help matters. The car turned onto a rough road, and he was bumped along for another few miles until the vehicle came to a halt and the motor shut off. Kyle lay very still, listening for whatever sounds he could pick up. If he could figure out where he had been taken, perhaps he could tip his father to his whereabouts during the standard ransom phone call.

The trunk lid popped open and brilliant sunlight filled the trunk cavity. Kyle let out a cry muffled by his gag and squeezed his eyes shut against the glare. Rough hands grabbed him and hauled him out of the trunk. He was tossed easily over a muscular shoulder and carted off into a house.

After passing through several rooms he was unable to see very clearly, Kyle was dropped into a straight backed wooden chair in the middle of a small, sound-proofed room. He glared up at the towering slab of Latin muscle that had carried him so roughly and blinked to clear the tears from his eyes. *Could it be? No. Why would he of all people abduct him?*

Kyle's abductor loomed above, looking him over with dark, narrowed eyes. After a few moments, the man reached out to abruptly pull the tape off his mouth. Kyle screamed into the rag in his mouth until it, too, was unceremoniously pulled free.

"Diego!" Kyle snapped. "What the fuck are you doing? Are you insane?" Kyle noticed Diego was holding a sweat sock and he felt his cock twitch again. "You used one of your socks for my gag?"

Diego raised a dark eyebrow and shifted his weight. "I had nothing else available."

"You asshole," Kyle said quietly. He wondered if Diego had discovered his foot fetish. He hadn't been as careful as he should have been some nights when he went to the club. Just the thought of those hot, hairy men sitting in the shoe shine chairs wearing their leather boots and nothing else made Kyle's cock once more stand straight up and beg to be released from his pants.

"I think you know that is an untruth." Diego turned and closed the door to the room then faced his captive once more. "You know, of course, that I was instructed by Armando to bring you here."

"'Bring me here'?" Kyle repeated in amazement. "You didn't 'bring me here,' Diego, you knocked me out while I was shopping in the marketplace and then stuffed me in the trunk of your car."

Diego shrugged. "Syntax."

Kyle shook his head then turned to expose his bound arms. "Can you free me up here?"

Diego shook his head. "Not yet." He strode across the room to stand before the chair, his crotch at level with Kyle's suddenly dry mouth. "Armando told me only to bring you here and secure you within this room."

"Diego," Kyle began, trying to keep his eyes away from the sight of the man's bulging crotch. "I'm sure Armando wouldn't want you to hurt me, and this isn't the most comfortable position."

Diego looked down at him, his dark eyes inscrutable beneath his heavy brow. His thick, dark hair was cut short, almost a flat top, and he had grown a neat goatee. Kyle thought back on all the evenings Diego had been to his father's house, acting as Armando's bodyguard. Kyle's father, the American diplomat to this country, had developed a good relationship with Armando Rodriguez, the liberal, democratic leader. Both men had, on more than one occasion, shown up for dinner in white dinner jackets and black bow ties. Kyle had never been able to eat very much during those dinners; his stomach had always crumpled beneath the sexual longing he felt for both men.

Where Armando was more polished in manners and conversation, a true leader who was easy going and articulate with a less muscular build; Diego was tough and silent, his clothes straining to contain his broad chest and arms.

"We have known one another for many years, Kyle Lassiter," Diego said quietly. "Every time I came into your home you always went out of your way to make me feel welcome. You brought me food when I was instructed to wait in the car. You even invited me to swim when Armando discussed politics in your father's study."

Kyle nodded, his eyes trapped by the intensity of Diego's gaze. He remembered each incident, every nuance of Diego's reactions to his overtures of friendship. The man had been uncomfortable, and Kyle had always thought his attentions were proving an immature distraction to Armando's bodyguard. But in truth, perhaps the distraction hadn't been immature at all.

Kyle took a breath and said, "You actually took your shirt off that day I told you to come swimming. I think it was the only time I saw you even partially relaxed in all the years I had known you."

"With you, I am never relaxed," Diego said with a smile. "You make me think of things I should not consider." Diego dropped a hand to his swelling crotch and squeezed the package beneath the straining fabric. "I have finally come to terms with my attraction for you, Kyle. I have wanted you ever since we first met, but I never approached you. I thought you would be disgusted by my attentions."

Kyle did not know what to say. He was sporting a potential railroad spike himself and, kidnapping or no, he was more turned on than he had been in years. "You want me?"

Diego hesitated only a moment, and then snapped, "Shut your fucking American mouth and pay attention." He quickly opened his pants and his long, thick cock sprang free.

Kyle stared at the monster before him, his mouth watering as he pondered how to take it all down his throat. The base of Diego's cock was at least two inches in diameter. The dark-skinned pole extended almost ten inches from the bodyguard's flat, hairy groin and ended in a blunt, uncut tip. The tan head poked out from beneath the folds of dark foreskin, glistening with precum. The man's balls were dark and hung low between his legs, shaved clean of the hair that covered the rest of his body, and Kyle entertained a brief image of Diego carefully shaving the stubble on his sac in the shower each morning.

"Give me that cock," Kyle said quietly.

"Before we get to that, I want you to worship me as you did those lesser men." Diego pulled his polo shirt over his head and Kyle moaned softly at the sight of his hard, hairy body. The man then pulled his pants off over his black, leather boots and stood authoritatively before Kyle. "Lick my boots."

Diego lifted a foot and placed it on Kyle's quivering thigh. Kyle lowered his head and ran his tongue along the leather, savoring the taste. He nipped at the top edges rimmed with sweat where it had rubbed against Diego's sweaty calf. He worked his way around the entire boot, spitting on the toe and then running the saliva over the rest of the boot with his tongue. Diego watched Kyle worship his boot, his cock throbbing, aching to release its load. But he held himself back, could not touch himself for fear of losing control. It wasn't time for that just yet. This man needed to be broken.

"Now the other one," Diego commanded and raised his other foot. Kyle repeated the process, licking the boot clean. At one point he let his tongue slip off the uppermost portion of leather and skim Diego's leg, groaning at the salty taste of his skin.

"No!" Diego shouted immediately. "You do not touch me yet. You touch only the boots. Do you understand?"

Kyle glowered up at him, silent and sullen.

"I asked you a question," Diego stated, his voice lower and more authoritative than before.

"Yes."

"Yes what?"

"Yes, sir," Kyle replied. His cock was cramped painfully inside his jeans. He wanted to pull it out and jerk his load off all over Diego's boots, then lick them clean again.

"Very good." Diego watched as Kyle completed cleaning his boot then lowered his foot to the floor. Looking Kyle in the eye, he asked him, "Do you want to suck my cock?"

"Yes, sir."

"Are you prepared to suck it?"

"Yes, sir." Kyle licked his lips. He had been prepared for this moment for over seven years. "I am anxious to please you, sir."

Diego smiled slightly and nodded. Kyle was catching on. "Very well then." He stepped forward, placing his legs on either side of Kyle's thighs, and slid his cock deep into Kyle's eager mouth. "Oh, yes, that's right. Get the precum out of it first."

Kyle worked on the head of Diego's cock, savoring the taste of the man's precum. He slipped his tongue under the foreskin and ran it around the head buried beneath. Diego groaned and reached down to pull back the skin and fully expose the meaty head of his cock. Kyle wrapped his lips around the sensitive tip, sucking hard on the exposed skin and relishing the grunts Diego produced.

"Now suck my balls," Diego commanded.

Kyle ducked his head and took the man's balls into his mouth, caressing their smooth surface with his tongue. He moaned as Diego lifted one leg and placed it on the back of the chair to allow him better access and he moved from one ball to the other, focusing his mouth on the smooth, hanging sac of skin.

Suddenly, Diego stepped away and moved behind Kyle, reappearing moments later with another chair. He placed this chair beside him, then turned his back on Kyle and placed his foot on the wood seat.

"Eat my ass," Diego instructed and leaned over, reaching back to spread his cheeks wide and reveal his dark, hairy hole. "Get your tongue in there and make me feel it."

Kyle dove into the crack of the man's ass, thrilling at the scratch of Diego's hairy ass cheeks along his smooth face. He worked his tongue deep into Diego's ass and then sucked on the puckered hole. Diego grunted and swore, the sweat running down his back and into the crack of his ass where it was lapped up by Kyle's obedient tongue.

When he could take no more, Diego suddenly straightened up and turned around, his cock jutting out of his large, dark hand like a mahogany baseball bat. He threw back his head and reached down to pull on his balls as they quickly retracted, preparing for his orgasm.

"Open your fucking mouth," Diego ordered, and Kyle quickly obeyed. Just as his cock started to spit its hot, thick load, Diego moved forward and stuffed it down Kyle's throat. The first shot landed on Kyle's face, covering his chin, and the rest filled his mouth then slid down his hungry throat.

Kyle swallowed every drop of the man's load, getting his tongue up under the foreskin again and licking the slick head clean. Diego pumped into his throat for a few moments, his hands tangled in Kyle's blond hair as he bumped his wiry patch of pubic hair up against Kyle's nose.

"I'm not done with you yet," Diego promised. "Do you understand me?"

"Yes, sir," Kyle managed around the man's softening cock.

"Good." Diego stepped back, his cock dropping from Kyle's mouth, and rounded the chair to peel away the tape binding Kyle's arms. "Release your legs and come over here."

Kyle obeyed and stood up, a little wobbly after being tied up for so long, and turned to face Diego. An iron cot with a thin mattress

66

stood against the wall. Diego stood at the foot of the cot, his hard on beginning to replenish itself.

"Take off your clothes," Diego ordered and watched as Kyle stripped. His body was smooth and lean, a swimmer's body, and Diego thought back on all the times he had sat inside the house watching Kyle swim laps. His tight, round ass and big cock packed into the thin material of a white Speedo. Now that cock stood straight up before him, the blond pubic hair surrounding the base sticky with precum. Kyle's dick jutted out seven inches, thick at the base and tapering to a point at the circumcised head. His balls were clean-shaven, and Diego felt his mouth water at the prospect of sucking the smooth sac into his mouth. He stared at the line of precum drooling from the tip of Kyle's cock and felt his stomach twist with nervous anticipation. He wanted to taste that precum so bad, but Kyle must know who was in charge.

"Now, get over here and lie on your back with your feet over your head." Kyle did as instructed, his bare feet lifting up over his head. Diego knelt before him and slowly, tenderly, ran his tongue along the sweaty crack of Kyle's ass and up to his round, hot hole.

"Oh, fuck," Kyle gasped as Diego's trim goatee scratched along the smooth curves of his ass. "Oh, eat my ass."

Diego immediately sat back on his calves, his eyes cold as he glared at Kyle. "You do not tell me what to do, is that understood? You ask if I will do something to you. And the word 'sir' always follows that request. Understood?"

"Yes," Kyle replied. He linked his arms behind his knees to hold his legs up higher.

"Yes, what?"

"Yes, sir. Would you please eat my ass, sir?"

"That's better." Diego bent forward to lick around Kyle's pink hole, his tongue flicking softly over the puckered skin. Occasionally, his bearded chin scratched over the surface of the hole, and Kyle gasped with pleasure.

When Kyle reached for his cock to start stroking himself, Diego snapped, "Do not touch yourself. I have not given you permission to touch yourself."

"Yes, sir." Kyle obediently moved his hand away and relished the feel of Diego's cheeks and tongue against his asshole. He wanted the man's massive cock to plunge into his ass, stretching his hole to its limits as Diego fucked him mercilessly. He wanted to feel the hot friction of that bare, dark-skinned cock pumping up inside him until it released a torrent of cum.

Diego moved up from Kyle's ass to suck on the tender sac of his balls, grazing his stubbly cheek along each thigh and then moving down to brush up against the sensitive perineum. He covered the taut, white skin with his tongue, spitting into Kyle's hole and working one of his fingers inside. He marveled at the contrast of his dark skinned finger sunk deep between Kyle's fair skinned buttocks and ran his mouth and tongue over each firm, round cheek. With his free hand, Diego grabbed Kyle's cock and stroked it in time to the rhythm of his finger fucking.

"Oh, yes sir! Would you please get another finger up my ass, sir?" Kyle said.

Diego worked another finger into Kyle's ass and increased the pace of his fucking and stroking. Kyle bounced his legs back in time with Diego's finger fucking and felt the pressure building up inside his balls. He was going to come soon, and if he didn't ask for permission first this might all stop. And God knew he didn't want it to stop.

"I'm getting ready to come, sir!"

"That's not how you were instructed to speak."

"May I please come, sir?" Kyle groaned, gritting his teeth as he reached critical mass. "Please?"

"All right, you may come on my chest," Diego replied and slid his fingers from Kyle's ass then leaned back to allow the young man to sit up. He kept his hand wrapped around Kyle's cock and used his free hand to pull his balls taut. Diego watched Kyle's tall, pink cock spurt out shot after shot of thick, white spunk.

While the majority of Kyle's load drenched Diego's chest, a few wads flew up to land on his face. He restrained himself from wiping it up and licking his fingers clean, deciding to leave that to Kyle. He would learn not to disobey.

"Oh, my God!" Kyle gasped and fell back against the wall, his body twitching as Diego continued to stroke his dick.

"You did not obey me, Kyle," Diego said softly.

"What?" Kyle sat up, his eyes filled with the fire of defiance. "What do you mean?"

"You did not come on my chest as ordered. You also came on my face." Diego raised his dark eyes. "Lick the cum from my face."

Kyle leaned forward and ran his tongue along Diego's goatee, cleaning the warm come from his chin. He then softly kissed the dimpled chin beneath the hair and slid his mouth to Diego's cheek. His lips grazed the permanent five o'clock shadow of the man's cheek and he felt his cock begin to stiffen once again as he licked up the last few drops of his wayward cum.

Before he could sit back, Diego turned his head and caught Kyle's mouth in a kiss. Their tongues twisted together, and Diego tasted his cum on Kyle's tongue. The kiss became harder and more intense, both men feeling their lust renew as their cocks hardened again. Diego's dick nudged up against Kyle's calf, and the American moaned.

Diego slowly raised himself up and eased Kyle back onto the cot, lifting his legs into the air with his muscular upper arms. Keeping his mouth over Kyle's, Diego reached up to run his fingers through the fresh load of cum Kyle had deposited on his chest. After smearing it over his cock, he reached down and used what was left to lubricate Kyle's greedy, gaping hole. Positioning himself with his cum-slicked cock just touching Kyle's asshole, Diego pushed forward and penetrated him with a slow, even pace, sinking his entire length into him.

"Oh, fuck!" Kyle exclaimed as Diego bore into his asshole. "Fuckin' fuck! Goddammit you are a big motherfucker! Oh, shit!"

Diego began to piston into Kyle's ass, his big cock diving between the tight pale ass cheeks faster and faster. Diego leaned even further forward, his mouth covering Kyle's, pushing into him with his cock and his tongue. Finally, unable to stand it any longer, Diego grunted against Kyle's mouth and shot another load of cum inside the younger man's ass. He slowed his hips, finally coming to a complete stop with his dick buried in Kyle's well-fucked ass.

"Oh, shit," Kyle gasped, his eyes closed, and his face bathed in sweat. He lowered his legs, resting them on Diego's shoulders, and began to stroke his cock. "Sir, will you please leave your cock in my ass until I come?"

"Yes, I will do that." Diego pulled on Kyle's balls and reached up to twist the young man's hard, brown nipples. When Kyle's balls started to pull up, Diego leaned down and took the tip of the man's cock in his mouth. The hot jets of cum that filled his mouth tasted good, and he eagerly gulped down each load. After swallowing the thick, hot fluid, Diego licked the shaft clean as Kyle groaned and thrust his hips up to meet Diego's face.

"Thank you, sir, for sucking me off," Kyle said quietly.

"You're welcome," Diego replied and stood up, turning to gather his clothes. "Now get some rest before Armando returns home."

"What?" Kyle snapped, sitting up and staring at the hairy man before him. "After all that, you're just going to lock me in here like a prisoner?"

"Yes, because that is what you are," Diego snapped. "And, remember how you speak to me from now on!"

"Yes, sir," Kyle mumbled. He got dressed as Diego left the room and slammed the door behind him. Kyle's mind whirled with possible escape plans and the terrifying consequences of each. How the hell was he going to get out of this mess?

II. Armando

Kyle Lassiter paced the confines of his room, his mind whirling from the events of the last few hours. The door was bolted and, more than likely, padlocked. The hinges were on the outside. There was no window and just a couple of hours ago he had been fucked hard and deep by the bodyguard of one of his father's old friends. This kind of shit was never covered when they were preparing diplomat's families for living abroad.

Kyle shook his head to clear out the thoughts of sex and willed his hard-on to go down. He had to try to find a way out of this place. Before Diego, Armando's bodyguard, had begun taking off his clothes, he had said that Armando himself had instructed Diego to bring Kyle to this house. That could only mean that Armando was intending on ransoming Kyle back to his diplomat father for a hefty price to fund his rebellion. Either that or persuade Turner Lassiter on some political agenda item Kyle couldn't conceive of at the moment.

"Fuck," Kyle whispered and sat on the cot he had only hours before been lying across with his legs in the air and a ten-inch cock up his ass. Again his cock started to twitch at the slightest thought of sex, and Kyle again redirected his mind to the more important topic of escape.

Armando had been a high-ranking official in this country when Kyle's father had been appointed diplomat for U.S. relations. Armando and Kyle's father had worked closely together for several years, each earning the other's respect. Armando and Diego had been guests in Kyle's home many times.

After four years, however, the country's ruling party had been overthrown by a military coupe, and a vicious dictator had taken control. This new leader was interested not in building secure, prosperous lives for his fellow countrymen, but rather in taking control of the surrounding countries and expanding his power.

Armando and Diego had fled into the thick jungle, Armando vowing to take back leadership of the country some day and liberate the people. Turner Lassiter had been instructed by the President of the United States to remain in the country and attempt to reason with the new leader, a man by the name of Carlos Santiago. He was a tyrant, known for his public displays of rage and paranoid-driven executions of members of his staff.

The deadbolt of the door slid back with a loud thump and the door was thrown open, causing Kyle to jump. He looked up to find Armando's body outlined in the doorframe. The man paused briefly, his face hidden by shadows as he took stock of his prisoner, then Armando stepped into the room, and Kyle came face to face with the man he had not seen for many years.

Where Diego was big and powerful, Armando was thinner, more wiry. He was more polished than his bodyguard, having spent his life working in politics and dealing with all types of people. His dark hair was swept back from his forehead, touched lightly at the temples with strands of gray. He had grown a thick, trim mustache since Kyle had last seen him, and it became him. The scar he had received at the end of a would-be assassin's blade two decades ago traveled down from the corner of his left eye until it stopped a few inches across from the tip of his nose. His full, generous lips, always Kyle's favorite part of Armando's face, were set into a line of determination, revealing what his dark, shadowed eyes would not.

71

"Kyle Lassiter," Armando said, his voice deep and smooth. The man's familiar accent proved a steadying balm to Kyle's fear.

"Armando, what the hell are you doing?" Kyle asked, struggling to keep his voice even. "This is no way to solve the political issues within your country."

Armando cocked a dark eyebrow and stepped further into the room. Behind him, Kyle could see Diego lurking in the hall, his thick arms folded over his muscular chest. Armando wore khaki-colored linen pants and a loose fitting white shirt that hung open to the middle of his torso, exposing his dark skin and darker chest hair. Kyle had to force himself to keep his eyes on Armando's strong face and off the man's body. He couldn't let his attention wander.

"I see you've kept yourself in shape over the last few years," Armando said quietly, and Kyle felt himself blush. Diego was a purely physical attraction, but Armando had the smooth talk and knowledge of many subjects that sparked Kyle's fascination and fantasies. This fact coupled with his physical presence made Armando a formidable opponent.

"Yes, I guess so. I try." Kyle cleared his throat and asked. "Can I get something to eat? It's been kind of a long morning."

"Of course." Armando turned and gestured for Kyle to precede him into the hall. "I will allow you first to wash up. You may use my personal washroom. Come."

Kyle stepped into the hall, his eyes catching Diego's as he brushed past the bodyguard. He could still feel the thickness of the man's cock as it plunged into his ass, and his own cock twitched at the memory. He mentally cursed himself and fought off the images and sensations as he followed Armando up a flight of stairs and down a long hall. They entered a large, magnificently adorned bedroom complete with a king size bed and several ceiling fans spinning slowly to circulate the air.

"Wow," Kyle said. "For being on the run from the government, you sure are living well."

Armando shrugged and picked a few grapes from a bowl of fruit on a nearby table. "I have several generous, wealthy contacts. The wash room is through those doors. Please bathe for as long as you wish."

Kyle entered the bathroom and stopped. It was large and filled with sunlight. To one side stood a deep marble tub and off in the corner was a walk-in shower with five directional showerheads. Kyle shed his clothes and stepped into the shower, turning on the water and basking in the cool flow as it washed off the dirt and dried cum. The shower was so deep there was no need for a door, so he didn't realize Armando was standing beside him until he turned and came face to face with the man.

Kyle jumped and cried out then laughed in embarrassment. "Armando! What the fuck are you doing?"

"I figured we could conserve water." Armando shrugged and Kyle noticed the man had removed his clothes and now wore only a white towel around his waist. "I needed to shower as well."

Armando dropped the towel and stood nude just outside the shower. Kyle's cock sprang to life as he looked the man over. Armando's dark skin glistened from the mist of the shower. His body was covered with a layer of dark hair that spread over his forearms, chest, and stomach before it blossomed into a thick patch of pubic hair at his groin. His cock was at half-mast, about five inches long so far, and thick. It wasn't as thick as Diego's, but it was uncut and waiting for some attention.

"I think you might enjoy it, Kyle," Armando said and that was all Kyle needed.

"I think you're right." He stepped up and set his mouth over Armando's beautiful lips, slipping his tongue between them. They kissed hungrily for several minutes, both men letting their hands wander over the other's body to explore crevices and muscles they had been fantasizing about for years. Armando's hands were large and strong, flecked with dark hair across the backs and knuckles, and from the feel of the muscles in his arms, he had been working out more regularly. Kyle raised the man's arm and slid his face down to bury his mouth and tongue in Armando's hairy, sweat soaked armpit. He ran his tongue over the soft, furry pit and licked up every drop of sweat he could find.

Armando groaned and raised his opposite arm, giving Kyle free access to that armpit as well. As Kyle was tongue-bathing his armpit, Armando reached down and grabbed both of their hard cocks in his large, dark hand and rubbed them together. The water sprayed over them as Kyle moved up to kiss Armando once again, allowing Armando to taste his own sweat.

Grabbing a bar of soap, Armando lathered Kyle's body, washing him head to toe. He knelt before the smooth-skinned, blond American and ran his hands around, under and over the pale cock standing straight up before him. Keeping the palm of his hand soaped up, Armando stroked Kyle's cock, increasing the speed as Kyle's entire body stiffened.

"Oh, fuck!" Kyle groaned. "I'm going to come, Armando. I'm going to shoot."

Armando leaned forward and let Kyle's load cover his face. Come clung to his mustache and eyebrows as Kyle released shot after shot of thick, hot spunk.

After he had spent his load, Armando turned Kyle's body into the spray and rinsed away the soap. Still kneeling before him, the cum dripping slowly down his face, Armando leaned forward and sucked Kyle's slowly deflating cock. He drank up the last remaining drops of cum from the head of Kyle's dick then expertly sucked him back into tumescence.

Standing up, Armando stepped up close to Kyle's sleek, wet body and took each of their cocks in his hands. He pressed the head of Kyle's cock against his own then slowly eased his dark foreskin up over Kyle's hard rod.

"Damn, Armando," Kyle said as he watched his cock disappear beneath the man's foreskin. "That is fucking hot."

"Fuck it like you would my ass," Armando instructed.

"I've been dreaming of fucking that ass for a long time now," Kyle replied and began to move his hips slowly forward and back. His cock slid in and out of Armando's foreskin and both men moaned at the sensations.

As he fucked Armando's cock, Kyle got a handful of lather going and ran his soapy hands over the man before him. He slid slick fingers into Armando's ass, exploring this previously unknown territory, and then lathered up the man's balls and groin.

After Armando released Kyle's cock from his foreskin, they rinsed one another clean and shut off the water to step out into the bathroom. Kyle immediately dropped to his knees on the bathmat to take Armando's long, uncut cock into his mouth. He slid his tongue beneath the foreskin and ran it around the glistening head beneath, tasting the precum he had fantasized about for so many years. Moving lower, Kyle massaged Armando's hairy balls with his tongue, sucking them each into his mouth and running his tongue over them. As he worked on Armando's balls, Kyle ran his hand along Armando's flat, hairy stomach and turned his blue eyes up to find Armando gazing down at him with a lazy, lustful look.

"Turn around," Kyle instructed. "I want to get at that ass of yours."

Armando turned and bent at the waist, his hands gripping his ankles to allow Kyle to get to his eager hole. He felt Kyle's tongue slide slowly along the crack of his ass and closed his eyes, waiting for the moment he got to the target. He could feel the hair on the cheeks of his ass scratching along Kyle's smooth face, and his cock stiffened even more. His load was building up; he would need to get some release soon.

Armando groaned at the touch of Kyle's hot tongue as it speared his twitching hole. Kyle's hands gripped Armando's cheeks and spread them wide, allowing him to get his mouth over the dark, puckered muscle that twitched at his touch. He darted his tongue in and out of Armando's ass, getting it as far up inside the man as he could. Just as he did in the shower, Kyle slid one, two, then three fingers up inside Armando's hole, working them in and out with a slowly building rhythm.

"That is enough," Armando suddenly said, his face red from hanging down by his knees for so long. "I want you inside of me. Now."

Kyle stood up and positioned himself behind Armando, holding his cock steady as he leaned forward and slid into his ass. Armando groaned loudly and straightened up quickly only to bend at the waist again almost immediately. Kyle got his dick part of the way up Armando's ass before he felt the man's muscles tighten up. Pulling the entire length back out, he moved forward again and this time buried his cock completely inside him.

"Oh, shit," Armando said with a grunt. "Get that cock up in there."

"You like that cock up your ass, don't you?" Kyle said through gritted teeth, moving his hips in rhythm to fuck Armando's ass faster.

"Oh, yes," Armando moaned. "Oh, get it up in there. Fuck that ass!"

Kyle reached up and put his hands on Armando's shoulders, feeling the muscles bunch from the exertion of his fucking as he pounded into Armando's hole. He could feel himself getting close again but fought to hold it back until Armando had a chance to come.

"I'm coming," Armando declared and stood up, his right hand working his cock as his left hand pulled on his dark, hairy balls. "Oh, fuck!" He bent his knees and shot load after load of spunk onto the dark tiled floor of the bathroom. Kyle watched Armando's cum shots in the mirror and finally let himself go, blasting his load within Armando's tight, hot hole.

Kyle slowly pulled his cock out of Armando's ass and wiped it off on a nearby towel. Armando turned to him and kissed him softly on the mouth then pulled him back into the shower to wash up once again.

After the shower, Kyle dressed in some of Armando's clothes that had been left on the bed for him. He walked downstairs, his mind relaxed and unconcerned with his current predicament. Looking around until he found the dining room, Kyle stopped in the doorway. Two men wearing army fatigues and holding automatic weapons surrounded Armando. Diego was seated nearby, the set of his jaw conveying his anger. He also was being held at gunpoint.

As Kyle entered the room, both Diego and Armando gave him panicked looks that screamed for him to escape. When he turned to flee; however, Kyle ran into the chest of a large, heavily muscled man wearing an army issue green T-shirt and fatigue pants. Before he had a chance to see the man's face, Kyle was knocked unconscious and sank down into darkness.

III. Prisoner

Kyle paced the confines of his stone walled cell. He had awakened, nude, inside this windowless, damp room at least two days before. It was difficult to gauge time when there was no way to see outside. A single light bulb hanging high out of reach illuminated the room around him, exposing an old, cracked toilet, dirty sink, iron cot with a thin mattress and rough wool blanket, and a thick metal door. It was through this door that Kyle's meals were delivered three times a day. Not the best in cuisine, but at least he was being fed. Although, why he was being held prisoner and by whom he had no earthly clue.

The door swung open behind him, and Kyle jumped, spinning around so quickly he became dizzy and sank to the floor with a groan, his head still aching from the blow he had received two days prior. Strong hands gripped him beneath his arms and lifted him from the floor, dragging him across the cell and to the cot. As he lay back on the coarse blanket, Kyle blinked up into the olive-skinned face of a beautiful young man.

He had black, wavy hair, eyes dark as charcoal, and full, soft lips surrounded by a two-day growth of beard. This was one of the two guards that brought him food. Kyle had noticed this guard watching him sitting nude on the cot while he had delivered his food, and he had tried to befriend the man. This guard was nicer and more attractive than the other. He would smile, revealing two deep dimples as he watched Kyle move back and forth across his cell, his dark, Latin eyes roaming his naked limbs and torso.

"Thank you," Kyle said and sat up slowly. "I still get dizzy when I move too fast."

The young man shrugged and rattled off a long, rambling burst of Spanish. Kyle shook his head, stunned. This was the first time either of the guards had spoken to him.

"You need to go slower," he said. "I know Spanish, but not that well."

"I am Berto, a member of the resistance army," the man said, enunciating his words carefully and kneeling by the cot. "We are fighting to regain our country and lead it into prosperity."

"Of course," Kyle muttered. "You and everyone else I've met in the last few days." He swung his legs over the edge of the cot and leaned forward, finding himself eye to eye with Berto. He glanced down at the leather military boots tied tightly on Berto's feet, green fatigue pants tucked into the tops.

As Kyle gazed at Berto's feet, Berto's eyes roamed his nude body, taking in Kyle's firm stomach, strong legs and arms, and stopping for a long, lustful moment on his cock. As Kyle realized where Berto's attention was focused, he felt his cock twitch and begin to harden with a will of its own.

"You like Latin men?" Berto asked with a sexy grin.

"Yeah, but usually not while I'm being held prisoner," Kyle replied.

Berto shrugged. "I did not put you in here. The leader did. I am merely watching and taking care of you."

Whoever "the leader" was, Kyle thought sullenly. From the looks of it, they were not in league with Armando's group, so Kyle did not understand how he had fallen under their control. *How many freaking groups of rebels were struggling to take control of this country?*

No matter how he tried to figure his predicament out and distract himself from thoughts of sex, Kyle felt his cock grow fully aroused and point straight out from his groin. It obviously had thoughts far and away from escape or understanding his dilemma. How he had the energy for a hard-on after being fucked by Diego and then fucking Armando, not to mention being knocked out cold and held in a damp cell for several days, Kyle didn't know. But obviously his cock was ready, willing, and more than able for a repeat performance.

"You want to suck my dick?" Berto stood up and began to shed his clothes, revealing a muscular torso covered with a layer of dark hair that gathered in a thick thatch between his solid pecs to run along his flat stomach and down to his groin. As Berto unbuckled his belt, Kyle nodded to the door.

"Aren't you afraid someone will come in?"

"They have all gone to get supplies. They will not be back for a long time."

Kyle thought about this, weighing his options. He could try to overpower Berto, take his clothes and escape. Although he did not know where in the country he was, or where in the compound, it would be preferable to being locked up nude in this damp cell. But then he turned to watch as Berto exposed his long, thick, uncut cock, and Kyle forgot all about trying to escape. Berto's cock was bigger even than Diego's, at least twelve inches long. The tan head poked out of the wrinkled sheath of foreskin, precum already gathering at the piss slit.

"You like?" Berto asked proudly. He obviously received many compliments on his tool.

"I like," Kyle replied and leaned forward to swallow as much of Berto's cock as he could. He gagged on the length, backed off to catch his breath, and then leaned forward again, gulping it down. Berto grabbed the back of Kyle's head and began to hump his mouth, pushing his hot, thick cock deep into Kyle's throat with each thrust.

"Oh, that feels good. Suck my cock," Berto moaned. He suddenly pulled his cock out of Kyle's mouth and pulled him up off the cot. Berto pulled the cot away from the wall and gently pushed Kyle back down to lie across it. Kyle flashed back to Diego commanding him to lie across the cot in Armando's house just before fucking his ass hard and deep and felt his ass twitch in anticipation.

Raising his head, he watched Berto strip completely and quietly moaned when the guard pulled his boots back on after removing his pants. Berto tied the long laces then moved around the cot so he was standing above Kyle's head. The guard leaned over into a sixty-nine position and plunged his massive cock down into Kyle's throat as he swallowed Kyle's own oozing cock.

Berto sucked Kyle's dick fiercely, hungrily pumping his mouth and fist along the shaft. Kyle choked down the entire length of Berto's foot long cock, his throat filling with its girth. He couldn't begin to imagine how much cum Berto would be able to spew down his throat, but he was eager to find out.

Berto's finger probed Kyle's hot, damp hole, enticing him to raise his legs and clamp them around Berto's back. He felt two then three fingers explore his anus and groaned around the cock in his throat.

"You like when I suck and fuck you?" Berto asked, raising his face from Kyle's cock but keeping up a steady rhythm along the glistening shaft.

"Uh huh," Kyle managed to grunt. He disengaged himself from Berto's cock, stroking him as he raised his head to look down at the beautiful man sucking his cock. "Eat that cock. Yeah, suck it. Get your fingers up my ass. Oh, yeah, that's it. Fuck that ass."

Kyle pistoned his fist along Berto's cock and shifted position to suck on the man's big, hairy balls. He savored the taste of sweat as he swallowed first one then the other. Running his tongue along them, Kyle drank up Berto's musk and continued licking him up along his perineum to his hot, hairy hole.

Out of the corner of his eye, Kyle saw Berto raise a booted foot to the edge of the bed. Keeping his hand on Berto's cock, he leaned over and began licking the dusty leather. He closed his eyes and worshipped Berto's boot with his tongue.

"You like boots?" Berto asked.

"Very much," Kyle moaned back.

"Then kneel at my feet and lick them." Berto stood up and moved around the cot to sit on the edge. Kyle knelt on the floor and leaned down to lick the dark, worn leather. He slid his tongue along the sweat-stained edges around Berto's muscular calves then moved up and licked the dark, hairy skin itself. Berto watched with half-lidded eyes as Kyle worshipped his feet, his right fist slowly stroking his gigantic cock.

Kyle had been jerking himself the entire time and felt his balls tighten in preparation for orgasm. "Uh, I'm going to come," he moaned as he moved to Berto's other foot.

"On my boots," Berto commanded.

Kyle straightened up and grunted through each burst of his climax. His cum splattered over Berto's boots and calves, the thick white fluid standing out against the black leather and olive skin.

"Now lick them clean," Berto instructed, and Kyle eagerly set to work. He licked up the cooling cum, relishing the mix of tastes and smells. As he was finishing the job, he heard Berto groan.

"Oh, I'm coming," Berto gasped. "Eat my cum. Suck it down."

Kyle sat up and opened his mouth, catching the first shot of Berto's cum on his tongue as the man aimed his cock down toward his face. He missed the second shot, getting it instead on his cheek, but managed to suck in Berto's massive cock for the final spurts of his orgasm, guzzling down his cum and draining every last bit from his amazing dick.

"You like how Berto tastes?" the man asked quietly, his dark eyes smoldering.

Kyle nodded, still sucking the last of Berto's juices from his dick.

"How about I fill you up from the other end now, hmm? Would you like that?" Berto asked. He wiped up the cum on Kyle's face and raised his fingers to his mouth to suck them clean.

"I don't know if I can take all of this," Kyle said, reaching up to tug on Berto's dick. "But I can try."

Berto stood and helped Kyle up, leading him across the room to the sink and toilet. Berto sat on the toilet and turned Kyle around to face the opposite side of the room. The guard then pushed on Kyle's shoulders until he bent at the waist with his ass in Berto's face. Berto leaned in and licked Kyle's asshole, spitting into the crack of his ass and using his tongue to spread the saliva around and into his hole.

"Oh, damn," Kyle groaned. "That feels good, Berto. Get your tongue and fingers in there. Oh, yeah, that's it."

Berto slipped a finger from each hand into Kyle's hole, stretching the sphincter muscle as wide as possible. He then slid his tongue as far up inside Kyle as he could, spearing the man with his tongue as he spat wad after wad of hot, slick spit into him.

"Now, sit on my cock," Berto instructed. Kyle turned to face him, straddling the guard's muscular legs, and then lowered himself slowly onto the rigid dick.

Closing his eyes, Kyle carefully impaled himself on Berto's cock. He eased himself up and down the dark, thick prick, feeling it stretch him further than Diego had just a day or two before. He had never had a cock this big up his ass.

"You're so fucking huge," Kyle gasped. "I don't know if I can take it all."

"Try," Berto said and raised his hips slightly to pump a little deeper inside Kyle.

"Oh, God," Kyle groaned. "You're so damn big. Shit!" He felt his thighs quiver as he raised and lowered himself along Berto's pole, his ass swallowing more and more of the massive cock with each downward thrust. Finally, Kyle felt Berto's pubic hair brush against his balls and forced himself down further still. He felt his anus widen almost to the point of tearing his rectal muscles apart deep within his body as he took in the final inch of Berto's hot, throbbing meat.

"Fuck!" Kyle shouted. "I can't believe I took all of you."

"I can," Berto said and pulled him forward for a kiss, sucking Kyle's tongue into his mouth. Berto pumped his hips as Kyle balanced above him, sucking the guard's cock with his ass. Kyle tightened the muscles in his rectum, and Berto groaned into his mouth, moving his hips faster and faster as he plowed into Kyle's ass. Berto wrapped a large, hairy hand around Kyle's cock and stroked him, pounding his fist along the shaft in time to the thrusting of his hips.

Before Kyle could come, Berto slowed his hips and pulled his long dick out of Kyle's ass. "Stand up," Berto instructed. "I want to fuck you from behind."

Kyle stood up, his legs a little shaky, and turned to face the sink. Berto stood behind him and ran his olive-skinned hands over his back and chest. Kyle moaned and closed his eyes, leaning forward and thrusting his butt back. In a moment, he felt the pressure of Berto's thick cock as the head butted up against his gaping hole. The big cock slid completely inside him on the first thrust, piercing him as he grunted and winced.

Gripping the metal sink with his fingers, Kyle lowered his head and opened his eyes. He could see Berto's leather boots between his own spread feet, and he felt himself grow even harder. Reaching down, Kyle stroked his cock, his eyes glued to those leather boots placed next to his bare feet. As Kyle jerked himself off, Berto's prick speared into him with an increasing intensity until he heard the guard's now familiar grunting.

"I'm coming," Kyle gasped. He felt his orgasm blast up from his balls and through his cock, each shot sending shivers up his spine. His thick cum shot down onto the floor, landing in thick puddles on the stones beneath the sink.

"Oh, God. Uh, uh, uh!" Kyle began to grunt with each of Berto's thrusts and felt himself building up to yet another orgasm. He had only experienced a double orgasm once before, many years ago.

"Dammit, I'm coming again." Kyle leaned forward and fired off another round of cum, again soaking the floor and this time part of the sink with his hot spunk.

"Oh, yes," Berto moaned and leaned his head back. Kyle let his head drop down and watched Berto's boots as he tried to catch his breath, all the while the guard pounded his ass faster and faster. "I'm coming!" Berto cried. "I'm coming!"

Kyle tightened his ass as much as possible after the fucking he'd been given and rode the man's cock, feeling him swell deep inside him and shoot a full load of hot cum. He knew it would be a while before his ass felt the same, but it had been worth it.

Kyle winced as Berto eased himself out of his red, stretched asshole. His sphincter felt as if it would remain gaping open and never close up again. He was going to need to sleep for a few hours to recover from this fucking.

Kyle staggered back to the cot and fell across the coarse blanket. He was bathed in sweat and exhausted. He wanted nothing more than a shower and some clothes.

"Do you wish to clean up?" Berto asked as he got dressed.

Kyle smiled with his eyes closed. "That would be Heaven."

"Come with me." Berto led him out of the cell and down a hall to a community shower area with faucets and showerheads placed every five feet around a large room. The walls were stone, just like his cell, and oozed dampness and a musty smell.

Kyle turned on the nearest shower and stood beneath the hot, prickling spray as Berto stood nearby and watched. He could feel Berto's cum dribbling out of his ass and down along his thighs, and he felt a tiny flicker of arousal course through him. Taking his time, he spent several minutes lathering himself, gingerly cleaning his ass and carefully slipping his soapy fingers up inside himself.

"You want Berto's cock up inside you again?" Berto asked with a low growl. His hand was clutching the unmistakable bulge of his erection in his pants.

"I don't think I could handle it again today," Kyle replied honestly even as his cock began to harden at the memory. "But sometime again soon."

"Very soon," Berto said with a smile. The sound of a truck came to them, and Berto jumped. "Hurry! Dry off and get back to your cell. They have returned."

Kyle grabbed a towel and walked quickly back along the hall to his cell where he stepped inside. Turning, he was about to ask Berto who had returned when the door was slammed in his face.

Drying himself off, Kyle wrapped up in the blanket and lay back on the cot, falling asleep immediately. When he awoke several hours later, a tray of food, several more blankets, and a pile of army fatigues waited just inside the door.

As he got dressed and gulped down bites of food, Kyle contemplated his situation. One group of rebels had abducted him,

Armando and Diego, and then a second, unknown group had taken him away from them. *And for what purpose?* He shook his head and finished up the food, putting two bananas aside for later. It was best to be prepared and ration his food.

While he was organizing the new blankets on his cot, he heard a key in the lock of the door. Turning, Kyle waited as the door swung open and his latest captor strode in, followed by Berto.

"Ah, Mr. Lassiter," the man said in Spanish. "How good of you to join us."

Kyle gasped as he recognized the older man standing before him in military fatigues. Things had just gone from bad to dangerous.

IV. Rescue and Return

Kyle stared at the man before him and tried to get his breath back. It was Domingo. He had been a powerful general leading the nation's army back before Kyle's father, had arrived as the U.S. ambassador. Domingo, however, had been removed from power, and it was rumored, had convinced a great number of his troops to leave the army and join him in the jungles to plan their resurgence.

"Mr. Lassiter," the man said in a deep, rich voice. He was dark-complexioned, and his black eyes shone with an almost religious fervor. A dark goatee surrounded his thin lips; some of the whiskers had gone gray and lent him a mature look. Kyle had learned about the man in his culture class and knew Domingo was in his fifties. "I'm glad we finally get a chance to meet."

"Hello, sir," Kyle managed to say through his suddenly dry mouth. "I've heard a lot about you."

Domingo leveled a cool gaze at him.

"I'm sure you have. Now thanks to your interfering father I'm stuck out here in the jungles stealing food and trying to keep my troops together." The man paced the room, and Kyle took the time to assess his body. He was in excellent shape for his age. The tight-fitting olive green T-shirt hugged his well-developed chest and arms as well as his hard stomach. His loose-fitting fatigues could not disguise the hard, round cheeks of his ass as he stepped back and forth across Kyle's cell. Most importantly, though, his feet were laced tightly inside what looked like size-thirteen military boots. Kyle dragged his eyes away from the sight of Domingo's boots and tried to follow what the man was saying. He was worked up, however, and the Spanish words were bursting out of him faster than Kyle could translate.

After finishing his tirade, Domingo nodded to Kyle, said in a cryptic tone, "We'll be meeting again, Mr. Lassiter," and turned on his heel to leave. Berto winked at Kyle and left as well, his sly smile a promise of more ass-splitting sex to come.

A few minutes after the general's departure, Kyle was thrown to the floor by a deep explosion. He got to his feet and steadied himself against the wall, listening as men shouted in Spanish and gunshots erupted from the hallway just outside his door. He looked around for a place to hide, but the cell was too small and open. He was trapped.

A key turned in the lock on his door and it was flung open. Berto stood there, his dark eyes alert as he held out a hand to Kyle. His other hand gripped an automatic weapon. "Come with me. I will get you to them."

"To who?" Kyle asked, staying where he was.

"No time. Come with me. Now!" Berto demanded, and Kyle took his hand. He was led through many corridors, passing men running with weapons and hearing the exchange of gunfire all around him. He kept his head down and his eyes on the black leather of Berto's boots, following as the man led him through the maze of hallways and out a small, steel door to the wilds of a hot, humid patch of jungle.

"Where are we going?" Kyle demanded and was brought up short by the appearance of a large, muscular American soldier. He towered over them, at least six and a half feet tall, and wore a khaki T-shirt stained with sweat under his solid arms and around his pecs. The soldier's brilliant blue eyes acknowledged Berto, then turned to Kyle as he reached out and grabbed Kyle's biceps. "Mr. Lassiter, I'm here to take you home."

Kyle glanced at Berto who grinned and winked. "I'll see you again soon. We have much more to accomplish." And he was gone, vanished into the deep green of the jungle.

"There's a truck back through here." The American pulled Kyle through the tangle of jungle and they crawled up into the back of the truck, moving away from the opening to the rear where they could sit side by side in the dark. Kyle fought to catch his breath and noticed the soldier wasn't even breathing heavy.

"What's your name?"

"Gunderson, sir."

"Sir? Please, call me Kyle."

Gunderson glanced down at him, and Kyle noticed those bright blue eyes linger on his crotch. His cock immediately responded, jumping to attention and straining against its material prison. Gunderson returned his eyes to the truck opening but dropped a hand to his lap, pressing his wide, sweaty palm against the crotch of his pants.

"Any way I can thank you for the rescue, Gunderson?" Kyle asked in a low voice.

"I can think of a couple ways you could thank me, sir," Gunderson replied. He swiftly opened his pants and hauled out a long, thick, uncut piece of meat. Stroking it to an even longer length, at least eight or nine inches, Gunderson smiled down at Kyle. "I've been awfully lonely out here in the jungle."

"Say no more, Gunderson." Kyle leaned down and swallowed the man's cock to the hilt. He gagged as the tip brushed the back of his throat but held his ground. He inched his lips down further along the shaft until his nose was buried in the soldier's sweat-soaked pubic hair. Kyle breathed in the sharp odor of Gunderson's crotch and felt himself swoon.

"Oh, that feels so fucking good," Gunderson groaned and leaned his head back. He planted a large hand on the back of Kyle's head and began to help him move his mouth up and down along the thick pole. Kyle reached down and grabbed Gunderson's hairy, sweaty balls and pulled them taut, twisting them in his fist as the man groaned and bucked his hips.

"Oh, fuck yeah!" Gunderson grunted. He hammered his cock up into Kyle's face with unrelenting force. "Take that cock and pull on those fuckin' balls. Pull 'em hard. Oh, fuck, that's it. Suck it!"

Kyle tightened his lips around Gunderson's prick and wrapped his free hand around the base. Squeezing tight, he jerked the man as he sucked him, stopping every few strokes to slip his tongue beneath the foreskin and lick up the copious amounts of precum oozing from the head of Gunderson's cock.

After a few more minutes, Gunderson bucked his hips faster and his breathing picked up pace. Kyle felt the man's balls pull up and knew he was preparing to come. He increased the rate of his sucking until Gunderson grunted and drove his cock deep into Kyle's throat, his thick load spurting into Kyle's mouth. He greedily swallowed each blast of semen, grunting along with his soldier savior until the man was spent.

Kyle raised his head and accepted a hot, fevered kiss from Gunderson. Their tongues collided and he passed some of the man's own spunk back to him. Gunderson swallowed the cum and licked up what he could find along Kyle's chin.

"I like the taste of cum," he said with a lazy grin. "Can I help you out now?"

Kyle stood up and slid his hard, dribbling cock into the soldier's mouth. Gunderson reached up to slip a finger into Kyle's anus and grabbed his balls with his other hand. Kyle fucked Gunderson's face, his cock slick with the man's spit as it slid faster and faster into his mouth. A few moments later Kyle blew his own load and watched as a portion of it ran out over Gunderson's lip and down his chin. The soldier kept his blue eyes locked on Kyle's face the entire time, his lips wrapped around his cock and his finger rubbing against Kyle's prostrate.

The sounds of returning soldiers prompted them to get dressed, and soon the entire rescue force was assembled and heading back to civilization. Kyle sat in the back with his leg pressed against Gunderson's muscular thigh, a smile on his face and the taste of the man's spunk in his throat. He stared at all the black leather boots assembled around him and tried to hide the bulge in his pants. So many military men, so little fucking time!

Kyle was debriefed at the embassy and returned to his parent's home where he was comforted by his mother and hugged by his father. In the days that followed his return, Kyle began working more and more with his father, discussing politics and some of the ideas that Armando had proposed so long ago. Turner Lassiter, impressed by his son's ordeal and the maturity it had brought to him, listened intently and agreed to meet with Armando. Kyle appointed himself mediator and set about to make the meeting happen.

Many weeks later, Kyle set out late at night and made his way to the familiar room where men sat naked, sweaty, and hard in shoeshine chairs. Their black booted feet were propped up on the metal footrests waiting for someone to worship them. Kyle walked past the row of chairs, watching with keen interest as men lined up to lick the boots clean and suck the cum from each cock that occupied the chairs. He made his way around men coupling in dark corners, listening to the sighs and grunts of sex, oral and anal, and found his way to a partially hidden door in the darkest corner. A man receiving anal sex to his left moaned and shot his load onto Kyle's feet just before he entered the door.

The room beyond was dark, illuminated only by tall candles. Several benches, an old shoeshine chair, and a table with chairs were scattered around. At the table sat Armando and Diego. Both men wore white tank tops and camouflage pants. Black leather boots covered their feet.

"Good evening, gentlemen," Kyle said with a grin. "Shall we get to business?"

"Always business first, isn't it?" Diego muttered and shook his head.

"Best practice, I've always thought." Kyle sat across from them, and they discussed strategies and concessions. Amazingly enough, General Domingo had agreed to join forces with Armando to work together to force Carlos Santiago from his evil reign. After almost two hours, Armando finally sat back and observed Kyle with narrowed eyes. "You are a shrewd mediator, Kyle Lassiter. You have matured much over the last few months."

Kyle shrugged. "I had a little help."

"Very good. This is settled," Armando pronounced. He looked at Diego and said, "Now, it seems my hot-blooded assistant is close to bursting with seed. He feels a need to spill it within someone."

Kyle stood up and moved to the shoeshine chair. He stripped and bent to tie his newly purchased black leather boots. Sitting in the chair, he propped up his boots and said, "Someone has soiled my new black leather boots. Both of you will need to clean them first."

Armando and Diego shed their clothes as they crossed the room, each retaining his boots. They knelt before Kyle and licked the polished black leather. Diego licked up the dried cum and ran his tongue to the top of the boot, darting it down between the boot and Kyle's calf. Armando ran his tongue slowly along the boot, tasting the dried cum as well and moving up Kyle's leg. Both men reached Kyle's prominent erection at the same time and took turns sucking him. They stroked their own thick, uncut cocks as they orally worshipped Kyle's cock and balls.

Reaching down, Kyle wrapped a hand around each of their cocks and slowly stroked them. He leaned his head back and closed his eyes as first Diego then Armando sucked his cock. While one was sucking the other would run his tongue along the shaft and down to his balls.

"Get up," Diego ordered, standing back by one of the benches. "And come over here."

Kyle walked over and lay along the bench on his back. Diego crouched over Kyle's face and planted his sweat-shrouded asshole over Kyle's mouth. As Kyle licked and sucked at Diego's hole, Diego bent to suck Kyle's cock. Armando stood watching for a moment, then stepped around and pulled Diego's hips back, moving his asshole away from Kyle's tongue. He pressed the wet, shrouded head of his cock against Diego's spit slick hole, and then pressed his hips forward to slide his cock completely inside Diego. Kyle sucked Diego's big, bull balls then reached up and pulled down the man's thick, ten-inch cock and swallowed it whole.

"Oh, fuck!" Diego groaned as Armando pierced his asshole. He gripped Kyle's cock tightly and stroked him faster and faster.

Kyle pulled the foreskin back from Diego's cock and focused all his suction on the head. Before long, he could feel his own balls tighten and the tingle in the head of his cock just before it started to erupt with cum. Diego swallowed each burst of semen, gulping it down as he grunted into his own orgasm. He drained his cock down Kyle's throat while Armando pounded into his ass from behind.

The sweat from Diego's crotch and thighs dripped down onto Kyle's face as Armando continued to pummel his ass. Kyle kept Diego's quickly inflating cock in his mouth, sucking him back to tumescence as Armando pulled out of Diego's ass and directed the bulging head of his cock at Kyle's face.

Releasing Diego's cock, Kyle opened his mouth and caught the majority of Armando's load in his throat. He swallowed it all and licked the long, clumping remnants from the surrounding foreskin.

They shifted positions and Kyle had Diego lay on his back on the bench. Reaching out, he found a can of shortening they had bought and smeared it along Diego's massive, hard pole. He greased up his own ass, slipping several fingers up inside himself, and then settled his body down on Diego's prick. Moaning softly, Kyle eased himself up and down along the rigid pole, feeling his ass loosen up as Diego's cock plowed into his ass. He picked up the pace and was soon bouncing up and down along Diego's granite-like cock. After several more thrusts, he leaned forward over Diego, kissing the man deeply as Armando stepped up to where they lay coupled.

Armando ran a hand along his own well-lubricated dick then crouched down and slid himself into Kyle alongside Diego's hot cock. All three men groaned as Armando penetrated Kyle to the core. They paused that way, both men buried deep within Kyle's body, and each caught his breath. They had only done this once before.

Slowly Diego and Armando began to pump into Kyle's willing, gaping hole. Kyle grunted and moaned, his cock bouncing on Diego's sweaty, hairy stomach with each thrust. Before long, the two men were moving in rhythm, faster and faster as they fucked the gasping American between them. All three were drenched in sweat that ran down their chests and across their faces.

Kyle came first, the force of his orgasm so strong his load shot up onto Diego's face. Diego came next, emptying his tightening balls deep into Kyle's ass as he grunted up into Kyle's mouth, their tongues jostling for space. Armando climaxed moments after Diego, his thick, hot load joining Diego's where it lay pooled up inside Kyle's body.

They stayed joined for several moments, all three catching their breath until Armando slowly eased himself free from Kyle's hole. Diego extracted himself as well, and they collapsed together on the bench, their limbs in a tangle as the sweat began to dry on their skin.

"I always enjoy our negotiation sessions," Armando said later as they got dressed.

"As do I, Armando," Kyle replied. He swatted playfully at Diego's hand as the big man reached out to squeeze Kyle's crotch. "I will let my father know the meetings can be arranged, and hopefully, we can come to some kind of agreement about how to go about effecting change for the country."

"I look forward to it." Armando stepped forward and kissed Kyle on the lips, his tongue making a slow, enticing circle in Kyle's mouth.

Diego kissed him as well, also slow and passionate, and then they were both gone. They always left separately so as not to be seen. Kyle waited several minutes, his eyes gazing dazedly at the bench where they had just finished fucking. He could feel a tiny trickle of cum dripping down the back of his leg and pressed his camouflage pants up against his skin to blot its course.

After an appropriate amount of time had passed, Kyle left the back room and made his way to the bar, which consisted of old crates and a bullet riddled door. He ordered a beer then turned to watch the men along the wall. Each of the chairs was occupied by a hard, dark-skinned man, and all but one had worshippers kneeling between their hairy, sweaty thighs. The lone man sat in the chair at the far end of the row, his face in shadow as he worked his hand along his slowly hardening cock.

Kyle moved closer and watched in amazement as the man's hard-on continued to expand. How big was this fucker going to get? By the time he had become fully erect, Kyle had gulped the rest of his beer and started shedding his clothes. He stepped up and knelt between the man's legs, opening his mouth wide to take the monster cock down his throat. He gorged himself on the man's hard timber, sucking for all he was worth as he worked his hands down the sweaty, hairy legs to the man's black, scuffed boots.

Releasing the cock from his mouth, Kyle leaned over to lick the black leather clean. He worked for several minutes, running his tongue over the smooth dark leather, and finally moved up along the man's legs to his low-hanging, hair-covered balls. He sucked the sack, pulling it away from the man's body and running his tongue down the perineum to the man's puckered hole.

The man lifted his legs and allowed him clear access to his asshole, encouraging Kyle to suck and lick at the twitching pucker of muscle. Slipping a finger inside him, Kyle found the man's prostate and rubbed the magic spot as he moved his mouth back up along the impossibly long shaft to the head peeking out from beneath a thick wrinkle of foreskin. He peeled the foreskin away from the head and clamped his mouth down over as much of the blood-gorged pole as he could. Moments later sweet, hot cum filled his mouth, and he swallowed each load with a sigh. Soon after Kyle brought himself to orgasm and emptied his load on the floor between the man's legs.

Keeping the softening penis in his mouth, Kyle looked up along the muscular body and discovered Berto, the guard from Domingo's camp, looking down at him. Kyle smiled and reluctantly pulled the man's organ from his mouth.

"How did you find me?" Kyle wondered.

"I've always known you come here," Berto replied. "I have watched you for a long time."

Kyle stood up extended his hand to help Berto out of the chair. They gathered their clothes, and Kyle led him along the shadows of moaning men to the back room.

"Come back here with me," Kyle said quietly. "I've got something to show you. And then we can talk about how you can help us out."

SHANK'S LESSON
Rick Polney

Two days ago in a longshoreman's bar in Thunder Bay, Ontario, someone passed out in a bathroom that smelled worse than babyshit. His nose was broken, covered in dry jizz, and he lay face down on blood-stained concrete, surrounded by bits of amps and guitars and broken chairs. His wallet and keys were long gone.

Two days later, hardened criminal Eddie Shank plowed down Toronto's University Avenue in a stolen, rusty, primer gray Ford pick-up truck. Toronto slept in late-January fog, a sleepy mist that looked comforting from the right angle. Shank took a truck that was painted earsplitting red, outfitted with chromed spike wheels and 72" speakers in the cab that would've shouted hellfire staccato, but Shank blew out the speakers, stripped the paint, and kicked the hubcaps within minutes of theft. Eddie liked grey and the cool rumble of V8 engines and the even cooler rumbling of his own brain for company. Just for kicks, he intentionally ground the gears so that the truck's ambient noise had the same affect on your back teeth that gnawing on gravel had.

Eddie had nothing to worry about though. It was Sunday, 4:00 am, and fog covered Toronto streets. His speed, his truck, and his noise bounced off curbs and nicked parked cars, while attracting whatever attention bums and methheads and burned-out club kids cared to give. All had their own fogs to worry about.

Here Shank was at the top of his form. Now all he needed was to punch another man senseless and then rape his ass bloody. It was going to be that kind of a night.

He turned left on Queen St., drove through each of the five traffic lights to Church Street, then headed north. The temperature was a few degrees above freezing, but Eddie wasn't wearing anything except his black paratrooper boots, denim jeans, and nipple rings. Eddie was a strange mix of Greek God, gutter slime, and sex-fiend with a hard chiseled body covered in hair the same color and consistency of used brillo pads. He was over six-feet tall and lanky enough so that you could see his ribs and clavicles, but years of hard living turned what could've been shaven sculpture into brillo-haired montage of knife scared facial features and a smile missing teeth, no left ear, and gray-green eyes. His chest and torso had a light layer of sag. His arms and legs were riddled with needle scars and cigarette burn abscesses, but they were strong. If he lived to fifty, he'd get lung cancer from smoking three packs a day, but he could run and fuck with blind rage vigor. Eddie's body was not a study in affectation; instead, it was the natural progression of a foul life.

To be sure Eddie liked his piercings, but his main pride was the crude Cyrillic-lettered tattoo on the left side of his neck. It bore the name of a prison in central Uzbekistan that had been shut down for brutality that made even police state professional sadists blanch. Eddie was one of the few men to walk out alive.

Under the Cyrillic were the Roman numerals XV.

The fists at the end of Eddie Shank's long arms were the living embodiment of every punk rock slamfest's morning after. These were Eddie's fists, the dangerous intersection of his body and mind's potential and hot ass-pounding action.

If Eddie's fists were the thuggish brothers of his aggression, then his cock was the howitzer because when it came it killed. It was the stuff of legend, seen as it was by bulge by most people; it was never unleashed except in dire moments. Eddie preferred to pound his men manually, i.e., with his fists. The cock came for special occasions and always only in the dark. As a matter of fact, Eddie's cock hadn't seen light of any kind in years. It might as well have had fangs (which it might) and be fearful of the crucifix (which Eddie might be, too).

Ed was a feared man, but it's better to be feared than loved.

The fog parted as Eddie slowed for the first time near the gay district at Church and Wellesley. He cruised the misty streets of Jarvis and Mutual looking for someone who needed a beating. Most of the men still alone this time of night were the wasteland's wasted, the unkempt gays too zonked out of their minds for sex. Others were the undecided, those kicked out of bed, and those who snuck out of bed. They were all fair game, but the Shank had an instinct for men who needed the shit kicked out of them. Men licked Shanks's balls and his weeklong unwashed feet or they swallowed their own teeth.

Shank traveled at gay cruising speed. He rolled through stop signs and traffic lights at 10 kph, pulling up to and driving onto the low curbs. Minutes of unwashed time passed as other cars just rolled past him. Eddie drove past a club that wasn't a club (red light behind cracked windows, pot and cigarette smoke dribbling in the mist, weather beaten rainbow flags stuck everywhere by sticky semen hands) on an alley that jutted north of Carlton Street. Walking the opposite way was a lone man. In the white haze penetrated by headlights the man was handsome. He was tall, thin, and Aryan, wearing faded blue jeans, a white sweater and a white woolen hat that covered bleach-blonde pointy hair.

Eddie's instinct for men kicked in. Eddie drove past the man, then right in front of an oncoming car, he popped the clutch and did a U-turn that sent the wheels screeching. Cinder ice and road salt flew everywhere. The truck skidded, bounced on to the curb on its two right-side wheels. Eddie pounded the brakes so that he stopped inches behind the man. The other car stopped.

Eddie leaned out his window and said in a voice that resembled a V2 rocket on takeoff, "Get in if you like it rough you Aryan youth-looking shithead."

The Nazi almost shit himself. He put up his left hand to the light, then in a weirdly exaggerated motion, put his right slowly on his jutting hip. The blonde said, "I take it any way you want for fifty bucks."

A goddamned hooker.

"You all man under those 501s?" Eddie asked. As he asked the question, he noticed the other car hadn't moved. For Eddie this was good news because nothing turned him into a fuckmachine like getting into real trouble did.

The man's right hand dropped to his pants and grabbed a bulge. "I'm more man than you are," the Nazi replied. "For seventy-five I might let you beat me in arm wrestling." Eddie liked a sense of humor. He glimpsed in the mirror. There were two people in the car behind him. The person on the passenger was getting out. Eddie smiled. "I need the money for, uh, college."

Eddie never paid for anything, but the cold air on his nipples, the chance to kick the shit out of at least one of the assholes behind him and a sure shot at raping a blue-eyed whore fueled Eddie's lizard sex mind.

Adrenaline Heartbeats Later.

"Get in," said Eddie to The Whore.

The man put his right hand in his back pocket and walked toward Eddie's truck.

"Hey asshole!" came the swishy yell from the car behind him. It looked as if it were coming from a man sitting in the driver's seat.

Eddie rolled his eyes. The Whore got in the passenger's side of Shank's truck. One of the men from the car behind Eddie stepped to Shank's window.

"My friend thinks you're an asshole, and he wants you to apologize," said the man. He was tall, brown, and handsome. He had that exotic tone of skin and shape of face that made it hard to figure out where he was from.

"Fuck him," Shank stared at the shorted brown man. "You're cute. Where are you from?" said Shank.

"I'm from Laos, but my family moved here last year," said the man.

"HEY ASSHOLE!" came the call from the car.

Shank shook his head again. "Do you like it rough?" he said to the Laotian.

"I don't know, I ..."

"ASSHOLE!" the call came louder. The driver of the other car was getting out of his car. He slammed his door shut and walked toward Shank's truck.

Eddie Shank got out of his truck, too.

Eddie smiled. "Let's take it easy." Eddie had turned down the rocket engine voice a few octaves so that he sounded almost human. When he got out, he got his first look at the other man. He was as tall as Eddie, had broader shoulders and wore leather chaps and a leather vest. "Watch this," Shank said to the Laotian. "You're gonna have a new boyfriend tonight." Eddie inhaled.

The tire iron came out faster than any human had ever carried it. Up and down first against the Laotian's skull. Eddie threw the tire iron like Hector defending Troy; the leather-chapped man fell harder than Patroclus.

The Shank didn't spend fifteen years in an Uzbek prison, didn't steal redneck pick-up trucks, and didn't go on shirtless hunts looking to anal rape castaways in the gay district to suffer challenges to his authority.

Eddie exhaled.

Then with the fluid motions of a man used to bagging and tagging, Eddie tossed the barely conscious lump of Laotian man into the back of his truck, tied his hands and feet with shoelace handcuffs. Eddie grabbed oily rags from the truck bed and didn't so much stuff the rags down the Laotian's throat as he did jackhammer them into place – expertly leaving the airway open through the nose. Eddie jumped out of the truck, thought for a split second, and then he jumped back in and punched his captive again. Just to make sure everyone knew who was running the game from here on.

The timid Nordic prostitute looked spooked. "Did you have to do that to the brown kid? He seemed nice."

"You're on the clock, Whore," said Shank as he choked out the boy whore with his right hand. "Shut up." The Whore slumped over and bashed his face on the dashboard.

Eddie drove away with the same smug smile any man with a truck full of cold, quivering captives would have. The other car's headlights were silently illuminating a knocked-out top spread-eagled in the street. This was a crime scene for someone to discover later, too late to do any good for the quivering captives. The Laotian was awake enough in the truck bed to hallucinate his friend's headlights as blue and red cop lights bleeding in the fog. As his vision dimmed, hope left his heart like a soul bound for Hell.

Shank rolled down the street thinking what to do now? How far could he get with two unwilling men in his truck? He just committed a violent crime and was driving with an unconscious whore next to him and a tied and gagged Laotian in the back, all of this in a stolen truck. Cops would be soon be everywhere thinking there was a violent abductor of gay Laotians and Nazi whores roaming the otherwise safe streets of Toronto. A new plan was needed.

Shank drove around the corners and down the alleys of downtown Toronto until he came to the corner of Carlton and Yonge. He saw exactly what he needed: a behemoth scaffolding, cranes and concrete. It was a construction site where parking garages had just been leveled to make way for two forty-plus story condo towers. It was a staging ground of vehicles, rebar, mounds of sand for concrete, stacks of iron eye beams, all surrounded by seven-foot walls.

Shank wanted to get rid of the stolen truck and hide for awhile. He pulled to the side of Carlton Street where he was about one hundred feet from the intersection with Yonge Street which for its own reason was coming to life. He turned off the lights, got out, and with the calmness that a professional weight lifter might carry sacks of potatoes to his kitchen, Shank hefted The Whore and the Laotian over his shoulders.

The construction site's boundary was defined in some places by chain link and in others was sturdier bright red and blue sheet metal. Shank didn't have any bolt cutters, so he would have to throw his friends over the fence. The Laotian was first. Shank picked him up to a fireman's carry position, and then pushed his captive over the fence. His slight body lifted and fell easily. He fell on the other side of the fence with a heavy thunk.

The Whore's face was smashed on one side, blood dribbling from his left nostril in two distinct paths. The first went into his mouth which made already ruddy lips even more garishly red. The second stream went from nose to the Nazi's left temple where it caked with close-cropped white hair. Even slumped on the dirt, the jeans and sweater fit nicely, the sharp Aryan features shined in mistlight. No, Eddie wouldn't pass this opportunity. To make the decision even more final, The Whore awoke for just a second, his not-swelled-too-badly right eye opened revealing perfect blue eyes that held all the clichéd adjectives about blue eyes and since there was only one working eye it might've taken on outrageous literary qualities, a singularity of blue in a storm of apathetic mist and surly construction grade concrete. Shank wanted to skull fuck that eye.

Shank bent over and put his hands under the Nazi, lifted and did a perfect standing power lift to propel the blonde up to the top of the solid fence. The Nazi balanced for a moment, and then fell on the other side. Shank had one more detail to take care of.

Shank picked up a bit of a cinderblock and grabbed another oily rag from the back of the truck. He wedged it as far as he could inside the gas tank and lit it on fire. He got in, started the truck and put it into first gear. He put the cinderblock on the acceleration pedal. Shank jumped out and ran back to the seven-foot fence and heaved himself over the edge.

The truck missed hitting any cars at the intersection but a bend in the road at Yonge Street took the truck directly into a Starbucks Coffee. The truck wasn't going fast enough to break though the store front, but the impact was enough to fuck up the fuel line, the gas tank, and the most of the undercarriage. Fluids dripped and drizzled everywhere. The rag flamed on.

Back at the construction site, Eddie dragged his new friends by their feet into the unfinished building. If Eddie had cared to look, he would've seen the semiconscious prostitute's cheeks and lips were turning blue. Eddie didn't care though. He was already hot, sweating now as the night's climax was approaching. Eddie Shank's predatory instincts took over. Everywhere he looked, he saw equipment for practical purposes (central air ducts and wooden crates for hiding) and toys for other purposes (exposed rebar, loose wiring, hand tools, plastic drop sheets). These were handy, but he couldn't stop yet. Here on the ground floor, he was still exposed. It was Sunday morning, so there probably wouldn't be any workers coming to the site.

The cops might though. He had driven less than ten blocks from where he knocked a man cold and maybe one- or two hundred feet from a Starbucks that had a stolen pickup truck sticking out of it. Eddie wasn't safe yet. He breathed in a deep breath of cold air that made his neck hair stand on end. As the chilled oxygen passed into his lungs, his already erect nipples tingled, his heart beat faster. The oxygen passed into his blood right down to cock, which stayed semi-erect. His lizard brain where primordial instincts were working was at full throttle.

Fuck and fight. Fight and fuck.

He knew what to look for. Outside the structure, the foggy night made the world dim, but visible. There was ambient light from the street lamps. Inside the guts of the unfinished building, it was almost absolute black. Almost, but for a dim light. In this blackness, even Shank's eyes almost failed. He stumbled once, twice on chunks of concrete. He took a few more steps and bumped his head on a low ceiling. Still, Shank kept his cool. If he couldn't find his way around this place at night, then no one else could either.

He rounded a corner and found what he was looking for: the elevator. Inside the car a single 40-watt light bulb brightened the elevator car, but not much else. He found something else useful: a small Maglite. With the light, Shank looked around at what he had avoided. He saw uncovered ventilation shafts, rebar hanging from ceiling, sharp metal sheets. At the very edge of the light shaft, were the two men he brought with him. They were slowly coming to life, coughing and shivering and moaning in cold consciousness. Shank made his way over to them, grabbed them by the feet again and pulled them back to the elevator. Door shut, he pressed the up button. He wanted to go to the top, naturally.

The elevator car was a large compartment since it was designed for men and material. It was also very Spartan with its single light bulb and particleboard wooden walls. The elevator began a slow ascent with Shank looking at the two men. He started with the Laotian. Shank removed the oily rag from the short guy's mouth. He leaned over and said, "Your name is Snowflake."

"Huh?"

"Shut up. Are you hard yet, Snowflake?"

"Jesus Christ NO, I'm not hard and what's with the name? Where are we? Where ..."

Shank punched him in the face again just as the elevator stopped at the top floor. Shank turned to the Aryan boy. "You're name is Whore. You'll both do what I say, when I say." Whore and Snowflake started to cry. This was exactly what Shank wanted. He reached down into his pants and felt his cock tingling, only it wasn't blood rushing, it was piss. Shank pulled the light string so the elevator was dark. Shank opened his zipper and let the stream of dark dank urine fly all over the elevator. Snowflake and Whore squirmed and bucked when they realized what was happening. In the dark, someone managed to stand and knock against Shank causing piss to go all over the place. While still peeing, Shank used both hands to reach in the darkness, finding a neck. He pulled the neck directly in front of his still peeing cock and roared!

"DRINK IT!"

Whoever he held clearly didn't want to drink piss because he pushed away, just making the piss go all over the place. Shank's grip tightened, but not to the point of suffocation; he wanted these people awake. Someone pulled at Shank's wrist, but was too weak to do anything about it. The useless hands stopped, fell away.

Shank turned the light on again, his dick was already back in his pants. At the end of his right hand, The Whore stared blankly up.

"You're still on the clock, aren't you?"

"I didn't think it would be like this."

Shank pulled The Whore up so that they were eye to eye with barely an inch between them. "You thought there would be more romance?" Shank asked. With his other hand, Shank grabbed Snowflake. "What about you? You got in a car with a man in assless leather chaps. Were you just ride-sharing? Splitting the gas money?" This little bit of levity eased the tension.

Shank shifted his grip on Snowflake from choking the Adam's apple to arm bar choke from the rear. Shank pushed lips full on Snowflake's right ear and nibbled a little, then blew softly. His grip relaxed a little to let Snowflake breathe. "Your hair smells nice," said Shank as he licked Snowflake's cheek. His breath was hot and reeked of stale cigarettes. Snowflake trembled a little from the cold, but he had no excuse for the blood rushing to his cock. Shank bit down on Snowflake's shoulder, then went to a wet sloppy kiss up and down his neck. Gooseflesh raised down Snowflake's right side. Far from being cold, every pore on Snowflake's brown body released enough sweat to cover him in a shiny film.

This whole time Shank's left arm was firmly around Shithead's neck. Snowflake was having a hard time deciding if Shank was going to kill them or just fuck them. Or both.

"Do as I say, and you might not get hurt any more than you have to. Shithead, I'm going to let go of you and you're going to suck Snowflake's cock. Do you understand?" asked Shank.

"Yes, sir." The Whore did as he was told. He unbuttoned Snowflake's jeans and pulled them down. Snowflake had an average cock, but it was getting hard. Whore kissed Snowflake's cock gently, licking the tip, taking in just the first inch. Snowflake's knees shuddered a little at the tease. The wooden elevator got a little warmer.

Shank saw what was happening and didn't like it.

"No tease. SUCK IT!" Shank pushed Snowflake forward so that The Whore's head banged against the elevator wall, which pushed Snowflake's fully erect cock all the way down The Whore's mouth, causing him to gag.

"Grab that whore's pretty white hair and skull fuck him." Snowflake did. He held The Whore's head and pumped his cock back and forth.

"Faster! Stick it all the way down. He's a whore and you're in control. Fuck his mouth!" Shank ordered. To help with this Shank used his own hips on the back of Snowflake's hips, which made The Whore gag. He threw up a mess of phlegm all over himself and Snowflake's pants.

The pounding continued. Shank used his free hand to rub Snowflake's nipples. More sweat poured out of Snowflake's body when Shank nibbled at Snowflake's neck. Snowflake was heavy mouth-breathing now, taking in the cold air and replacing it with his own hot mist. He was giving The Whore a mouthful with every thrust. Snowflake looked down at The Whore, at the phlegm and the pained look on The Whore's face whose eyes were closed shut, not just closed, but clenched shut in a face that looked every bit as much as if he were suffering from jagged broomsticks fucking his ass as he was about to have a body orgasm explosion.

Not that it mattered.

Shank knew Snowflake was close. His hips were bouncing faster than any man's hips should move. Shank moved his free hand to Snowflake's asshole, which by now was oozing sweat and ass juice. Shank massaged Snowflake's ass cheeks in time with the thrusting. When it was close to the end, Shank made a cone with his five fingers and pushed them up and into Snowflake's asshole all the way to Shank's knuckles.

Snowflake exploded and melted.

The Whore took the load like a champ, swallowing every drop. Shank took his fingers out of Snowflake's asshole and put them in The Whore's mouth who dutifully licked them clean, and promptly threw up every bit of food he'd eaten for the last two days. The Whore collapsed crying on the floor. For a few odd moments, the elevator was silent. The 40-watt light bulb kept the scene in underlit freakishness.

Snowflake looked at The Whore and The Whore's mess in disbelief and got the awful feeling that this was his fault. He reached out to The Whore.

"No pity, Snowflake. Just retribution." Shank released his choke arm on Snowflake to stop any tenderness between his two prisoners.

"What do you ..."

Shank elbowed Snowflake in the head, knocking the little Laotian down.

"Stay down Snowflake," commanded Shank. "Get up Whore." Shank pulled The Whore to his feet by his hair. The Whore was covered in puke and phlegm and probably some sperm, too. He was drenched. As the adrenaline decreased, The Whore's body temperature dropped. His body-warm puke was turning cold.

"Your turn," said Shank. "Pull down your pants, Snowflake."

For the first time tonight, Snowflake and The Whore made eye contact, each pleading something from the other, but afraid to speak it. If there was a way to convey Snowflake's guilty pleasure from The Whore's pain or The Whore's shame at his own raging hard-on, there was no way to confirm it.

Shank saw The Whore's bulge. "Pull down your pants, Whore." He did. He was huge. The Whore was a full eight inches long and very thick. And shaved. And he was hard, fully erect.

"Good Whore. Now facefuck your Snowflake. Fuck him right in his pretty brown face," said Shank. "Now Snowflake, lie still and face up. Whore get on top, sit on his face."

The Whore straddled Snowflake's face so that he was facing Snowflake's feet like they could almost go right into a sixty-nine. The Whore's massive cock immediately gagged Snowflake who had never sucked off a man so big. Shank pushed The Whore's hips to make them go faster. Snowflake gagged more and harder, much worse than The Whore had.

"Look what you're doing to your friend, just like he did to you, but you're making it worse for him."

"I can't fit it all the way in, he keeps gagging," said The Whore.

"Oh really?" said Shank. Shank hammerfisted Snowflake square in the gut, forcing all the air out of him. When he tried to take his first breath, Shank pushed with his right hand down on The Whore's hips so that his cock was three full inches down Snowflake's throat. The danger was obvious.

"FUCK HIM FAST OR YOU'LL KILL HIM," yelled Shank.

The Whore looked back only once at Snowflake's face. His eyes were wide with terror. Whore pushed harder, maybe he would've pulled out, but when Snowflake's throat reconstructed he was in he tightest, wettest hole he'd ever felt in his life. Before he could stop himself, he slid in and out of Snowflake's trachea. It was too awful to think about what he was doing, but he did it anyway.

The more Snowflake spasmed, the better the fucking felt. Feeling the best physical pleasure and the most revulsion he'd ever felt about anything he ever did in his life. Even when Snowflake went limp, The Whore continued, and finished. Then he pulled out as fast as he could.

Snowflake gagged up the semen, then threw up himself, which in turn caused The Whore to throw up again. All the while Shank laughed.

"Now it's my turn for some fun," Shank said as he opened the elevator door. Shank took them by his favorite method, by grabbing their hair and dragging them into oily dark night. Although they were on the top floor, they weren't at the top of the building, which is where Shank wanted to go. They stumbled in the dark until he found the stairwell to the top.

Just as he expected, there were several safety harnesses just inside the door leading to the roof. He strapped one around his waist and used a harness with a D-ring to secure himself to a safety rod attached the ground outside the door. It was a little lighter in the sky and not as misty as before. The sun came up late this far north of the equator, so Shank had a few minutes before he had to get inside.

The Whore and Snowflake were quiet the whole time. They'd had their orgasms, had been throat-fucked to near death and were getting cold again in the winter air. It was too much trouble to speak, much less to ask any questions.

When Shank had put his equipment on he said, "Come here boys, look at me." The boys came and they looked at him. Shank promptly knocked their heads together yet again and dragged their limp bodies to the building's edge. Just as Shank thought, the safety wires allowed him to get right to the edge, but would prevent him from falling over. Shank let a drooping Snowflake fall at his feet as he hoisted The Whore in front of him on the ledge. Shank pulled down his own pants, then The Whore's. With no ceremony, he unleashed his own massive manhammer. Shank grabbed The Whore with one hand on his neck and the other around Whore's waist. The he fucked him.

The Whore had dried up a little, but a little Shank spit got things lubed up right away.

Whether it was the massive schlong in his asshole or the just above freezing weather or that dream that people get that they are about to fall off a building that fully awoke The Whore is not important. What is important is that he woke up forty-three stories above Toronto with a huge shlong in his ass and the only thing keeping him from falling was Shank's grip.

The Whore never remembered if he himself came, he only remembered Shank's laughter and that his heart stopped dead cold for a few brief seconds then just started ticking again. Once the ticking restarted, The Whore saw just how beautiful Toronto looked from so high at night. He could clearly see the lights at Eaton Center and the noble glass cubes that stood for office buildings. The Whore also remembered how good the cold air felt on his body and that his ball sack must've looked like a tiny walnut out there in the wind. He wished he could see better why there were so many fire trucks and sirens wailing below. He was certain it wasn't for him because below was only more oily night. Once the fear was over, once he realized that he had no choice but to trust Shank's grip, he thought it an amazing experience. When Shank shot a gallon of sperm in The Whore's asshole, The Whore never thought about condoms, or about payment only about what Shank must've gone through to get the way he was.

When Shank was done, he tossed The Whore next to Snowflake who looked like he'd already seen Shank's way of seeing things. too. Shank walked past them unbuckling his harness.

"Let's get inside. It's cold out here, "Shank said. They took the elevator down to the first floor and went outside. Shank helped them both over the high metal walls, and then went over himself. Down the block was a burned-out Starbucks. The three walked a little way when Shank stopped. He took out his pack of smokes and a lighter, and then tossed two twenty dollar bills at the boys.

"I don't care how you get home. Take a taxi if you want," Shank said. Shank walked over to a nondescript gray sedan, broke a window and opened the door. Seconds later, the car started. Shank drove away from the dawn. He'd be horny again soon, and he wanted to be in a position to do something about it.

HUDSON WOODS
K. Appleby

Josh slowly began to feel again; the surface he was lying upon felt hard and rough. A question gradually formed in his mind, what was he doing on the floor? A throbbing pain in his head replaced his thoughts. He instinctively put a hand to the back of his head and ran his fingers through his soft short spiky blonde hair. The fact there was no wetness and therefore no blood comforted him. The comfort soon left him as the realization formed that the pain was inside his head. Josh tried to stand, but his body was too weak to move, every muscle ached as if he had run a marathon.

Panic flowed through his body. His arse ached and his throat was sore. He managed to roll to his side as he tried to focus; his eyes slowly became accustomed to the darkness. There was a faint light coming from outside through a nearby window; it was moonlight. His sight was returning slowly, but his vision was still quite blurred. He could make out the wooden floorboards that he lay upon and could just see the rough wooden walls of the room. He was in a crude shack. What was he doing in here?

He heard noises behind him. Something was moving on the other side of the shack wall. As Josh turned around, he noticed a door between him and the disturbance. He froze as he listened to the approaching noises, straining his ears to make out the sounds of a conversation.

"Excellent, we caught a real good one," a rough harsh voice stated, coming from somewhere behind the door.

"I know, but we still got to gut it," another, softer voice replied.

The unidentified voices were getting closer. Josh could hear their footsteps approaching the interior door.

Josh looked around the room, his vision slightly clearer. He could see a wooden hobbyhorse beside him, and scattered around the floor of the dim room, he saw orange rope, some rags and what looked like a pile of dildos and dongs in the corner.

That was all the motivation Josh needed. He forced himself up off the floor as adrenalin filled his body and overcame the numbness in his limbs. He looked around frantically and saw an open window just as he heard the men moving even closer.

"I'll gets the knife for you," the gentler voice uttered as it approached from the other side of an interior door.

Within seconds, Josh was climbing through the open window. His naked parts scraped roughly against the windowpane. With no thoughts for his safety, Josh jumped out onto the dirt. His bare feet jarred with the impact but he ignored the pain and sprinted into the all-consuming darkness.

Josh ran naked through the trees, leaving the derelict cabin as far behind him as possible. He ran as fast as he could through the woods, not knowing where he was heading. The cool night air left goose bumps on his lightly sweating flesh. His long thick flaccid penis ached with every strike against his taunt stomach muscles and thighs as he raced wildly through the dark trees running for his life.

Josh ran until his heart pounded in his chest. He was not sure how long he had been running. He might have fled through the woods for an hour, or it could have been four hours. His athletic body was exhausted and tired from the tension. Tiny nicks, scrapes, and cuts covered his muscled arms, chest and legs. He stopped to catch his breath leaning his supple exposed form against the coarse trunk of a large tree.

Josh could not think clearly. He couldn't remember how he had gotten into that cabin. He knew his name was Josh and that he lived just outside an outback town called Bamy. He had finished work and returned home, but it was so hard to think clearly. His head ached as he tried to remember the events that had led up to this moment, but he was becoming more and more exhausted by the cold and the recent exertion.

Josh gulped in breaths of air and tried to compose himself as he sat down with his back against the tree trunk. As he cradled his muscled legs close to his bare chest for warmth, only one thought kept tumbling around his mind... *What happened?*

* * * * *

Josh had been at work; it was a warm summer's evening. It was Friday afternoon, and he had arranged to go to his friend's house. Billy had a pool, and Josh was anticipating a relaxing swim. Josh had been excited to spend time with Billy again; he had been looking forward to it all day. They had not seen each other all week, as they had both been too busy with work.

Josh checked the time on his watch as he entered the front door of his home and found it a little after six o'clock. Work had run longer than usual, and he wished it hadn't. He stripped off his shirt and pants, leaving his wallet, keys and watch on the wooden bookcase beside the front door. Pausing for a moment, he smiled at the metal phallus on his key chain that Billy had made for him in metalwork class back in high school. He just laughed to himself while he kicked off his shoes and pulled off his socks. His tired feet felt much better out of his footwear as he approached the stairs. Josh practically leapt up the stairs, taking two at a time in his excitement.

He walked up the hall and into the bathroom stepping out of his tight-fitting blue briefs that showed off his bubble butt exquisitely. Removing his underwear released his impressive manhood. His cock was rather thick but was more impressive due to its length. It swung more than halfway down to his inner thigh. He fleetingly glanced at it admiringly in the mirror before stepping into the shower.

After turning on the taps to a comfortable temperature, he grabbed the soap and started to lather it over his smooth buff body. His delicate but still manly hands ran the soap along the muscles of his arms coating his soft smooth skin and the thin layer of supple blond hair that lightly covered parts of his body.

Moving down to his feet, he rubbed the bottom of his soles clean slipping the soap between every toe. Once he had cleaned his feet, he lathered the soap up his leg to his well-formed calf muscles. He then turned his back to the flowing water and rubbed the soap over his bubble-shaped butt. He gently soaped his firm bottom, allowing his hands to part the cheeks before rubbing the bar gently over his taut arse hole.

Satisfied, Josh turned around and moved the soap to his sculpted abs and his protruding chest. As he got to his sensitive nipples, his cock twitched. He lingered, rubbing the soap from one rapidly erecting nipple across his broad chest to the other, his cock growing steadily in appreciation. Josh continued until his cock was nearing full erection, it rose proudly past his navel and against his six-pack stomach.

He sighed deeply, wanting so much to grab his aching cock and stroke it until the swollen organ released a mighty week's worth of love juice. He had to restrain himself though because he had promised Billy to save it up for him, and Billy had promised that he was doing the same. Josh quickly rinsed off the lather of soap covering his body, and stepped out of the shower. Grabbing the towel, he dried himself vigorously, the warmth of the evening speeding up the process considerably.

Moving across the hall to his bedroom, he had dressed quickly, eager to meet up with Billy. He wore a fresh pair of underwear a little too tightly, showing the bulge at his front, a tight white T-shirt that made his muscles stand out prominently, and loose-fitting grey camouflage fake-army cargo pants. He wore the pants low. so they sagged just enough that he could see the top of his underwear stretched over his perfectly rounded arse. Josh had decided to wear the bright red sneakers Billy thought were so hot even though they were a little louder then the clothes Josh would usually wear. He glanced once in the mirror and was satisfied.

Josh raced down the stairs grabbed his keys, wallet and watch from the bookcase before he dashed out the door, locking it behind him. Josh was in his car in seconds, starting the engine. It was not too far to Billy's place, and he would get there just after nightfall.

Josh turned on the radio and wound down the window. It was a warm summer night, and he was already starting to sweat lightly. He tried not to think of Billy, as whenever he did his cock started to grow in his tight underwear and become uncomfortable. Josh smiled to himself as he realized that he would be nearing Hudson woods soon, which was about the halfway point to Billy's place. The closer Josh got to Billy's place, the harder it was getting for him to control his already straining jocks.

* * * * *

CRACK! A noise startled Josh from his memories. As he listened intently, he wondered – was it a branch cracking underfoot of one of those horrible men from the cabin? Josh hoped that noise might just have been an animal going about its own business. He steadied his breathing as he tried to quiet his pounding heart. Josh alerted his senses to the darkness all around him straining for any sight or sound that he could detect.

The cold night air was making the light blond hairs on his naked flesh stand on end though the fear of the unknown could also be responsible. He did not know where he was, who his pursuers were or how he had gotten here. He did not even know how he had gotten naked. His senses strained into the cold darkness as he could hear something approaching through the bushes.

"Hey, you there, come here!" A loud exclamation came from within the bushes just a few feet away from him as a huge bear of a man came crashing through them.

The large man reached menacingly toward Josh. Josh hesitated for only a second, the voice might be different from the others he had heard in the cabin, but he could not be sure. He forced himself up, swung around the tree trunk and bolted for his life.

"Don't make me chase you!" the mountain of a man yelled as he crashed through the bushes in pursuit. Josh fled for his life for the second time that night. He ran through the woodland, dodging trees and jumping fallen logs. It was not long before the sounds of his pursuer ceased, but he continued at a breakneck pace. Suddenly Josh broke through the woods into a clearing. He paused, unsure of what to do with the sight that confronted him in the dim moonlight. There was a small and decrepit shack in the clearing. Relief struck him as he realized that it wasn't the same cabin he had fled from earlier that night.

Josh shivered in the cool night air as he crept toward the partially open, old, rotting door of the hovel, crouching behind it. With his long flaccid cock resting on the small veranda, he listened intently for any signs of movement from within. He could hear nothing that would indicate anyone was inside. Gaining courage from some unknown reserve, he peered through a crack of the rotten door. The shack was dark and creepy, with shadows playing on the table and chairs within; he saw no signs of movement.

He stood, reached for the door and pulled. The door opened fully, shuddering on its rusty hinges. Josh looked within, ready to run at the first sign of trouble. Relieved upon seeing the shack was empty, he crept inside. Straightaway Josh noticed the warmth coming from an old potbellied stove. He thankfully looked around the room, glad to be out of the cold night air. The hovel was dirty and old. A table and chairs sat in the middle of the room being the main feature. There was a metal framed bed to one side and the lit stove was to the other.

Josh raced around the old table and stood in front of the stove, feeling its warmth radiate over his cold naked body. He rubbed his hands together and held them close to the heat. After a few minutes, his front had warmed, so he turned around to warm his back, that is when he saw the massive moonlit shadowy shape blocking the door.

Straining his eyes Josh could see this was the large man from the woods. He would have been around his early forties, had stubble on his face, and was attractive in a rough and rugged way. The man was big, both tall and muscular. He stood with his massive arms on his wide hips.

"You shouldn't have made me run. Were you so eager to enter my home?" the giant man bellowed. Josh was terrified; he had nowhere to run.

"I'm sorry Mr. um … I just wanted warmth, I don't know where I am and I need help," Josh pleaded.

The man just laughed heartily, then stood smiling for a moment. "Don't be scared mate, we're all in this together. We can help each other out, I am sure." His smirk took an almost sinister form, as if he knew the joke, but Josh did not.

Josh gulped, walking toward the man holding out his hand in a gesture of friendship.

"My name's Josh, do you have a mobile phone I could use?" Josh offered, summoning all his courage. Something about this man's voice seemed familiar, but Josh could not tell why. The big man advanced on Josh, grabbing his offered hand.

"Josh yes, g'day Josh. You remember now, me name's Mark. Sorry to tell you this, but the mobile networks went down," he said in a masculine, booming voice before taking a step back and looking his guest up and down.

"You must be cold. Go get a blanket from me bed and I'll put some soup on the stove for us." Mark suggested firmly, pointing toward the rusty metal bed.

Josh turned and walked over to it. He grabbed one of the blankets and wrapped it around himself; then turned to face the large man. As Josh watched, Mark put a pot on the stove, pulled out a chair from under the table and sat in it near the table facing him.

Josh found his groin beginning to stir under the large man's piercing lustful gaze.

"Mark, could you maybe point me in the direction of the nearest town?" Josh peeped before clearing his throat.

"I can take you there if you want. After the soup that is." Mark laughed and then he hesitated, giving Josh a strange look. "Perhaps you could give your good friend Mark some payment for his aid?" Mark requested as he undid the buttons of his pants.

Josh hesitated, something about the man made him think he should trust him, something oddly familiar. But something else told Josh that it was not really a question, and that Mark would not appreciate his refusal. Josh also did not want to go back into the cold night alone. Meanwhile Mark sat staring and motioning for Josh to come closer.

Josh moved over to Mark and lowered himself to his knees. Mark pulled his pants down to his ankles revealing a large thick-veined cock. Josh glanced quickly up into Mark's eyes; Mark nodded his head in affirmation. With that, Josh took Mark's thick cock into his mouth and sucked, moving his mouth up and down over it. Its thickness and length strained his mouth, but he endeavored to go as deep and give his rescuer as much pleasure as he could muster.

Suddenly massive hands held Josh's head in a familiar forceful way. Mark abruptly started to face-fuck Josh hard and deep. Josh was finding it hard to breathe with Mark's hard tool hammering down his throat. However, just as Josh was about to protest, Mark's enormous cock pushed its way so deep it was touching past Josh's tonsils. The massive dick shuddered, and Josh had no choice but to swallow repeatedly the thick, acidy cum thrashing deep down the back of his throat. Josh's nose filled with the musk of the large man's pubes, and he could hardly breathe – he could only swallow.

"Oh yeah, drink my seed," moaned Mark as more and more of the thick jism filled Josh's throat.

Josh swallowed again as the last remnants of fluid oozed from the cock as it lessened in size and was slowly removed from his mouth.

Josh smiled, licking his lips; he had never drunk so much cum before. He was not sure if it was just his imagination but something about this man's cock and semen seemed familiar as well.

Mark smiled back, putting a hand on Josh's head affectionately.

"Thanks mate, I needed that, don't get service like that very often. I am actually very tired. You help yourself to the soup. I'm going to have a rest," Mark said, as he did his pants back up.

Mark stood, took a spoon from an old tin can beside the stove and handed it to Josh. Mark then strolled over to the bed, took off his thick jacket, and tossed it onto the table.

"Wake me when you're ready to go to town," Mark said as he lay down on the bed.

Josh quietly took the pot from the stove and sat it on the old wooden table. He noticed Mark's jacket and grabbed it putting it on quickly. Then Josh sat and filled his belly with the warm watery soup, washing down the last traces of Mark's thick cum. When he was done, Josh looked over at Mark, who was snoring lightly. Josh realized he was rather tired himself, being unsure of how long he had actually been awake. Josh rested his head in his arms on the table. They would both wake in the morning, and he would finally go to town. Once in town, Josh hoped that this horrible experience would be over.

Sometime later, Josh awoke to Mark's heavy snoring. He stood up and noted the thickness of the jacket he now wore. The old jacket was a few sizes too big for him and covered half his hands but it was still not long enough to conceal all the length of his cock. Josh decided he would have a look for some pants, and wondered how long he had slept as it was still night or was it night again? He discarded the thought for the time being. Firstly, he would find some pants and then wake Mark, so they could go into town.

As Josh glanced around the small cabin, something caught his attention. A pile of clothes was under the old rusty metal bed, finally he could get dressed. He slowly approached the bed not wanting to wake Mark while he was still half naked and feeling vulnerable. Josh reached under the bed and pulled out the bundle of clothing. All of it was old and dirty being little more than rags and rubbish. That is when he noticed the orange ropes attached to the bed head. The same type of rope he had seen in the cabin where he had awakened on the floor.

Josh's head cleared, and his mind was filled with a vision or memory. He was laying on his back as a large man towered over him, holding his head back and plunging his thick veiny cock down into his mouth. Josh shuddered, dropping the clothes and staring in puzzlement at the sleeping giant. Had he been imprisoned here also? Was Mark one of his abductors?

Josh turned to flee the cabin, suddenly frightened that Mark would awaken. He quickly reached the cabin door and forced the door open. Terrified, he darted outside again into the cold night air. He left the door open and traveled again away from that first cabin and this new hovel of horror.

Josh tried not to think of what might have been done to him and of what would be done to him if he were recaptured. He wondered how long he had been imprisoned. Where was he? It was midsummer but the cold night air felt more like winter. He either had been taken somewhere cold or had been captive for many months. Either of those single thoughts terrified him. What had they been doing to him all this time? His arse did feel like it had received a forceful shafting recently. Was that from his captors, or had he been with Billy? As Josh wandered through the woods, his endless questions stimulated memories from his mind.

* * * * *

The drive to Billy's house had been mostly uneventful. Josh listened to the radio as the anticipation of their reunion stirred his loins into a semi. His cock strained as it expanded, filling every available inch of his already tight underwear.

However, something odd did happen. As he was halfway to Billy's near Hudson woods, the radio lost signal. The music was suddenly replaced with static. A cacophony of songs and conversations filled the car, and at the same time, the engine sputtered, and the lights dimmed. Josh was worried slightly by this, as he could not afford to replace the electrical wiring in his car right now. The worry passed quickly with the electrical disturbance just as his car left the forested area of Hudson Woods. He thought little of it at the time, an interesting bit of conversation to talk to Billy about before they got down to business.

Before long Josh was at Billy's front gate. He got out of the car, opened the gate, and drove a little ways and then closed the gate behind him. As he was walking back to his car, he saw headlights on the road behind him. He was about to get in his car when he heard beeping as a Landrover pulled up abruptly outside the gate.

"Hey mate! I'm John, do you know where Hudson Woods is?" called a young man from the passenger seat in a rather gentle and smooth voice. John was thinly muscled – he wore no shirt and Josh could imagine that his stomach was flat and smooth, and he had shaved his light hair very short. Josh could not make out much of the driver, though he looked handsome and more thickly muscled and had dark hair.

"Just down the road as you were heading, on the left, you can't miss it," Josh replied in the most masculine voice he could muster.

"There's a rave on this weekend in the woods; if you drop in look around for me and Gus!" John yelled as he put his head back in the Landrover.

Josh could hear excited laughter from the Landrover as it sped off, screeching its tires and sending a small dust cloud in Josh's direction. Josh coughed and returned to his car. He drove down the driveway slowly to allow Billy to anticipate his arrival as much as he was.

Driving up to the house, Josh remembered all the good times he and Billy had experienced there. From young friends at school, they had grown up together, and eventually as they aged, friendship had grown into something more. As young adults, they explored each others bodies, noticing every change as manhood replaced adolescence. However, lately they would usually get together at least thrice a week to down a few scotches and then go down on each other. They did not have anal sex much, but when they did, it was sublime.

Billy did not have the biggest cock, but his arse was so tight it got Josh hard just thinking about it. Billy always complained that Josh was too big and that every deep plunge was too much, but Josh knew that Billy really loved it. He loved to be fucked by Josh's long thick cock, and really got off on the way it stretched his arse muscles to almost the point of pain. Billy especially loved it when Josh got caught up in the moment and would ram and hammer Billy's arse with no restraint.

Josh's cock strained in his pants as he exited the car. He had to readjust himself as he strolled casually toward Billy's house. He walked to the front door, knocked and waited a few seconds and knocked again. There was no answer, but obviously, Billy must be out the back in the pool. The summer heat was stifling. Josh could do with a swim and he walked around the house to the pool.

* * * * *

Despite the cold of the woods the thought of his sexual exploits with Billy had filled Josh's cock. His manhood pointed out and up, proudly swinging from left to right in front of him with every step. His cock led the way in front of him as he walked briskly through the woods, lost in his memories.

Josh was so preoccupied with trying to remember, that he realized too late his foot had not met with the ground. He fell forward into a wet cold ditch. Now covered in mud he looked over the edge of the ditch. No, he realized as he composed himself, it was not just a ditch. He was in a drain by the side of a dirt road. His heart soared with thoughts of rescue and the safety of civilization. He climbed out of the drain and onto the road. He stood looking left and right. Trepidation replaced his elation as he stood wondering, which way should he go?

Josh did not know where he was in relation to the closest settlement or station. The wrong choice could see him walking for miles deeper into the outback and away from all hope of survival. Nevertheless, he had to make a choice and soon. Those redneck kidnappers could be just through the trees drawing closer and closer with every moment he hesitated. With that thought sending shivers through his already cold and wet body, he took decisive action. He would go left, he was not sure, but that just seemed to be the way to go to move further away from the initial cabin.

Josh walked for a few hours, the exercise barely battling the numbing cold. When he saw lights coming from behind him, he suddenly felt very exposed and vulnerable. His worried mind feared it could be one of his captors. He quickly leaped over the drain and dived into the bushes of the woods. Looking back, he saw the lights, they were high, it must have been a semi trailer truck. There was no truck noise, though there was a high-pitched whirring sound. Was that one of those roo deterrents? They were fixed to vehicles in the bush to scare kangaroos away; a head-on with a roo could be deadly for both the driver and animal.

The noise was hurting his head now, the same place it hurt before. With a "whoosh," the lights darted over his head and into the woods at his back. His mind reeled, was it a helicopter or an ultra light plane? He suddenly felt foolish. Was it a search party out looking for him? He worried that he had just hidden from his only chance of rescue!

He sat in the bushes for a moment feeling scared and very alone. Only the cold forced his tired body to continue moving down the road. Josh had wondered if he should try to follow the lights but decided the road was the safest option. He walked for a long time before spotting a metallic object about the size of a car on the side of the road.

Josh moved back over the drain and into the bushes approaching as quietly as he could. Upon getting close, he could see more clearly. He recognized it as the same make and model as his car. However, this car had rust where paint should have been. The glass had been shattered, perhaps broken long ago by vandals. Even the tires were missing. The old bomb looked like it had been there for years neglected and silent.

Josh peeked into the car through the broken drivers window – the inside was ripped and stained, but would protect him from the cold wind. He forced open the door and climbed inside, closing the door behind him. Lowering himself down onto the floor of the front seat to better keep out of the cold night air. As Josh huddled out of the chilling breeze, he suddenly felt very tired, so very tired. As he drifted off to sleep, his mind cleared somewhat and he remembered.

* * * * *

Josh walked around the side of Billy's house to the paved entertainment area. Opening the gate, Josh heard splashing. He looked into the pool, and Billy was there swimming. He had not noticed Josh yet. Billy's thin-framed body flexed every one of his small but prominent muscles of his arms and back as he splashed and swam in the water. His longish black hair was wet and stuck to his head and neck. His deep olive skin glistened in the underwater lights of the in-ground pool.

"Hey babe!" Josh called as he closed the gate and headed over to the pool.

Billy's head bolted up to where Josh stood. A look of shock was apparent on his face.

"Shit Josh, you scared the hell out of me!" Billy gasped.

Josh just laughed as Billy turned to face him, his thick chest and broad shoulders protruding from the water. Billy was not as muscled as Josh, but he held enough balance of muscle and fat on his petite body to have a certain youthful attractiveness.

Josh noticed his dark brown nipples standing erect as Billy bobbed up and down in the water.

"Come on in; it's the right temperature for a skinny dip," Billy suggested.

Josh needed no more prodding he pulled off his shirt with one hand and flung it aside as the other undid his pants. He kicked off his shoes and with a few steps toward the pool pulled off his socks and then his underwear. Josh's manhood liked the view of Billy playing in the water and sprang out erect and eager to explore Billy's hidden regions.

Josh dived into the pool, the cool water refreshing his body. He swam under the water a few strokes enjoying the relief from the heat, until he came to within a few inches of Billy. He forced his upper body out of the water and grabbed Billy by the waist.

"You're a bit late, thought I'd take a dip," quipped Billy, smiling cheekily.

"I had to work late again. Sure has been a scorcher today," replied Josh as he lowered his right hand onto Billy's butt cheek and cupped it tightly.

Billy gasped lightly and moved closer. Josh could feel Billy's penis growing hard against his upper thigh. Josh leaned in and kissed him deeply, and Billy returned the kiss passionately. As their tongues intertwined, Josh moved his hand closer to Billy's hole and started to rub his finger along the puckered entrance. Billy moaned with delight at the attention his hole was receiving.

Josh could wait no more – he lifted Billy up by the waist, holding him close as he carried him over to the side of the pool. Josh gently placed his burden on the edge of the pool's ledge. Josh knelt going further down into the water until his face was centimeters away from Billy's penis. It was hard and fully erect. Josh smiled as he admired it. Billy's dick was only about half as long as Josh's, but it was smooth and soft. Billy's silky dick was definitely one of the most beautiful cocks Josh had ever seen.

Billy looked down at Josh sheepishly, anticipation written all over his face. Billy was obviously eager for Josh to touch his cock. Josh was happy to oblige him; he leaned forward and licked the tip of Billy's knob. Billy's entire body shuddered, and his cock spurred to life. Josh pulled Billy's cock into his mouth and sucked, licking around the shaft with his tongue. Billy's cock was just the right size for Josh's mouth. Josh took full advantage of the fact that Billy's cock size allowed Josh to work it fully with his moist tongue, and caressing the throbbing soft flesh. He reveled in every ecstatic throb that started in Billy's knob and seemed to move down the shaft until it made his entire body shudder. Josh felt the shaft grow thicker and more rigid as it filled with Billy's love juices. As the knob started to pound against his throat Josh knew he must stop before Billy blew his load.

"I'm close, suck me Josh, drain me," Billy moaned.

Josh carefully raised his head, removing Billy's throbbing cock from his mouth; he glanced down to see it rigid and still pulsing with the nearness of release. A small glob of glistening precum oozed from the engorged tip.

"Not yet, Billy, not like that," Josh teased, smiling.

Billy moaned in frustration as Josh climbed out of the water. He grabbed Billy, lifting him and carrying him to the outdoor table. Josh laid Billy down on his back with his small round butt just hanging off the edge.

"But Josh you're so big, you just won't fit," Billy protested meekly.

"Oh I'll fit, don't you worry about that!" Josh glowered as he started to rub his own knob against Billy's tight warm pucker.

Though he knew that nothing could prepare him for Josh's immense girth and the hammering he was about to accept from it, Billy still tried to ready his body for the shafting he was about to receive as best he could.

Josh pushed his engorged cock against Billy's arse but the small entrance was locked tight. Josh glanced around and saw on the table a bottle of tanning oil. He quickly flicked off the lid and dribbled the fluid over his rampant hard-on before dropping the bottle onto the tiles. Josh stroked his pulsing cock with the makeshift lubricant quickly before pressing his dick against Billy's quivering hole. As Billy moaned quietly and trembled with anticipation, Josh forced his shaft into Billy's arse with one powerful stroke.

"Ahhhhh fuck!" Billy cried out as the full length of Josh's long thick cock harpooned him.

Josh grinned – he loved it when Billy reacted like that. Josh pulled out slightly and again thrust into his tight arse repeatedly, Josh's cock was unrelenting. He allowed his thick cock to punish Billy's arse with no restraint. Billy's body flexed, and he moaned with every penetrating stroke.

"Oh you're so big. Too big, Josh!" Billy bleated.

Josh paused and slowly withdrew his bloated manhood from Billy's small arse, until only the tip of his knob was clenched tightly by Billy's pink ring. Josh marveled at the fact that Billy did not look big enough to accommodate his flesh sword, but his large cock somehow found somewhere to go inside Billy's small frame. Billy looked at Josh longingly.

"Give it to me, Josh," Billy begged.

"Take it, Billy, take all my cock!" Josh commanded as he forcefully reinserted his cock and continued his frantic pounding.

"I … I can't! Oh, it's so good … I can't take it" Billy cried as his whole body was banged against the table by Josh's merciless drilling.

"I'm going to come!" Billy roared as he grabbed his own engorged dick and started to stroke it rapidly.

"All right than you can have it all!" Josh warned just as he pushed his cock fully balls-deep into Billy's weary arse. Josh re-doubled his assault on Billy's aching passage, his balls now slapping against the other young man's arse with every thrust. Billy moaned and gasped in ecstasy as he wanked on his own cock and took Josh's assault deep inside him.

Josh thrust violently as his cock expanded even larger, and he filled Billy's already-bursting arse with a mighty load of his jism. As Josh slowed his pace and emptied his cock within Billy, Billy came, too. Spunk gushed from Billy's dick and oozed over his shaft and hand. Josh collapsed onto Billy, and they finally caught their breath, exhausted after their energetic fuck.

* * * * *

Josh awoke with an engorged hard-on; he had trouble realizing where he was at first. Then he felt the stinging cold and the hard rusting metal floor of the wreck. It was still dark, or had he slept all day again? Josh slowly raised himself onto the ripped and torn front seat of the car, the abrasive ripped fabric gently scraping against his bare arse. He looked around sleepily and noticed the stereo had been removed long ago, he wondered lazily if it had been anything like his stereo, the car itself certainly would have been very similar in its day.

Josh stretched his legs, his unprotected toes clanged against something angular and metallic on the floor. He reached down feeling around in the darkness, until finally he found and grabbed the item he had kicked. Now holding it up into the moonlight, he saw it was an old set of keys, he stared at the rust encrusted key chain and confusion griped his mind. There it was – the metal penis Billy had made for him, still attached to the key chain, Josh's key chain! He blinked dumbly and stared – they were his keys, but now they and the key chain were encrusted in a thick layer of rust. How was that possible? How long had he been in captivity?

Josh's hard-on quickly diminished as his mind filled with unanswered questions. He had to know for sure, and he remembered one way to find out. He felt under the withered dashboard. Up and around the back there was a little ledge, his fingers strained and he touched the tube, and clasping it in his trembling hand, he brought it out. He held it close to his face to see it clearly in the moonlight. It was the tube of lube that he had always kept in the car for emergencies, but now it was covered with dirt. The plastic lid was corroding as he rubbed it with his cold, trembling fingers. The tube was old, but he had only just replaced it. This was his car and it had been here for years! In shock, he dropped the lube onto the floor.

Josh suddenly had a horrifying thought. He looked around the floor of the car, and reached for a broken piece of mirror. Being careful not to cut himself, he picked it up and with a deep breath held it to see the reflection of his face. He breathed a sigh of relief when he saw that he was still young and handsome. How could it be his body had not aged, but his car and its contents had?

He shook his head and stroked his cock subconsciously. He had to think, he had to get help, and he had to continue on to the nearest town. He reluctantly opened the door and started walking in the same direction as before. Josh hoped that with his car being here he must be close to his home. He reassured himself that eventually he would see a landmark he recognized or maybe stumble into a town.

Josh walked for a long way down the middle of the road. After some time, he wondered why he had not seen any traffic. This dirt road was in bad shape and was probably one of the many back roads that converged on the towns. He was sure he would see a car eventually, the driver would stop to help him, and they would all be embarrassed by his nakedness. He smiled at the thought that with only an old jacket to cover his body he would feel foolish.

That is when he saw it, dull and dirty in the night. Standing a few feet in front of him was a sign, a road sign. Josh ran to the sign, his heart pounding. He quickly slipped his hand into the jacket sleeve and used it to wipe some of the dirt from the sign. His smile broadened and he let out a laugh – the sign said simply "BAMY."

Bamy, his hometown. He ran a few feet past the sign and yes, there it was, another sign that if he wiped of the grime would say, "BAMY CREEK." He kept going until he felt the rough bitumen under his tender, uncovered feet. Josh started to run, his tired limbs fueled by the realization that he was almost there. He ran until he reached the main street.

The Bamy Pub was on the corner, where it had always been. Josh bounded for the door. Shock stopped him in his tracks, as the doors were boarded shut. He looked around, panicked and bolted for the store; it, too, was boarded shut, but what remained of the door was wide open. He cautiously stepped inside, and his heart sank, as it was derelict. Rubbish and broken shelves lay haphazardly around the store.

He sat on the floor, an old newspaper protecting his naked arse from the cold tiles. Josh put his hands over his face in desperation and tried to comprehend what had become of his world.

* * * * *

Josh and Billy lay on the table in each other's arms. Their naked bodies were already starting to sweat from the summer night air, the warmth from their closeness and their recent exercise.

"Josh, I love you," Billy said tentatively.

"Oh come on, Billy, don't ruin what we have," Josh argued.

"But I do," sighed Billy.

"Look, we are good friends, and I like to fuck you, but that's it!" Josh chastised.

"I know that's not true, Josh," Billy said with sadness in his voice.

"Can you please just drop it already? I don't want to have this argument again!" Josh asserted.

He was getting annoyed. Billy did this occasionally; he would get all overly affectionate, and it would annoy him. Josh did not feel he could love anyone, not even Billy. He wanted to go out into the world and experience life. Josh did not want to be tied down to someone else.

"Josh ... what's that?" Billy asked as calmly as he could.

Billy's question jolted Josh back from his thoughts. He rolled fully onto his back, to see what Billy was referring to. Josh could see lights coming closer from the direction of the driveway.

"Maybe it's the guys I saw earlier; they asked for directions at the gate." However, before Josh had even finished the sentence, he knew it wasn't those guys.

Josh and Billy watched in amazement as the lights were hovering over the front yard now. They both lay there, fascinated by the strange lights. An intense blue light emanated from the other lights. The blue light surrounded Josh; it burned his skin and hurt his head.

"Josh!" Billy cried out "No!"

However, Josh couldn't see or feel anything – it was as if he was floating. The blue light consumed his entire body. He reached for Billy but found only empty air. There was nothing he could do.

Then just as suddenly, there was pressure on his back. Josh was lying on something cold and metallic. As the blue light started to lessen in its intensity, Josh saw vague grey shapes moving around him. His head really hurt, and the bench he lay on was so cold. As much as he tried, Josh couldn't move. He wasn't restrained but was somehow paralyzed. There was a pain in his arm like a needle, and he started to panic, his mind screaming for release. As much as he tried, he couldn't make a sound. Josh thought he would soon slip into insanity.

Then the pain was gone, and his vision slowly returned. As grey figures turned from him before walking away, one of them was holding a vial of blood. The other beings left the room via an arch that then kind of bled or melted into a solid wall. There was one shape remaining, standing close to him. It was grey-skinned and inhumanly thin. Its large elongated head had huge black almond eyes, a tiny nose and a mere slit for a mouth. Josh didn't know exactly what this creature was, but it definitely wasn't human.

"Do not be afraid." It did not speak – the words just seemed to form in Josh's mind and suddenly all fear left him, instead, he was curious and calm. The communication was odd; Josh had to assume it was some form of mental telepathy. He could feel this creature's alien presence inside his mind. "We see what you have done. We wish to do this." The words again formed in Josh's head, but the meaning was unclear.

Josh's legs then parted and rose. No hand or machine moved them. He tried to resist, but he had no control over his body. Josh suddenly realized the meaning of the creature's words as his body moved to make his anal opening more accessible. The creature then held up a device. The device was like a dildo but with many different little extensions coming off it in all directions. Josh was starting to get scared again; that dildo thing looked nasty, and he didn't want it inside him.

The creature moved in close to Josh's head and cocked its own head to one side in a curious manner something like a dog.

"We agree, this is not for you." Formed in Josh's psyche as the creature showed its hand revealing that the probe had gone.

The creature then moved between Josh's parted legs and unseen forces maneuvered Josh's body again. His mind spun – he really was not into this; sex with an alien just seemed so *Springer*.

"You are aroused," thoughts again shaped in Josh's head as his penis filled with blood and came to a fully erect posture. In fact, his cock was more erect than it had ever been – it ached with the strain of its own erection. As Josh lay watching his dick grow to never-before-seen girth and length, he was puzzled but suddenly horny, eager for this creature to take him.

Josh willingly awaited the creature's probe; Josh strained to see its manhood. He became disappointed and confused as he noticed the creature had no cock. Then Josh saw a slit appear between its legs and a tiny tentacle-like thing wiggled as it slowly poked its way out. The tendril didn't stop; it kept emerging until it was as at least twice as long as Josh's cock, and at its base at least as thick.

The tendril brushed against his anus, it felt soft and moist like a tongue, and it started to rim him. The being's strange cock's attentions caused Josh's anal muscles to relax. Josh moaned at the warm wet rimming. Suddenly, the tendril found the opening and wiggled its way inside him. The feeling was like nothing Josh had experienced before, like a tongue fuck but with a penis. It was as if the creature's cock had a mind of its own as it wriggled and squirmed its way deep inside Josh's tight hole.

The creature just stood there only moving its head slightly like it was nodding. However, its penis was going wild inside Josh – it writhed and coiled around in his arse, and it pulsed, expanding and contracting. It was like nothing Josh could ever have imagined.

The being reached out and started to tweak Josh's nipples gently. Its touch was inhuman, cool and rubbery; more like a plant than an animal. Nevertheless, Josh enjoyed the attention. He had very sensitive nipples, and the creature seemed to know exactly how to manipulate them.

Josh was in ecstasy, he couldn't tell how long this went on, but the alien eventually released his nipples. Then the creature's body started to spasm slightly, and its cock inside Josh's arse grew into a wild frenzy of motion. The feeling was intense – both horrible and incredible at the same time. Josh had just about had all he could take when the creature stopped and withdrew its tentacled dick, which quickly wiggled its way back inside the alien's thin grey body. The creature turned to leave, then looked back quickly before leaving the room.

"Release," twisted itself into in Josh's head as the creature turned back momentarily before leaving the room.

As the word forced itself into Josh's consciousness, his cock flared to life, and he came. Repeatedly, his jism oozed out of his cock and just kept coming until finally with a few spurts he was fully drained. His own spunk covered his entire chest and dribbled down his sides. Josh's arse ached from the internal thrashing it had received. He lifted his arm to his head, which also ached inside, and he suddenly realized he could move again. He raised his torso and spun his legs off the bench; he almost fell to the floor his legs were so weak, and his head was still spinning.

Josh looked around and saw that the archway had formed again. He walked cautiously forward and peeked out into a hallway. He could see an exit into a forested area to his left and bolted for it. Josh made it out of the strange laboratory and ran for his life running naked through the woods. He didn't stop to look back. He must have run for hours, and it was cold and dark. He had no idea where he was, and the more he ran the worse his headache became.

Josh was near collapse when he stumbled upon the old derelict cabin. He checked the window and found it was unlocked. He used all his strength to lift it open and then climbed in. His brain burned and he collapsed onto the wooden floorboards.

* * * * *

Josh awoke in the abandoned shop, he was cold and it was still dark. He remembered his abduction, and wondered if somehow time was shorter in that bizarre lab, if he been gone for many years but had only experienced a few minutes?

He got up from the floor and noticed the old newspaper he had been lying on. It was ripped and dirty, but he picked it up and left the shop. Upon walking out into the moonlight, he strained to read the headline. He could pick out a few words – ORBIT SHIFTS and GLOBAL PANIC!

He strained to read more but couldn't. He turned the paper over but nothing was readable there either. What did that mean? Mark had said the mobile network was down and his car looked ancient. It felt as if he hadn't seen daylight in days; then there was the cold. Where was the summer heat?

His thoughts returned to Billy. Billy was at the pool when Josh had been abducted. He could still be at his house. Josh decided he had to find Billy to make sure he was safe. Josh had been so cruel to Billy. He had to find him and make it up to him. Josh ran as fast as he could, out of town and back down the road that he knew would lead to Billy's house.

As he left town and made it to the dirt road, he saw the lights again. The aliens were after him! Josh darted into the woods beside the road, and ran wildly with the lights in pursuit. Josh ran dodging trees and ducking behind them hoping to lose the aliens. Then he dived into a ditch hiding in the shadows. He waited as the lights approached in the sky hoping he hadn't been seen. His head started to hurt again as the blue light hit him. Josh panicked, realizing they had found him. He tried to climb from the ditch but couldn't move. The blue light penetrated him and consumed him before he lost consciousness again.

The mist in his mind parted, and he remembered.

* * * * *

Back in the first cabin, not long after climbing through the window and blacking out, Josh awoke with hands on his body. He opened his eyes and tried to focus but couldn't. He tried to resist, but he didn't have the energy. Someone held up Josh's legs, and someone else was holding his arms down. He became aware of voices and laughter.

"We're in this together, we all get a turn, mates!" A man bellowed from near Josh's head as something large pressed against his exposed anal hole.

He just managed to get a glimpse of the man that was threatening to violate his arse – a heavily muscled male with dark hair. It was the driver, Gus, from the car outside Billy's place.

Large hands held onto Josh's mid-thighs as what must have been Gus's cock pressed harder into Josh's hole. Then it entered, and it was so big! Josh had no control – he tried to squirm away, but the massive cock just kept pushing further and further into his arse.

"So glad you could join our party!" yelled Gus as what had to be the last of his length filled Josh up. The grip on his legs was like a vice, and Josh could do nothing but accept the tool inside him. As he realized he was helpless, he became aroused.

"Please more!" he whimpered.

He felt more hands, and they held Josh's head, pulling it back. He shook his head in a futile attempt to dislodge the large hands from it.

"Come on mate, don't make me chase you," bellowed the man.

Something pressed against Josh's mouth, but he refused to open it. If these guys were going to abuse him, he wasn't going to make it easy for them.

"I'll get it open for you, Mark," said Gus as he lessened the pounding on his victim's arse.

The cock inside Josh slowly withdrew, so just the tip remained inserted. But as soon as Josh relaxed the dick was forced back in with one mighty blow. Josh gasped. Just as suddenly, the cock at his face took advantage of his open mouth and filled his throat.

"Thanks, Gus," Mark moaned as he forced his cock deeper down Josh's throat.

Josh struggled to breathe as the cock filled his airway. He couldn't breathe! He started to panic as the man's large testicles hung over his nose and covered his eyes.

"Its all right, mate," Mark said as he withdrew out of Josh's throat slightly.

Then the dick in Josh's mouth started pounding his throat, and he could manage a few gasps of air through his nose when it withdrew slightly, just before being pushed back in so far and hard it almost made Josh gag.

"What about me?" Another voice chimed in from off to the side.

The voice also sounded familiar. Josh turned his head slightly, just long enough to see the thinly muscled body and shaved head of the other guy from the Landrover, John. Before his vision was blocked by another powerful thrust of Mark's cock within his mouth.

"Why don't you get on there, John?" Gus suggested.

Now Josh was being fucked at both ends. He was no longer being forcibly restrained, but the hands were still there holding him. He could barely breathe, and his already foggy mind was reeling. He had had dreams and fantasies of this situation but had never had the courage or opportunity to try one.

Then a weight pressed on top of him, and he could feel the man's breath on his neck. The cock pumping his throat remained and the weight on his chest made it even harder to catch his breath. John, the man on top of him, rubbed Josh's cock with a slippery gunk and slowly inserted Josh's cock into his arse. He sat on Josh's cock riding it up and down and playing gently with Josh's highly sensitive nipples.

Time seemed a blur of pleasure and pain. His nipples twisted as his cock throbbed inside an unknown arse. Josh's own butt was being fucked raw – Gus showed no restraint. Josh couldn't see much other than Mark's nutsac. Josh could smell the unmistakable scent of man sex, an intoxicating mix of sweat and precum. Moans and groans filled the room as the men reached their peaks of ecstasy.

An unknowable time later, the cock down his throat stiffened and the pounding of his arse grew rougher. Suddenly, cum was gushing down his throat and exploding within his arse. A few more powerful thrusts is all it took for Josh to come, too. He came inside John's arse that rode his cock, as John's jizm squirted over Josh's chest and neck.

John released Josh's cock from his butt, climbing off him. Gus removed his manhood from Josh's arse as Mark finally withdrew from his mouth. A trickle of come drizzled from Josh's arse as he was lowered onto the floor.

"We should go fishing; our friend is going to need to eat," said one of the men, possibly John.

"He really needs to lay off those mushrooms!" Another replied, as Josh slipped into unconsciousness again.

* * * * *

Josh awoke to find the alien being again standing above him. He was cool, but the chilling cold was gone.

"Be calm, we are taking you home," Again, the alien words mysteriously filled Josh's head. Josh instantly became calm. He realized he could move and sat up on the metal examination table. He was naked again and clean. All the cuts, scrapes and bruises from this long night were gone.

"That place was not for you, rest, and you will be home again." The alien's thoughts twisted into his mind.

With those words came a vague understanding. Josh knew that their were many realities or dimensions and that these creatures traveled the different possibilities, studying how alternate events affected the same individual from different dimensions. Josh realized that he had fled into a world that was not his own and that his counterpart on that world probably knew Mark and the others quite well. He knew now he was silly to flee from Mark. If he had stayed in that first cabin maybe they would have helped him. Josh suddenly felt very tired and lying back on the bench, he quickly fell into a deep sleep.

* * * * *

Josh awoke slowly. His head was clear, and he could feel the warmth of Billy's naked body lying in his arms. Opening his eyes, he saw he was lying naked on the bed in Billy's room. Looking over Billy's nakedness brought Josh's cock to life. It quickly stood to attention, and he pressed it against his friend's side.

"You're not the only one who's awake I see?" Billy remarked cheekily, referring to Josh's stiff manhood.

Josh smiled and held him tightly in his arms. He kissed Billy's neck and felt his body with his hands.

"I got a little something for you, Billy," teased Josh as he quickly lubed up his cock and pressed it against Billy's tight little pucker.

"There's nothing little about your something, Josh!" Billy giggled.

Josh held Billy's cock gently stroking it as he slowly inserted his manhood into Billy's taut hole, enjoying every moan Billy made as his stiff dick slowly edged its way deep inside Billy.

Josh quickened his pace slowly and steadily making sure that Billy had enough time to accommodate his thrusts.

"I'm going to come ..." moaned Billy.

Josh thrust his engorged cock into Billy's sweet tight arse quicker and harder and stroked Billy's erect dick faster. Then with a final thrust, they both came simultaneously. Josh's jizm filled Billy's anus, and Billy's sprayed all over the sheets.

Josh stayed inside Billy, both of them lying on their sides. He held Billy tight not wanting to ever let go. Josh finally knew in his heart, he didn't need to go out looking – he had already found the man of his dreams. Billy had been right here waiting for him all along.

"I love you, Billy," Josh whispered into Billy's ear.

"I love you, too, Josh. I think I always have," Billy replied as he snuggled further back into Josh's embrace.

Slowly, Josh drifted off to sleep holding Billy close, his cock slowly going limp inside the other young man's warm hole. As Josh relaxed, he thought of his love for Billy and the great times they would have over the warm summer days ahead. One last thought entered Josh's mind before sleep finally took him ... that Billy might like to go to Hudson Woods tomorrow and see if they could hook up with John and Gus at the rave.

PASSPORT TO FREEDOM
Lew Bull

Wars have been fought throughout man's history, and in them, traumatic and often degrading acts have taken place. It's almost as though man is hell-bent on either trying to annihilate his fellow man or reduce him to a crumbling insignificant creature. Wars in the Middle East are no different from those that are conducted in Africa or other parts of the world, and it was during one of these occasions that I found myself in Central America, caught up in guerilla warfare.

I had been sent to Central America as a war journalist, reporting for a German newspaper. My time wandering through jungles had generally been uneventful, but one day, the vehicle in which I and three other journalists, two German and one British, were traveling became stuck in the mud along a narrow road, bounded on either side by dense forest. Three of us climbed out of the truck and began to push. Out of the dense jungle foliage emerged twelve armed men, each pointing an AK-47 rifle at us. They were clad in green camouflage kit and varied in age. They shouted something to us in what I thought was Spanish, so we froze where we were, in the mud. Although we were journalists and therefore regarded ourselves as being neutral, it was a frightening experience to be confronted by these men, as we weren't sure for which side they were fighting.

"Journalists!" shouted Heinz, one of the Germans, in an effort to defuse the situation, and raising his hands at the same time.

Instinctively, we all followed suit.

Everyone seemed to be shouting at once, so it became confusing, this cacophony of noise. The circle of men closed in on us like a pack of hyenas ready for the kill, until they were face-to-face with us, then one of them spoke in English.

"Who are you?" a grizzly-looking man said, jabbing Manfred, the other German, in the stomach with the barrel of his rifle.

"We are journalists," replied Manfred.

"Who you journalists for?" barked the grisly man.

"For a German newspaper," I answered.

"You Americano," he blurted, turning on me.

"Yes," I replied, not sure of whether I had said the right thing.

He spat on the ground at my feet, so I took that to mean that I was not popular with him. This action confirmed for me that they were the rebels. The grizzly man turned and walked away from us, and as he did so, barked out an order in Spanish to his men. Just then, an army truck rounded a corner and came to a stop next to us. We were shuffled to the truck, and it was indicated that we should climb up into the rear of the vehicle. We did as we were commanded, and the other men joined us.

As we started our journey to who-knew-where, I looked around at our captors. Most looked young with a couple of men who might have been in their mid to late forties. The older men either had beards or moustaches, while the younger ones tended to be clean-shaven.

The four of us were seated on the floor of the truck while the men sat on benches along the sides of the vehicle. My eyes traveled down one row of benches and then the other. Even at this fear-provoking time, I was still able to take cognizance of some good-looking faces among the soldiers. They were all Latinos, some darker tanned than others, but none had the semblance of a smile on his face.

The German guys broke into their native tongue and communicated with the British guy and me through this medium, in the hopes that the rebels wouldn't understand what we were saying.

The journey was long and arduous. We were never sure whether government troops might attack us or whether the rebels might kill us for the mere fun of it. The truck slipped and slid along the narrow muddy track until we reached another side road. We veered off the main road and headed down into a steep valley. After much meandering, we reached a clearing alongside a river. There were a number of crude huts made from wood and iron in which the men probably stayed. The truck came to a halt, and we were ordered out. The rebels once again surrounded us while old grizzly went off to one of the huts. After a moment, he and another man appeared.

An instruction was barked, and the soldiers surrounding us lined up and stood to attention. The two men from the hut moved toward us. Grizzly stopped while the other, a tall, elegant-looking man continued walking toward us. His thick black hair lay greased to his head, and his small moustache had been trimmed smartly. He was swarthy with a Y-shaped upper torso that streamlined to a trim waist. His tight combat fatigues hugged his body, and I couldn't help but notice a pleasing bulge in the front of his crotch. He walked past each of us, surveying us carefully.

"You speak English?" he queried in his broken English tinged with a Spanish accent.

We all nodded.

"I am told you say you are journalists. Is that so?"

Again we nodded.

"You!' he said pointing at me. "Do you have a tongue?"

"Yes," I replied a little timidly.

"What is your name, Americano?"

"Gary," I answered.

"Well, Gary, I am Captain Miguel Lopez. I am leader of this band of liberators. Who are these others?"

"This is Manfred and Heinz, from Germany, and Bill who is British."

"And what are you men doing here? Spying for the government?"

"No. We're just reporting on the conflict that's taking place." I thought I would flatter Captain Lopez. "We are reporting on how well your rebels are doing."

"I told you we are liberators, not rebels," he barked with annoyance in his voice.

After a little more of what might be called mild interrogation, we were led off to one of the huts, which were sparsely furnished. There were three beds, a table and two chairs, and a drafty, broken window through which rain and wind would no doubt fly. The door was slammed behind us, and we heard the click of the key as it locked the door. We were their prisoners.

"We've got to get out of here before they kill us," said Bill, pacing the room like a caged tiger.

"Well, we could easily break out of this window," suggested Heinz, but before he could continue with his escape plan, I interrupted.

"Have you seen outside? There are guards everywhere. We'd probably get shot the minute the first person left the window. No, we're going to have to find another way of getting out."

Heinz looked around the room and said, "How are we going to sleep? There are only three beds."

Each of us looked at the other, but nobody came up with a suggestion.

"We'll have to draw straws to see who sleeps on the floor," said Manfred, stoically, almost sounding as though he was destined to be the one to sleep on the floor.

"Why not throw all the mattresses on the floor next to each other then we can all sleep on them," suggested Bill.

"Trust the British to come up with a plan," I commented. "The only thing they can't plan is our escape."

The two Germans laughed heartily at my dig at Bill.

Rather indignantly, Bill reminded Heinz and Manfred that during the Second World War, it was mainly the British who found ways to escape, to which Manfred replied, "Ja, it was only because we Germans kept catching you."

This banter seemed to break the tension that surrounded us.

The door to the hut was unlocked, and a young rebel, whom I had noticed on the truck, came in bearing a tray of food and drink. He placed the tray on the table, stepped back and said, "For you."

We hadn't eaten all day, so hunger pains were manifesting in our stomachs, making us ravenous. Our young captor stood and watched as we gobbled the food, each grabbing as much as he could. Occasionally I caught him watching me, and when I did, I would smile. To my surprise I noticed a slight smile emerge across his face.

Our captor couldn't have been more than twenty, athletically built with typically Latino features. His dark eyes flashed when he gave me the odd subtle smile, and I could see that when he folded his arms as he stood and watched, his biceps were bulging, just like the package that he had hidden in his pants.

Darkness was beginning to overcome the jungle, and soon a few dim lights could be seen around the camp, but our hut had no illumination of any kind. Because of this, we all decided to settle down for the night and await the next day to see what would happen to us.

The claustrophobic air that surrounded us was stifling. I peeled off my jeans and lay down on the mattress in only my Calvin Klein briefs. Manfred came and lay next to me, having also removed his jeans. Soon all four of us had stripped off our outer clothing and had huddled together on the three mattresses.

As we lay in the dark, talking quietly to each other, wondering about our fate, I could feel Manfred's hand gently touch my side. This touch awakened a sensation within me, and I could feel myself getting hard. I adjusted the lie of my cock in my Calvin Klein briefs and then turned on my side so as to face him. As I did so, I know that my hardened cock rubbed against his leg. Once I had got comfortable, Manfred rolled onto his side to face me. I could feel that he, too, had an erection, which rubbed gently against mine. Neither of us touched the other with our hands because we didn't want the others to realize what we were doing. Instead, we just let our cocks rub and throb together. As we were lying there, enjoying each other's company, the door to the hut flew open and the young soldier who had brought us our food entered again.

"The man called Mr. Gary. Who is he?" he asked, his voice revealing a touch of deep masculinity, yet his earlier appearance seemed that of a young man.

"I am Gary," I said. "What do you want?"

"The Captain wants to see you now!"

He emphasized the word now, so I left the comfort of Manfred's company and rose from the mattress. The young soldier stared down at my crotch. My erect cock was tenting the front of my briefs, making it clear the length, shape and girth of my cock. A wry smile emerged across his face as he escorted me from the hut toward the Captain's hut.

As the door to the Captain's hut opened, and the Captain saw me, my young soldier smiled to the Captain and said, "La tiene bien grande."

I smiled, too, and replied, "Thank you my friend, I think we can all see that I'm well hung."

"You understand Spanish?" inquired the Captain.

"A little," I answered.

My erection was still very evident as I stood in the light of the doorway, my white briefs revealing my excitement.

"Come in," said Captain Lopez. "Have a seat."

Both the soldier and I entered together. The Captain told the young man to sit to one side while he and I spoke. I sat down in the chair offered to me while Captain Lopez sat on the edge of his desk, facing me. His legs were spread apart and I noticed how the bulge in his crotch was outstanding. My erection never diminished, and a wet patch had developed on the material of my briefs near the tip of my cock.

"You say you are journalists."

"Yes, that's true."

"And you say you are covering the war here."

"That's also true."

"What aspects of the war are you covering?"

"I think we've tried to cover every aspect."

"Even how kind and gentle we rebels, as you call us, can be?"

"That I can't say because I haven't had first-hand experience of that."

"Pedro, show our guest how gentle we can be."

The young guard stood up, advanced toward me, stood between my legs and then sank to his knees. He was now eye level with my burgeoning crotch. He stretched out a hand and gently traced the length of my cock through my Calvin Klein briefs. I gasped as his gentle touch sent shivers of exhilaration through my body. Captain Lopez remained seated on the edge of his desk, watching the two of us. Pedro then lowered his mouth to my outlined cock and ran his wet tongue along my shaft. As he did this, so I noticed how Captain Lopez ran his hand across his hardened cock, which was now tenting his pants.

Pedro continued to saturate my briefs with his tongue and mouth until the wet outline of my cock became apparent, then he stopped, stood up and went back to his seat.

"I see you have a good weapon on you," said Captain Lopez, still stroking his shaft. "Pedro was right when he said you were well endowed. Was Pedro gentle enough to you?"

I couldn't deny Pedro's technique with his tongue and mouth.

"He was very good," I replied.

"That is why I keep him to myself," said Captain Lopez, rising from the desk, crossing to Pedro and standing before him.

Pedro extended a hand and rubbed the engorged length that was presented to him. Then slowly he unbuttoned the fly to his Captain's pants. Underneath the Captain was bare. His tanned skin glowed, and as Pedro revealed the Captain's swollen cock, my eyes lit up. A long, fat cock emerged, its foreskin still covering the head like a hood until Pedro slowly pushed it back to reveal the glistening pink mushroom-shaped glans. Once he had done this, Pedro lowered his head and opened his mouth. In one move he had engulfed his Captain's cock right down to its base. Captain Lopez exhaled a sigh and gave a gentle thrust into the back of Pedro's throat.

I sat and watched as Pedro pleasured his master, allowing Captain Lopez to thrust deeply down the depths of his open throat. All the while, my cock throbbed and oozed precum. After three or four minutes, Captain Lopez removed Pedro's mouth from his cock, helped him to his feet and ordered him to take me back to my hut.

"You have seen how we so-called rebels can be gentle to others, now go and sleep and think on these things. Goodnight, Mr. Gary."

I rose from my chair; the front of my briefs soaked in precum, and thanked the captain. As Pedro and I made our way back to the hut, I was almost tempted to take Pedro in some bushes and finish off what he had started, but I was afraid that the other guards or the captain might see me doing it. I wondered how Pedro must feel because at no stage had either the Captain or I even touched him.

When I entered our hut, Manfred was still awake.

"What happened?" he asked as I lay down on the mattress.

I wasn't sure that I should divulge what had happened; instead I snuggled close to Manfred and let him feel my wet briefs rub up against him. A searching hand felt between my legs and found the wet patch. His hand traced along my length, squeezing my shaft as he stroked me. After what I had experienced that evening, I was desperate to shoot my load, so I let him have his way with me.

The following day, each of us was taken out separately to Captain Lopez's office and interrogated. When it came to my turn, Captain Lopez was waiting for me.

"I hope you enjoyed our display of friendship last night?" I smiled and said that I had. "You will stay here with us until the world knows that we are not rebels. We will hold you hostage until your countries acknowledge our cause."

"And what is your cause?"

"You are a journalist, you should know," he scowled.

"Yes, you're right. It is freedom for all oppressed."

"That's right. Do you feel oppressed, Mr. Gary?"

"The only oppression I feel is being held hostage here by you."

"Have I or my men oppressed you in any way?" he asked, walking around me and surveying me from every angle.

"No."

"Then maybe we must oppress you then you will have something to complain about."

I sensed that he was perhaps a little angry by my answers and brusquely ordered me out and back to my hut. When I arrived back, the four of us began asking each other what sort of questions had been asked. Manfred sidled up to me and whispered so that the others wouldn't hear him, "What's he like?"

I looked at him, smiled and then whispered back, "*Ein großer schwanz*".

"Is his cock bigger than yours?"

"Just as *großer*," I joked.

While Manfred and I were enjoying a close relationship in this camp, Bill and Heinz centered their activities on trying to develop an escape plan.

After a week, our countries' governments had realized that we were being held hostage but seemed to be doing very little to get us returned home. Every day, we had been interrogated, and every night I had been taken to Captain Lopez's hut to witness the kindness shown to him by Pedro. Apart from Manfred, who knew what happened on my nightly visits, the other two became suspicious of my nightly departures and wondered whether I was playing into the rebel's hands.

One evening, when Pedro had come to fetch me to go to Captain Lopez's hut, I spoke to him on the way there.

"Pedro, does the Captain never give you pleasure?"

I saw a sign of resignation cross his face. He hesitated then answered a subdued, "No!"

"Would you like to have some pleasure?" He smiled and nodded. "If I were to give you some pleasure, would you help us to escape from here?"

Panic was written right across his young face.

"I could not do that."

"No one needs to know. I will give you happiness, and then in the dark of night, we can escape from our hut and head for the government forces."

"You will bring them here to kill us. No!"

My plan wasn't working so I decided to take a different approach once I reached Captain Lopez's hut.

When we entered I was surprised to see the Captain sitting behind his desk, shirtless and with his feet up on the desk. I stood in front of the desk while Pedro went to his customary chair and sat. As I stood looking down at the Captain, I watched as he constantly ran his hands over his crotch. He was teasing me once more.

"Drop your jeans, Mr. Gary," said the Captain, smirking at me.

I unzipped them and let them fall to the ground. I kicked off my shoes and stepped out of my jeans. My cock lay flaccid within the confines of the cotton material of my briefs, but not for long. I could feel an erection starting, just admiring his well-defined body. I also thought of a plan.

I shucked my briefs to my ankles and stepped out of them, allowing myself total freedom. I stared at the Captain as he admired my body, which I had managed to keep in good shape, and then I gave a command.

"*¡Mamámela!* Suck me!" I said, with conviction. Both Captain Lopez and Pedro stared in shock. I stood there gripping my long shaft in my hand and said, "You want this, then suck it!"

Captain Lopez removed his feet from his desk, rose and walked around to confront me. "You have cheek, Mr. Gary," he said, grabbing hold of my cock and balls and squeezing them. I cried out as I felt the pain shoot through my body. "Not so tough now, hey?"

He released his grip, and as quickly as he had done that, his fist flew through the air and connected me on the mouth, cutting my lip in the process. The shock of his action stunned me, but also sent a pleasurable sense through my body, causing my cock to throb involuntarily as I tasted the blood trickling from my lip.

"You think you are big?" said the now strutting Captain as he undid the buttons on his camouflage pants and dropped them to his ankles. He kicked off his boots and removed his pants. He turned to face me, and I saw his massive weapon, erect and proud. Pedro's eyes lit up, and I must confess, so did mine. Now that we were both naked together, I looked at our cocks and realized that he was bigger than I. His foreskin had rolled back, and his cock-head was engorged and getting fatter all the time.

"This is big," he said, waving his bargepole in the air. "Now you suck on this."

Quickly I retorted, "If I do that for you, then you must do something for me and the others."

"What!"

"Let us go. You said you were fighting for freedom, so you can set a good example of that ideology by setting us free, and we could also write about the good that your men are doing in our various newspapers."

I felt sure that this was an offer he couldn't refuse. Either way he scored: He could have my ass and get free publicity for his cause.

"¡Cógeme! Fuck me!" I exclaimed.

Pedro's eyes widened with delight, while Captain Lopez strolled around me surveying the prize meat that he was deciding on whether to take advantage of or not.

"¡Bonito fundillo! A nice ass," said Pedro, licking his lips.

Captain Lopez stood in front of me, his cockhead touching mine. The drop of precum, which had risen up my shaft and exited from my piss slit, lubricated the head of his cock. He swiveled his hips, making his cock swing against mine, hitting it, then he walked behind me. I felt a firm hand on my butt, and then he slapped my ass. The sting reverberated through my body, causing my cock to jerk spontaneously.

Just as the stinging sensation was beginning to subside, I felt the tip of his tongue venture into my ass crack. It was such a cooling feeling, and it felt so relaxing, that I automatically bent over, allowing him easier access to my ass. My pink bud winked at him, and he licked my opening, softening me up for his planned attack.

Out of the corner of my eye, I watched as Pedro frantically rubbed his erection within his camouflage pants. I could see that he was desperate to be part of this action. I moved my head, indicating that he should come and join in. Without hesitation, Pedro rose from his chair, unbuttoned his pants, stepped out of them and headed toward my head. My mouth was waiting for his cock.

Pedro's cock was fatter than the Captain's, but shorter. His foreskin had also shucked back along his shaft revealing a glowing head waiting to be lubricated by my mouth. I engulfed the young man's appendage as Miguel Lopez sank his thick, hard cock slowly into my warm chute. I held my breath as I felt his huge cock being pushed slowly inwards.

"Aargh! You are so tight!" he exclaimed as his cock sank deeper into me.

The feeling he was creating was one of ecstasy for me. I pushed back onto his bargepole, allowing him deeper access, until I felt his heavy balls nudge up against my tensed ass. His hands clasped hold of my nipples, and he pinched them, creating an orgasmic rush through my body. As this happened, my mouth sank deeply over Pedro's thick cock, causing him to gasp with pleasure.

Miguel knew exactly how to use his cock and please a man. I could feel my eyes almost roll into the back of my head, as his cock seemed to stretch my ass. In fact, it felt as though he was splitting me as his cock rhythmically ploughed back and forth into me. His strong arms held me firmly so that I didn't fall over from his manly thrusts.

Suddenly, Pedro felt he wanted to be an even bigger part of the passion. He spun around, took hold of my cock and guided it toward his tight little ass. I felt myself slide effortlessly into his waiting entrance and then felt the tightness close around my shaft. He clamped firmly on my length and squeezed his ass as I entered him. I thought that my cock was being strangled and as this sensation ran through me, so I tightened my grip on Miguel's weapon. With the three of us now conjoined, we ploughed into each other, our bodies slapping and sweating against each other.

I turned my head slightly to be able to see Miguel, and as I did this, so his mouth found mine. His tongue entered and searched my mouth, finding my tongue and dueling with it. With our lips clamped together, and him tasting my blood, he thrust more frantically, causing me to also plough into Pedro.

Pedro was the first to come, and as he shot his load, tightening his ass muscles in the process, I could feel myself rising to the edge of no return.

"I'm coming!" I gasped as Miguel increased his speed and depth of thrusts.

His breathing became more intense and then he growled a deep guttural sound, shouted "¡Me estoy viniendo! I'm coming!"

Our bodies rocked and shook as we each unloaded the mass of pent-up lust that lay waiting to escape. As our breathing began to return to a form of normality and our throbbing cocks began to subside, Pedro slipped from me and then I slipped from Miguel. He turned me around to face him.

"Your mouth, it is still bleeding."

I smiled. "It's from where you hit me."

He kissed me long, but gently "You are a good fuck," he said, pulling me closer to his chest.

"So are you," I replied.

Pedro in the meantime had returned to his chair and was sitting watching us, his cock still leaking the last few drops of his love juice.

"I hope that I have pleased you," I said, looking deep into the Captain's eyes.

"You have," he answered.

"Does that mean that you would consider the offer I made to you about us going free?"

He obviously didn't like the reminder, as he sulked back to behind his desk and sat down, looking angry. I remained staring at him, waiting for an answer; even Pedro sat alert waiting to hear the outcome. I could see that he was contemplating the outcome for him should he release us.

"If I let you go, the army will be in here before you even reach your home, which is not good for us. On the other hand, if I keep you here, I can use you to bargain with."

"But if you let us go, we can broadcast to the world your cause and that you are only concerned about the freedom for the oppressed," I retorted.

"I shall sleep on it. Now go. Pedro, take him to his hut."

Pedro and I got dressed and the two of us departed. On the way, Pedro stopped and said, "Mr. Gary, thank you for the pleasure you gave me."

"Pedro," I said, "it was my pleasure. Not only did Captain Lopez give me pleasure, but also so did you. You have a beautiful ass and body that you must be proud of." I could see that these compliments made Pedro happy. "Pedro, where are your family?"

"Puerto Rica."

"Why don't you come with us, and we can all escape, and you can return to your family?" I was hoping that if Captain Lopez wasn't keen on letting us go, perhaps Pedro might help us to escape.

I could see that he was intrigued by the offer, but also afraid that he might be caught and punished for helping us to escape.

Two days later, Pedro came to our hut at lunchtime with our usual ration of food. He placed the tray on the floor and stood watching us, instead of his usual leaving. I watched him with interest, and when we had finished eating, I offered to help him clean up the plates at the tap outside of the hut. Together we stood next to the running water, washing the plates.

"Did you want to say something to me, Pedro?"

"Tonight, Mr. Gary, you will be called to the Captain's hut, but on our way back to your hut we must make our way to the jungle. A truck will be waiting there for you and your friends."

"But what about you?"

His face became depressed and a forlorn look appeared.

"I will waylay Captain Lopez for you. You must tell the others to be prepared."

I thanked Pedro and went back inside to the others.

"What was all that about?" enquired Bill, who had been watching from the window.

"Tonight we're escaping," I said in a sotto voce.

"How?" interrupted Heinz.

"Tonight we are going to go to a truck, which will be hidden somewhere out of the camp and taken to safety."

"When is this going to happen ... tonight? asked Heinz.

"I don't know, but we'd better get ready for whenever it happens."

An element of excitement mixed with tension brewed among us as we waited for night to arrive. At nine that evening, I was fetched by Pedro for my nightly visit to Captain Lopez.

"When I leave the hut, I will leave it unlocked and you three must slip out, head in a northerly direction for about five hundred meters through the jungle until you come to a small clearing. There will be a truck waiting for you there. As soon as Mr. Gary gets to you, you must go," said Pedro, with a touch of sorrow intertwined with anxiety in his voice.

Pedro and I made our way to Captain Lopez's hut. When we entered he was already naked and sitting on the edge of his desk. I studied his solid, beautiful body and thought how I was going to miss him and our nightly fun. He sat stroking his long, tanned cock, and I watch its steady growth. I didn't need an invitation, but immediately took it into my mouth and started lubricating it with my tongue. Pedro sat silently on his chair, watching my actions.

Once I had gotten Miguel hard enough, I gently pushed him so that he was lying across his desk, then I sat astride him and lowered my waiting ass onto his bargepole, impaling myself on him. The pleasure that ran through my body as I sank down his length was most satisfying. Once he was embedded in me, I began to ride him, sliding up and down his full length. We continued like this for quite some time until I could feel my balls rising as they readied themselves to fire my load.

"I'm going to come," I warned him.

Miguel thrust up into my innards, hitting my magic button that set in motion a flood of warm cum that coated his chest and stomach. When I had emptied myself of all my juices, I slid from his throbbing cock and told Pedro to take my place. Pedro smiled at the invitation and stripped off and did as I told him.

I guided Miguel's cock into Pedro's waiting ass and watched as the young man slid down to rest on Miguel's crotch. The two had often done this and both enjoyed each other sexually. Pedro leant forward and began kissing Miguel, passionately. This was my sign to escape.

I grabbed my clothes and quietly and stealthily left the Captain's hut and darted through the dark in the direction of where the truck should be. I ran through the jungle, being slashed by sharp branches and leaves until I reached the clearing and there was the truck. I saw the others in the back and leapt in to meet them. As I did so, the truck started up and we headed away from the camp.

"You're naked!" said surprised Bill. "Why?"

Manfred laughed quietly and sidled closer to me.

"I was your passport to freedom," I said.

"What were you doing?" enquired Heinz.

"Don't let it worry you. Just be grateful that we're on our way home."

Manfred knew exactly what I had been doing and whispered to me, "I wish it was me with you in there."

I squeezed his thigh and answered, "When we get to safety, it will be."

We sat in silence as the darkened truck heaved its way up the hill to safety, but one thing worried me – Pedro. Through the jungle we traveled until we made a sudden stop. The four of us remained still, waiting to hear or see what was happening. The back of the truck was flung open and we froze. In the dark we made out a silhouette climb in the back alongside us, but no one spoke.

"Mr. Gary, are you here?"

"Pedro, is that you?" I asked, excitedly.

"Yes."

"How did you manage to get away without Miguel harming you?"

"He made it clear to me that he was tired of me and that it was your ass that he longed for, so after I had gained some pleasure from him, I fled into the jungle to meet up with the truck."

"But how did the driver know to pick you up?"

"He's my brother," came the reply.

I put my arm around the naked Pedro and our two naked bodies huddled together, warming our souls and ourselves as we headed for freedom and a new life for my young friend.

THE AFTER-WORKOUT
Milton Stern

Bobby always worked out at 5:00 am, walking from his home in Columbia Heights in Washington, DC, down 16th Street, to Results the Gym on U Street, in the dark, early morning hours six days a week. His friends worried that he would get mugged one day, but Bobby wasn't worried. Even though he was only five-foot-five, he weighed in at almost 170 pounds, and all of that was solid muscle. Some joked that at least twenty of it was cock as Bobby was known for his endowment, which would make a horse envious. This was another reason he chose to work out so early. Results had open showers, and Bobby grew tired of all the stares he would get while showering since his dick hung at least to mid-thigh even under the coldest spray. When he was done working out around 6:00 am, he was usually the only one in the shower, which suited him just fine.

This particular morning, Bobby was shampooing his hair after a grueling chest workout when he heard a showerhead being turned on, then another. Great, he thought to himself, more gawkers. Bobby turned around, so his back was to the wall as he rinsed the shampoo from his hair, and when he opened his eyes, he almost gasped at what he saw. He blinked twice to be sure he was not hallucinating. Standing across from him, using adjacent showers were identical twins, and these were no ordinary twins. They were blond, blue-eyed Adonises, over six-feet tall, with god-like physiques and hanging between their legs were the largest dicks Bobby had ever seen soft, with the exception of his own of course.

The twins pretty much ignored Bobby as they soaped up and rinsed off. Bobby decided to do the same, but he had to face the wall, for staring at the twins would surely cause his cock to swell, and there would be no hiding his hard-on. The three men finished showering at the same time, dried off and made their way to their lockers to get dressed. Bobby finished dressing first, and after deciding against introducing himself, he left the gym and proceeded to walk back home up 16th Street.

As he crossed Florida Avenue, Bobby noticed a car across the street that was moving in the same direction he was but rather slowly. He thought nothing of it, figuring it was probably one of the newspaper delivery drivers making his early rounds.

He walked just a few more yards more when the car sped up, then made a sudden tire-squealing U-turn and stopped in front of Bobby. Before he could react, the passenger side door opened, and a man grabbed Bobby, placed a hand with a handkerchief over his mouth and threw him into the back seat of the car. Then, the car sped off.

Bobby blinked open his eyes and did not know where he was or how long he had been there. He tried to say something, but he had a ball-gag in his mouth, and when he looked down, he saw that he was naked and strapped to a table on his back. He looked around the room and noticed it was a basement with little to no furniture that he could see from his vantage point. He started to panic and hyperventilate just as one of his captors entered the room.

It was one of the twins from the gym, and he was now standing over Bobby wearing nothing but a pair of *lederhosen*. The Adonis noticed Bobby was hyperventilating, so he removed the ball-gag and put a paper bag over Bobby's mouth. Bobby breathed into the bag, and his captor kept the bag there until his breathing calmed down.

Once the bag was removed, Bobby started shouting, "Where am I? Who are you? What are you doing with me?"

The twin said nothing. He placed a finger over his mouth to indicate that Bobby should stop shouting. Bobby calmed down and waited for the blond to say something. But, nothing was said. Then, the other twin entered the room, dressed in identical *lederhosen* and stood on the other side of Bobby. The twins looked at each other then the twin to his right spoke.

"If you promise not to shout, we will make this as pleasant as possible, but if you do shout, you will regret the day you were born."

Quietly, Bobby asked, "Make what pleasant?"

"This experience, of course," the other twin said. "We just want to have a little fun with you, and if we enjoy ourselves, we will let you go when we are done, but if we find you tedious, we will torture you until you beg for your own death."

Bobby didn't have to think long about his options. He was apparently strapped tightly to the table, and even if he did manage to get loose, these guys were twice his size.

They looked at Bobby and smiled, then opened their lederhosen, pulled out their enormous dicks and proceeded to piss all over Bobby. The little muscleman was no stranger to water sports, so this did not bother him as long as they avoided his face, and fortunately they did even though they seemed to piss a gallon each. The stench of their urine permeated the room, and Bobby could only wonder what was yet to come as he had never before been in a situation such as this. Once their bladders were empty, they removed their lederhosen and ran their hands all over Bobby's thickly muscled body working the piss into every pore.

One grabbed his balls and gave them a good yank, causing Bobby to grunt, while the other squeezed his dick, which was now starting to fill even though he tried to keep it from getting hard. But, it was to no avail, as the hands torturing his cock and balls were doing more to turn him on than frighten him, and within a minute, his dick was at its full ten inches, which on his five-foot-five frame brought the mushroom head to right below his pecs.

The twin to his right hit a button under the table, and suddenly Bobby's legs were being pulled up and apart by some sort of pulley device he had not noticed before, and the contraption did not stop until Bobby was suspended by his ankles with only his shoulders on the table. Then the twin to his left hit a button and the same thing happened to his wrists until he was suspended by his wrists and ankles, spread eagle from both ends with no support for his back. He thought he was going to be quartered, when the twin to his right reached up and pulled down a leather strap, passed it under his back to the other twin, who then connected it to a hook in the ceiling, thus supporting Bobby's back. The table was then rolled away, and Bobby was lowered until he was just below waist level of his captors.

The twin on his right then moved down to his feet and positioned himself between his legs while the other one went to the other side of the room to get a cart and wheel it over to where his brother was standing. In spite of all this, Bobby's dick refused to go down. He wondered if he was suffering from Stockholm Syndrome. *But, didn't that take a few months or even years?* He thought.

Bobby could not see what was on the table, but guessed at least one of the items was grease or lard, as he felt his ass being slathered with something thick and gloppy. Then he felt the intruder – one, maybe two, maybe even three fingers being forced into his ass, twisting and probing with no finesse at all. Bobby gritted his teeth and took the intrusion like a man as the other twin walked over to his left and stood by his head.

Bobby looked over and saw that he now sported a huge hard-on that rivaled his in size, and it was sticking straight out at his face with precum practically pouring from the slit. Bobby involuntarily licked his lips, and this captor shoved his enormous meat into Bobby's mouth without ceremony. Bobby figured if they were going to kill him, he might as well go out with a smile, so he sucked hungrily on the huge cock in his mouth, which continued to leak pints of precum that tasted better than he would acknowledge to these two bastards.

As he was chowing down on the manmeat, he felt the fingers exit his asshole, only to be rudely replaced by the other huge cock in the room, all greased up and practically up to his nipples within seconds. Then the pounding began – from both ends.

The twins showed no mercy as they used the little muscle man for their own pleasure as if he were just a hole to be plugged and filled with cock. No attention was given to Bobby's dick, which now ached it was so hard, while his huge balls drew up, ready to explode.

The twins had great staying power and pumped and pumped for quite a while, or at least it seemed quite a while, until the one in Bobby's mouth exploded with a yell, and shot pint after pint of his thick cum down Bobby's throat, which he didn't lose a drop of. Then, his brother yelled identically and left his own quart of milk in Bobby's ass, causing Bobby to shoot a load to be envied all over his torso with a few shots hitting his chin.

The twins exited their respective holes, and Bobby thought *that's it?* And, with that, a hand with a handkerchief was placed over his face again.

Bobby opened his eyes, and after looking up, saw that a couple of people were staring down at him, including a police officer. He shook his head, and after looking around, realized he was in Meridian Hill Park.

The police officer helped him up and asked, "Are you OK? How long have you been lying there?"

"What time is it?" Bobby asked.

"Around 8:00 am," the officer answered, and Bobby took a good look at him. He was over six-feet tall, blond and obviously built and hung. He then looked out to 16th Street at the patrol car and saw an identical officer waiting for his partner.

"Only two hours?" Bobby asked. "That's the best you can do?" And, Bobby walked away with a smile.

INTERVENTION
O.H. Fowler

It wasn't about sex. I could have had him without all the trouble – I did, in fact.

We met at a party. One of those invitation-only bacchanals I had no idea even existed until after my public troubles. A few rich old queens scattered around the Northeast have them regularly, though that one was my first and last.

My recent notoriety made me an attractive guest for certain elements of the community, though probably not the ones you think. With the ink still fresh in the headlines ("Dirty Doctor Awarded Undisclosed Settlement,") my presence proved an added enticement to those invited, I'm sure.

I'm not certain why I went, to be honest. I suppose I was still reeling from the loss of everything that had given my life structure. One day, I was a founding partner in one of the largest pediatric practices in Boston, respected but relatively anonymous, and the next I had become a notorious pervert. It was like being swept away by a flood – I was still hurtling down stream, wondering how long I could keep my head up.

When I pulled into the circular drive, I had no idea what awaited me. Life in the conservative suburbs had not prepared me for bare-chested valets in leather pants with feathered masks hiding half their faces. One dark-skinned beauty smiled and greeted me by name. I remember hoping he could see properly through the eyeholes; I'm rather fond of my car.

The host greeted me and made a few polite introductions before melting away. A sharp-faced man inquired about the size of my settlement, managing to make it sound obscene.

"Enough to keep me comfortable," I answered. My former business partners had not admitted wrongdoing in forcing me out of my own practice, but they paid me what it was worth and then some. I'd been happy enough to let it go; thinking that part of my life was over.

Years of dedication and study, gone at the stroke of a pen. "The papers didn't say because all the parties involved agreed not to discuss it."

"A gag order, hmm?" The others grinned at his innuendo.

"Something like that." I smiled at them and saw the effect it had. I had been little more than a curiosity to them, but I saw their eyes on me and realized I was not without power here, even as fresh meat.

The talk went on in the same vein, playful and sly, but their hungry faces did not interest me.

I slipped off to a quiet corner as soon as I could manage it. If this was the loving embrace of the gay community, then I was more screwed than I had thought.

Sure, I'd won the legal battle and a great deal of cash, but I'd lost my practice – the only thing that had ever really mattered to me. Perhaps that was why I had stayed in the closet, though coming out quietly would have been better than an arrest for lewd conduct in a public men's room. No desperate, anonymous hook-up was worth the price I'd paid.

I had known my father would never speak to me again once he found out I was gay, and the circumstances didn't help. I had hoped that my sister would be more understanding, but three years' worth of returned Christmas presents sent a pretty clear message. I sometimes wondered if her kids ever asked about me, and what she had told them. The women I had seen socially took it rather well – perhaps I had not deceived them after all. At least, I hadn't had a wife and kids to drag down with me.

My life had stopped, and I couldn't imagine how I would start it again. Not if all I had to move on to were parties full of hungry-eyed men who thought they knew me because they'd seen my picture in the tabloids.

Staring out a window at the gathering dusk, I pondered how much freedom I had now. Nothing of personal importance left to lose, and a lot of money. All I had to do was decide what I wanted. Nothing came to mind.

I heard a sound behind me, a glass settling onto an occasional table. I had been brooding at the window for ten minutes, and thought myself alone. I turned and saw someone had been there all along. He was almost hidden, slouching behind the wings of a hard-looking chair, legs curled up and a book open on his knee.

He looked young – too young for me, judging by the boyish profile. His hair was long and stylishly unkempt, falling in sections of three distinct colors – electric blue locks hung across his forehead to the left and honey blond to the right, with the rest an unnaturally uniform black. He wore torn jeans and a hoodie with too-long sleeves. With one sock-clad foot perched on the edge of the chair and the other under him, he radiated relaxed comfort. He could not have been more different from anyone I'd met so far that evening.

He must have sensed me watching him, because kohl-rimmed eyes of an intense blue flashed up at me. He said nothing, but held my gaze. At a loss, I glanced at the book he had been reading.

"Leaves of Grass," I said. "You like Whitman?"

He shrugged. "Better than talking to the trolls." I must have blanched at that because he added, "I don't mean you, Dr. Turrow."

So he recognized me. I steeled myself for another tactless inquiry into my personal business, but it didn't come. He closed the book with his finger inside to mark his place, and looked at the cover, brows knitting.

"I prefer Robert Frost, actually," he said. "I know rhyming poetry is unfashionable, and some say simplistic, but I think that only shows how small minds have gotten."

"How so?" I took a seat opposite him, pleased by the prospect of a conversation without the same uncomfortable questions, repeated ad nauseam.

"It's simple orthodoxy." He picked up his glass and took a sip of amber liquid. "Something is good because people say it's good. That's over-simplifying, but poetry is like wine – the fun is in deciding what you like and why. I think modern poets are lazy because rhyming in English is a bitch. In rhyming poetry the rhyme schemes also make for more subtle layers of meaning."

I smiled. He spoke so confidently, his appearance in stark contrast to his refined topic. So self-contained. "Layers of meaning?"

"Sure." Smiling, looking me in the eyes. "Take 'Stopping by the Woods on a Snowy Evening' for example. On the face of it, it's a nifty little poem about watching it snow. But," he said, pointing the book at me for emphasis, "look a little closer and it's about duty, responsibility and an unfulfilled longing for death. Totally emo." A sly grin showed the barest edge of teeth. "In a good way."

I smiled back, feeling the nervous knot inside me loosen a little. "I see you've given this some thought."

He shrugged, uncommonly fluid in the gesture. "The modern stuff, though…" He paused, flashing me a sharp look from shaded eyes.

"You don't like it," I said.

"I find it pretentious," he corrected me with a grin. He reached for a magazine, one of several highbrow titles arranged for display. Grimacing, he flipped through and then tapped the page. "This one, for example. A modern thing, no rhyme and little attention to meter. The subject matter is heavy and unpleasant. War, and what it takes from the soldier when he kills. Look deeper at that and what do you get?"

"I assume you're going to tell me."

"Yes." He grinned broadly this time, displaying white, even teeth. "You get a preening poet, wallowing in the importance of his message, showing us how deep and angsty he is."

"Totally emo," I said, deliberately mocking him, just to see how he'd take it.

My elfin companion showed his dimples, tilting his head forward and looking at me from under fine, quirked brows. "But not in a good way."

I laughed, pleased to have met a man with a wit so much sharper than his appearance would suggest. Before I had a chance to speak, our host entered the far end of the room.

"There you are," he said as he rushed in; I realized he was not speaking to me. "I'm not paying you to drink my scotch and molest my books."

The poetry critic stood and placed the book and the magazine neatly on the table before handing me his glass.

"The scotch belongs to the good doctor." He leaned toward me and said in a conspiratorial tone, "His decorator bought the books by the foot."

He gave me a wink and a grin just as the host grabbed him by the arm. "Hurry up, now. Johnson will show you the way."

"See ya 'round, doc." He turned and followed another man out the opposite door. My host had replaced the magazine in the display and was now looking over his shelves with the book in hand.

I heard him mutter, "Dark blue, dark blue … there they are," as he replaced the book.

I couldn't help but smile as I glanced toward the door.

"Is he a musician or something?" I asked my host, nodding toward the door. That made sense; I could hear a band warming up, though I hadn't noticed it before. "An entertainer?"

"Something like that." My host grinned in a way that seemed to be at my expense. "Blue is more of a … party favor."

Though by that time I felt certain my host and most of the guests despised me, I found the prospect of intimate time with "Blue" intriguing enough to stay for a while. It was not difficult to slip off in search of him. I happened to see the host's servant come out a doorway. I waited until he had gone before I entered the room.

What I found there surprised me, though I suppose it shouldn't have. I recognized him by his hair. The blue and the blond stood out in the moody lighting, augmented by the flickering of many candles. He was not so much bound as on display, pale flesh glistening with oil. The sight took my breath.

I had never seen anything like the apparatus that held him. Bent at the waist, leather straps held his knees apart, bound to a polished wooden framework. His arms were secured elbow to wrist behind his back, and two leather straps around his upper arms kept his shoulders level with his hips. The sight of his firm little ass presented for use had me hard, though I tried to ignore it at first.

To my right sat a small table laid out with a variety of condoms, oils and towels. A box of latex examining gloves rested beside the towels, familiar but alien in this context. Such things were not a regular part of my sex life, which had consisted mostly of rushed encounters in places meant for other purposes. I had not returned to those haunts since my arrest and the public shaming that followed. Whatever desire I might have felt since then had not been enough to make me seek out my own kind. Until now.

Even in this place, I didn't feel entirely sure of myself. Was he really willing? I couldn't imagine how he could be, yet I was in no hurry to release him. I moved around him slowly, taking in every inch of him, the smell of oiled leather, wood polish and candle wax. Even his balls were bound up to the shaft of his cock with crisscrossed leather. I winced at the color of the flesh that showed between the strips.

As I moved around him, I saw his supple mouth stretched around a red ball gag, and a blindfold over his eyes. His breath quickened as I came closer; I could hear it whistling through holes in the ball.

I touched his hair, and before I knew what I was doing or why, I knelt by him and removed the gag. Maybe I simply wanted to talk to him again. He was, after all, the only man here who had not treated me with subtle contempt.

As the gag slipped free, he whispered, "Doc?"

I was touching him by then – running my hands over his shoulders and back, stroking a thumb across his swollen lips. I couldn't help myself.

"How did you know?" My question came in a whisper, punctuated by the hollow thumping of my heart.

"Lagerfeld," he answered, his voice strained. "You're wearing Lagerfeld."

I traced my tongue along his ear, tasting the metal of at least three piercings and the bitterness of hair gel. "I might not be the only one."

"Wishful thinking, then." He kissed my thumb as it passed across his lips, nibbling on the tip.

I ran my other hand slowly across his chest, though I had to crouch even more. It seemed a shame to have so much of him out of easy reach. I didn't dare remove the blindfold, though. I'm not sure why, but I didn't want him to see me.

"Why do you do this?" I asked.

A broad grin marked his cheek with a dimple. "An Ivy League education is an expensive thing."

"That's not the only reason," I said, biting gently at his neck.

"You're new at this, aren't you?" I heard the smile in his voice, the playful mockery. "Too much talk kills the mood."

I thought I understood – he needed to keep his head in the right place for this sort of game. I stood and walked around him. "You'll earn your money tonight."

I smacked his bottom hard, just to hear him gasp. He seemed so self-assured, even held open like that. My life had been ruled by fear – fear of what I was, fear of people finding out – and here was this man ten years my junior, still confident and relaxed under such circumstances. Helpless, awaiting the pleasure of some twenty-five rich old men.

One of whom was me. I reached for a condom and some oil. He must have heard what I was doing because his breathing changed. As I slipped on the condom I heard him mutter softly, "The gag. Please."

I ignored the request, whether out of haste or some perverse spite, I can't say. I only knew that I wanted him and I could have him. Nothing seemed to matter beyond that.

Our first transaction ended with embarrassing speed; I thought I heard him chuckling when it was over. I cleaned up and tossed the refuse in the bin. As I settled my clothes back into place, he spoke to me.

"Could you put the gag back before you go?" His voice cracked, and he cleared his throat. "Please."

I walked around to his head, the gag in my hand. Tiny droplets of sweat covered his brow, plastering blue and blond strands to his face around the blindfold. I felt suddenly possessive of him, jealous of the others who would use him, who had used him. This world was new to me in many ways – the freedom to take felt alien, and his surrender seemed the most beautiful gift I had ever been given. But had he really given it? I hesitated, catching sight of the grin on his face. The wry, superior smile did not seem so intriguing when I was the subject of his scorn.

I smoothed the hair away from his forehead. Without warning, I grasped a handful of blue and pulled his head back, stopping his startled cry with my lips on his. He tried to turn his head away, but I wouldn't allow it. Kisses hadn't had a place in my sex life for a long time, and he wasn't going to deny me one now.

His lips felt soft and moist, if a little cooler than I had expected. I licked them and he opened to me, passively receiving my tongue. My grip on his hair tightened as I kissed him; soon, his passivity ended in the velvet heat of a kiss returned. When I released him his head dropped forward, his breathing ragged.

"I can take you with me," I whispered, though uncertain whether it was true. "I can pay you more than he is."

I could pay more, I felt certain, and I was sure there had been a connection between us. He swallowed hard, and said nothing for a moment. I did not expect the laughter that finally answered me.

"The Dirty Doctor wants to be my sugar daddy." He continued to chuckle until it sounded almost like sobbing; head bowed, his shoulders shook with it. "You're so cruel."

Cruel? His laughter was more cruel than anything I had done. I was hard again, embarrassed and angry at having my offer rebuffed. He was laughing at me, just like everyone had since my life became a bawdy punch line.

"All right," I said. "Have your gag."

I shoved the ball back in his mouth and tightened the straps as far as they would go. It must've hurt, from the way he squeaked. I expected the gag to quiet him, but it didn't. The intensity of the sounds he made didn't change, but now they sounded less like laughter. I liked it that way.

I crossed to the table and picked up a leather flogger. I had never used one before, but I warmed to it quickly. I beat him without hesitation, until his buttocks and legs were flushed red, and he shivered at the slightest touch. I had never done anything so violent to another person, and it surprised me how much I enjoyed it. I was so hard my balls ached. I opened my trousers and put on another condom as if in a trance. It felt unreal that I could do what I had done, and so very good.

I grabbed a handful of his hair and the straps of his gag, and pulled them as I thrust into him. I rode him hard, and lasted much longer than I thought I could. It was like something out of a dream; I came harder than I had ever come in my life.

When it was over, I cleaned us both and used a fresh towel to dry some of the sweat from his body. Wouldn't want him to catch a chill.

He made urgent noises behind the gag, turning us head as if trying to see me through the blindfold. There was nothing he had to say that interested me – I'd had enough derision to last a lifetime; I had no reason to take more of it from him.

Still, I took a moment to stroke his hair, and when I touched his face he pressed a hot cheek against my palm, like an affectionate cat. I ran a finger along his lower lip where it touched the gag.

"Thank you." I left quickly, without looking back. I didn't trust myself not to do something foolish if I lingered.

When I entered the hall, my host was waiting, looking especially smug.

"Have a good time, Doctor?"

I answered with a smile and a nod, feeling relaxed for the first time in months. The insinuations in his manner no longer bothered me, and I didn't care to examine why. "You certainly know how to entertain."

"Thank you." He returned my smile, and this time it seemed genuine, perhaps even compassionate. "Life has a lot to offer a man in your position – more than you know."

I wasn't sure what he meant, but I nodded.

The other guests seemed more relaxed around me when I joined them. There was music and food, and the liquor flowed freely. A few made jokes about interstate rest stops and the like, but it seemed benign enough. Guests slipped away discreetly to various rooms, making it clear boy Blue wasn't the only party favor on the menu. I felt no need to sample the others, and if some of the guests had designs on me, they were disappointed as well.

Despite my new ease with the company, I left as soon as politely possible. The valet clasped my hand with both of his when I tipped him, caressing my wrist. The contact made me tingle; something had changed in me – I felt reborn.

Driving north from Boston in the wee hours, I had time to think over everything. About Blue, about my money and what I could do with it. How free I was, now, to indulge my desires.

Of all the men I had met that night, no one had interested me half as much as Blue. I envied him, to be so comfortable with himself. As I settled into bed his sharp, mocking smile seared itself into my brain. Dreams of struggle filled my head that night, sensual and unsatisfying.

The next day, I set about the business of unpacking some boxes. I had not been in my house long, and there was still much to do.

As I filled the shelves around my hearth with books, arranging them by topic, I thought of the study in my host's grand house and his rows of color-coordinated, unmolested books. It made me chuckle, to wonder what Blue would think of my books. Though I didn't want to admit it to myself, I wanted him to see my home – to see my books in all their mismatched glory and know that they were there to be read.

After lunch I rang up my host to thank him and to ask about Blue. "Do you know which university he attends?"

"University?" He laughed. He told me the area where I could find him – or a variety of other street hustlers. "If you are so inclined."

I bore the insinuation in his tone because I could not deny the accuracy of his assumptions – I'd had a piece, and I wanted more. He gave me what I needed to find Blue; that was all that mattered.

Still, the revelation stung; Blue had deceived me. Hearing it from a man I despised did not help matters, but neither did it change the fact that I wanted to see Blue again. More than that. Now that I knew the persona he had worn was an affectation, I had to see the reality.

Finding him proved easy; then I started watching him. I even drove the SUV on the off chance he would know the car I drove to the party. Several days and nights I tailed him as he worked the streets, keeping myself hidden. I watched him suck the cock of any fat old wretch with a bit of cash, astonished by how much it angered me. I followed him to the hovel where he crashed with some six other young men – none of whom seemed especially friendly toward him. I saw a life that, despite its outward differences, felt quite familiar to me. A life of solitary misery, without meaning or joy.

Drugs were a part of that life, and soon enough I found his dealer, a wary man known only as Jay. After a little bribery, I found out what he used and how much. He hadn't been using long, at least as far as that dealer knew. He always paid in cash.

I knew where Blue's life was headed, and it tormented me. I had seen the spark of a lively mind inside that multi-colored head of his, and I didn't want to see it smothered by hopelessness.

There was one thing more I could not deny – I wanted him. Not for a night, or a weekend. I wanted him to be mine; I wanted to see everything he hid from the world, everything he was inside. To breach the wall of brittle pride and condescension he had built around himself, to show him he was nothing. And everything.

The plan formed in my mind easily enough. Legal or moral concerns did not dissuade me; I worked like a man possessed. Buying or building the things I needed, I made the preparations as quickly as I could. I still had my license to practice medicine, so I got the paperwork in motion to have a clinic at my home. Of course, my home was now a comfortable place tucked away in the Maine woods, but there were things I needed that I could not get without the proper documentation. I made some changes to my house as well – closed circuit security monitors, soundproofing, everything I would need.

With the preparations in place, I watched and waited for the right moment. The seasons had changed from autumn to winter, and he spent more time indoors or in his johns' cars. I wasn't sure what I was waiting for until it happened.

As he walked home one night, some guys jumped him. One grabbed him from behind and the other started punching. I couldn't really see much, but I knew something bad was happening. I sprinted across the street and into the alley, and heard them calling him "faggot" among other things. The same bastards who hounded me out of my old life, wearing different faces.

He was down before I got there, with both of them kicking him. I yelled at them and they ran. They might have been able to take me, but I guess they didn't want to risk it. I can be an imposing figure when I want to be.

When I got to Blue, he was out cold.

I couldn't examine him in the alley, but I had to know how badly he'd been hurt. I carried him to my SUV and climbed in the back with him. He moaned once or twice while I checked for injuries, but didn't seem aware of what was happening. There were some bumps and bruises, but his pupils were responsive and he didn't have any broken bones. Once I felt certain he didn't need any more treatment than I could give on my own, I searched his pockets.

He didn't have much; I found a small bag of powder and an expired driver's license in the back pocket of his jeans. His wary face peered out at me from a New Hampshire license issued in the name Edward Staunton. He would be twenty-two in just over a month.

"This is no kind of life for you, Edward," I whispered as put the license and the bag into my own pocket.

I didn't want to use a sedative on him when he was barely conscious, so I bound his wrists and ankles with cable ties and put a burlap sack over his head. I left him on the back seat, and drove the speed limit.

It was a long ride, and my concern for his health abated somewhat when I heard him moving around. He hadn't spoken, but when I glanced back I saw that he had worked the sack off his head and was slipping his legs through the loop of his arms to get his hands in front. I found a spot to pull over, but by the time I stopped the car it was almost too late.

I dove over the seat and caught him before he could get past the child safety locks on the doors. He would not have gone far with his ankles tied together, but someone might have seen.

He wriggled around to face me and got his legs up, landing a hard kick to my chest. It knocked the wind out of me, but I had been a competitive grappler as an undergrad and pride would not allow me to let a tied-up rentboy half my size get the better of me. Once I got on top of him, it was all over but the cursing. There was a lot of that, especially on my friend Edward's part. It was dark, but he recognized me.

"New at this, too. Aren't you, Doc?" He was trying to choke me, pressing cord that bound his hands against my throat. He scratched at my neck, but couldn't get a good grip.

I pulled back out of his reach, holding him with my weight on his upper thighs. "I think I'm doing all right."

He bucked, trying to throw me off while I got the syringe from the case in my pocket. I kept my seat, just barely. His fear thrilled some dark place in my psyche; I'd shattered his composure, if only temporarily.

He continued to curse at me while I caught his hands and pressed them above his head. I took the shield off the needle with my teeth, and pressed it into the exposed skin where the side of his collar fell open, into the muscle. It would take longer, but I hoped the needle would do less damage there, what with him thrashing so much. He struggled a little bit longer and then began to slip away. As his eyes fluttered closed, he whispered, "Fuck."

"In due time," I said. I had had the dosage ready – enough to keep him docile for the whole trip, and we were almost there.

When we got to my place it was late and much colder than in the city, and he wasn't dressed for it. The chill and being carried over my shoulder roused him and he started struggling and screaming. Not a big deal for me, since my nearest neighbor is at least ten miles away. When I moved here I thought I wanted to live quietly, away from people. Luckily for me it was also a good place to commit a felony or two.

Now that I had an unwilling guest, it didn't seem so quiet. He did his best to hit me, but his leverage was bad in that position. The ties around his ankles made kicking difficult, but I still took a couple of knees to the chest before I got him inside.

If all had gone the way I wanted, he would have had no idea where he was or who had him at this point. I had a feeling he was less afraid than he would have been if he hadn't known who held him. He'd stopped speaking to me – he just screamed for help and cursed at the top of his lungs.

"Keep that up and you'll lose your voice." He stopped screaming, and I dropped him on the floor near the hearth on the main level. The bedrooms were upstairs, and I had a garage and partial basement underneath. That was where most of the modifications had been done, but I thought it would be best to start out in a more hospitable atmosphere.

While he tried to get his feet under him, I found it fairly easy to press him to the floor and pin his arms above his head. He was still a little drugged, and I enjoyed feeling him struggle against me. He must've noticed how hard I was, because he relaxed suddenly, and smiled at me in a way that was both sensual and unfriendly.

"So, what do you want," he said, voice just above a whisper. "I can give you the best blow job you've ever had. Or is it my ass you're after?"

I chuckled. He was all street hustler now, miles away from the man who spoke so passionately about Robert Frost at a rich man's party less than two months earlier. "Do you really want to open negotiations by offering me something I can take any time I want?"

His lips pressed together in a hard line, and he looked away. I had him a little off balance, and that was where I wanted to keep him. He barely flinched when I rolled up his sleeve and gave him another injection. He stared at me, eyes cold, until the weight of the sedative dragged his eyelids down.

I scrambled to my feet. That was a very small dose; I had a lot to do and not much time.

He was still out when I left him in the new room in the basement, naked and bound in a more flexible way. Lockable leather cuffs linked right wrist to right ankle, left wrist to left ankle, and a leather collar chained to a ring embedded in the concrete floor. He would be uncomfortable when he woke up, though I made certain the room was warm, and left the light on.

The light was for my benefit; the closed circuit camera didn't work in the dark, and I wanted to keep an eye on him. I went upstairs and took a long, hot shower, beating off a few times, just to keep my head clear. He expected me to fuck him, but I planned to thwart his expectations. The next time I had him, I wanted him to be mine body and soul.

After my shower, I dressed and watch him on the monitor. He was awake, and apparently calm. I went down to speak to him; it was time to begin.

He turned to face me when I entered the room. "What is it you want?"

"I want to talk to you," I said. "Tell me a little about yourself, Edward."

He glared at me when I said his name. "Fuck you."

"Why did you lie about being a student?"

"I never lied." He spoke defiantly, chin up, looking me in the eye. I doubted I could lie so convincingly were I naked and chained to the floor.

"Yes you did. When I asked why you did that sort of thing." I'd have blushed if I had the complexion for it, just at the prudish ring of the words.

"I said that an Ivy League education is an expensive thing," he answered evenly. "That is a perfectly true statement."

I laughed at my own presumption. "Clever."

He shrugged. "Cleverness doesn't pay as well as sex, but it has its uses."

"Why didn't you want me to know how you live?"

"How I live is none of your business," he said, shuffling to find another comfortable position that was possible the way he was bound. "Besides, how do you know I wasn't a student last term?"

"Ivy League to street whore is a long way to fall." I said it as gently as I could.

"So it is," he said, settling on his knees. "Not as far as respected doctor to Jay Leno punch line."

I sat on the floor a few feet away. "You know all about my fall," I said. "Care to tell me about yours?"

He turned his wrists to me in a pleading gesture, but his tone was harsh when he spoke. "Do you mind?"

"Not at all." I made no move.

After a pause, he snorted at me. "You're a real comedian."

"You haven't answered me." I was determined to hear his story, one way or another.

"I don't owe you anything." He looked away. "But if you unlock these cuffs, I'd be grateful."

"I may be new at this," I said. "But I'm not stupid."

"I'll tell you what you are." He said it with passion. "You're a coward who lost everything because you tried to be something you're not. You think you can kidnap me and be my master or some shit, but you can't. You've never even mastered yourself."

"Ouch." I smiled when I said it, though the words were too true not to hurt. "Maybe you can help me with that."

I stood and went to the locked cabinet by the door. "After all, I brought you here to help you."

I took out the little bag I'd found in his pocket the night before. He looked away, lips pressed to hard line.

"I talked to Jay." Mentioning his dealer's name had the desired effect. He shot a look at me, one with real fear in it. "He says you don't have a heavy habit. Yet."

I took a syringe and a little bottle from the cabinet; he watched every move, but said nothing. I took some medicine from the bottle with the syringe, cleared it of bubbles and replaced the cap.

"How long do you think it will be before you start to feel it?" I looked at him evenly. "Withdrawal, I mean."

"You'll just have to wait and see, won't you?" He was trying to be cool, but I could tell I had shaken him.

"No," I said, holding up the syringe. "This is Naloxone. It's an opiate antagonist, used to treat overdoses. It blocks the opiate receptors while the drugs metabolize. It can also induce withdrawal that is rather more sudden and severe than usual."

He started shaking his head and edging away from me, though I hadn't taken a single step toward him.

"You don't have to do this." He swallowed hard. "We can talk – I'll tell you whatever you want to know. You can help me off it slow. I know you can. It doesn't have to be bad."

I bit my lip. What he said was true enough. "I think it does have to be bad, Edward. It's the only way you'll take me seriously. I'm going to let you suffer the consequences of your actions. We all have to do that sooner or later."

"No." He was breathing faster, but his face still looked calm. He glanced at the toys and other implements that hung from a rack on the wall. "What about that stuff? You could use it on me, tie me up and fuck me. I could suck you off – I'm really good at that."

I put the bottle of Naloxone back in my cabinet with his heroin, and took the syringe. I took a chair from the corner, placed it near him and sat in it.

"That sounds like a good deal," I said, opening my trousers. "Show me how good you are."

With his hands cuffed to his ankles, he used his lips and teeth to free my erection, and set about pleasuring me. He had not lied about his skill.

When he had swallowed everything I had to give him, he sat back on his haunches. I put my clothes to rights, and knelt beside him, running a hand through his hair. I grabbed a handful of silky hair and pulled his head back. I kissed him, tasting my semen on his lips. The injection was quick, but not so quick he didn't notice.

He gasped and pulled away, but it was done. He glared at me, but I could tell he was afraid. "We had a deal."

I went to the cabinet to dispose of the syringe. "Actually, I said it sounded like a good deal. That is a statement of opinion, not an agreement."

I left, then, closing the soundproofed door against his angry shouts. Upstairs, I turned down the sound on the monitors, and went to bed.

I couldn't sleep. Despite the things that had been said of me recently, I had never been less than a dedicated physician; I had certainly never used my training to inflict unnecessary pain. I wanted him to be clean – I wanted to free him from that trap before it claimed his life. But what I really wanted was his surrender, his obedience, perhaps even his love.

He was right – I was a coward. I envied the peace he had, the way he faced every moment of a bleak existence with calm. I wanted to break that cool, superior shell so much that I had broken the only vow that had ever been sacred to me.

I lay there watching shadows of branches sway upon the wall until the sky began to lighten. Then I got up and looked at Edward Staunton on the closed circuit screen. Blue. He had a story, and as much as I wanted to know it, I couldn't bear to force it from him this way.

I dressed and went to him. He lay curled up on the floor, shivering at the end of his tether. Beads of sweat stood out on his back and shoulders. In the night, he had vomited and crawled as far away from it as he could get.

When I got close, he flinched away from me. I opened the locks that held his cuffs together, and the one that secured his collar. Then I carried him up to the first floor, to a room where a hospital bed waited, a testimony to my good intentions. His blue eyes blinked at me, dulled by pain.

"I'm sorry," I said. "I'll take care of you until it's over." I put him on the bed, and closed the lock on his left wrist cuff to the bed rail. I couldn't risk letting him get away just yet. I would face that decision when the moment came. I pulled the blankets over him, and asked if he wanted an electric blanket.

He turned his head and stared out the window as if I hadn't spoken.

For the next few days, I did what I could to keep him comfortable, and a lot of patient care I hadn't done since medical school. I helped him bathe and changed his sheets. I brought him warmed milk and whatever food he said he wanted. I kept him hydrated with an IV, and took a few blood samples and sent them for testing. Once enough time had passed for him to have metabolized the Naloxone, I treated him with small doses of buprenorphine, which seemed to relieve his symptoms. He didn't fight me; we both knew that something had changed between us.

Sometimes, I would sit by his bed, and we would talk about trivial things. Sometimes, I read to him or brought him books we had talked about. I didn't press for details of his life, though he occasionally spoke of people he had known or things he had done in childhood. When I washed his hair I saw the roots coming in honey blonde. He'd kept a stripe of his natural color. I thought it suited him and told him so.

On the fourth day I brought him some clothes and shoes and took him for a short walk in the woods on my property. It was cold and dry; leaves crunched with every step. That evening, I started a fire, and we sat together by the hearth for some time. Edward picked through some old volumes of poetry I had chosen for him from my collection. He asked me to read a few aloud and made fun of me when I did. I took it in good humor and made some stew for dinner. We ate by the fire and didn't talk much, staring unto the flames.

Things seemed so normal between us that it felt strange. I wondered if he had grown accustomed to me, or if he would leave at the first opportunity. He seemed content to be here with me, but he had given me no reason to hope for more. I supposed I didn't deserve to hope. I hadn't forced the issue and I wouldn't, but my home would feel empty without him. I was almost ready to tell him, so when he broke the quiet, pulling me away from my tangled thoughts

"I knew you," he said, putting aside his dish. "When I saw you at the party, I knew you."

I cast him a puzzled look. "Everyone at that damned party knew me."

"I knew you from before," he said, softly.

I stared at his face, willing myself to remember. Edward Staunton, honey blonde hair ... I couldn't remember, so I asked. "Were you a patient?"

"No." He looked down at his hands. They were well-kept, almost elegant hands. Part of my mind wondered if he had ever played piano and whether I should buy one. I was anxious to hear what he had to say and terrified at the same time. "Not really. I was kind of old for a pediatrician. My dad caught me fooling around with a guy from prep school. He took me to see one of the doctors in your practice because someone said he'd recommended a place that could fix me."

I remembered now – not Edward, but the incident he was about to relate.

"We were all in his office, but the door wasn't closed all the way. Maybe you heard something, I don't know. You came in and yelled at the other guy, Dr. Mitt ... Mitch ..."

"Mitley," I said, clenching my teeth at the memory.

"Do you remember what you said?"

"Not specifically, no." I'd had a lot to say that day, most of it about how no one in my practice was going to send patients to one of those places. I hoped I'd been more controlled in front of patients and family members, but I simply did not recall.

"You made the other doctor step out in the hall, and you yelled at each other for a while. Then you came back in alone. You said that kids do things when they're young, and you told my dad if he made too big a deal out of this one thing, then he would lose me. You told him he should be proud of my accomplishments, and not fixate on some childish indiscretions." There were tears making tracks down his face, but his expression remained placid. That same self-assurance, that same strength, still evident in the line of his body, the tilt of his head.

"Did it help, what I said?" I had wondered at the time. Even as conflicted I had been about myself, I never considered supporting the gay rehab movement, especially in the case of teens, who were often given little choice in the matter.

He broke into a smile and then began to laugh – a real, clear laugh, so unlike the cynical chuckle that had become so familiar to me.

"Not at all," he said. "At least not like you mean. He sent me away that summer, just like he planned. But I remembered what you said – what it meant for someone to stand up to him, and tell him he should be proud of me. I remembered, and that helped."

I couldn't speak; I tried, but the words wouldn't come out. It wasn't what most people would remember about me, but I had tried to do the right thing for my patients. I had made some small difference to Edward, and that made a difference to me. He slipped his arms around me and kissed me on the lips.

When he pulled away, he whispered, "You're a good doctor, and a good man. Don't let anyone tell you otherwise."

I couldn't imagine what he'd been through in his life, how he had come by that impenetrable self-assurance, the sanctity of his soul.

"How do you do it?" I whispered. "How do you know who you are?"

"You just know." He smiled and gave one of his elegant little shrugs. "Or maybe the right person has to tell you."

He leaned in to take another kiss, and I was glad to give it. The taste of his warm lips reminded me of blueberries. He sighed and settled in close beside me, but something caught his eye.

"Look, Doc," he said, pointing out the window. "It's snowing!"

I turned to see the large white flakes falling, as thick as goose down. They wafted through the trees, slowly forming a pristine blanket over the soil. Maybe in the morning we would venture out, not caring where we went, leaving tracks wherever we'd been. But the morning didn't matter now, and neither did the past. The moment was everything, as the two of us watched the woods fill up with snow.

THE K9 PROJECT
Christopher Pierce

Phase I. Subject Acquisition

After an extensive search, we have finally chosen a Subject for the K9 project, a 25-year-old Caucasian male named Randy. (Due to the nature of the project his last name is irrelevant.) Randy is homosexual and has been observed patronizing several gay bars in his local neighborhood. The establishments he frequents most are known in the gay community as "leather bars." Of particular interest to us is the fact that Randy has attended several "puppy events" at the above-mentioned bars. At such gatherings submissive men are encouraged to demonstrate canine personas, in effect becoming "human dogs" for the duration of the event. The significance of this for us is obvious.

Monitoring of Randy's activities has allowed us to extrapolate a schedule for him. On weekend nights after he's been to the bars, he drives his motorcycle out of the city into the abandoned farmland beyond. After a circuit through the deserted area's roads he returns home to his apartment. We believe this setting provides the opportunity we need: with the correct preparation and methods, we can acquire Randy without being detected or inflicting any damage on the Subject himself. We have selected a man within our organization we believe can perform the capture successfully.

A report on the acquisition attempt follows.

Report on Acquisition of Subject: Randy.

I guess the Directors of the company chose me because of my size (6'1" and 250 lbs) and strength compared to that of the guy I was supposed to grab for them (5'7" and 140 lbs). My instructions didn't say why they wanted me to kidnap somebody for them, and I didn't ask. I didn't want to know. The Directors sign my paychecks, and I've got a wife and kids to feed, so I just said of course, I'll do it. There's all kinds of things going on in this company that I don't know about. But like I said, I don't want to know. I just do as I'm told.

So I followed the instructions. At about midnight, I drove out past the city limits to this old road out in the middle of nowhere. I pulled the truck they had provided me off the road. (They told me they didn't want me to use my own car in case someone saw me and got the license plate.) I got out and lifted the truck's hood. I waited about fifteen minutes, then saw a single headlight heading toward me. It was the guy, riding his motorcycle, just like they said he would be. I leaned under the hood and pretended I was trying to fix something in the engine. Sure enough, the guy slowed down and stopped his bike next to my car.

Transcription of recording made from wireless microphone hidden in acquirer's clothing:

Randy: Hey there!

Acquirer: Hi, am I glad to see you.

Randy: Havin' some trouble?

Acquirer: Yep. Engine just died on me and my damn cell phone battery crapped out, too. You got a cell phone?

Randy: No, but I might be able to help you with that engine.

Acquirer: Yeah? That'd be great.

[Sounds of Subject getting off his motorcycle, putting the kickstand down, and walking to the front of the vehicle.]

Randy: Let's see what we got here.

Acquirer: I think it's the damn carburetor.

Randy: That's – hey! Wh–

Report continues.

Grabbing him from behind, I held the rag soaked with chloroform over the guy's nose and mouth. He struggled, but there was no way he could break the hold I had on him. Within a minute, he'd breathed in the fumes and slumped forward, totally knocked out. After making sure there was no one around to see us, I lowered him to the ground and tied him up with the cuffs the Directors gave me. They looked sort of like the kind cops use, but they were bigger and heavier. After the guy's hands and feet were locked together I picked him up, threw him over my shoulder and stashed him behind the seat of my truck. I threw a blanket over him, so he wouldn't get cold, and no one would see him. Then I put the tailgate down and pulled down the ramp that was in the bed of the truck. I rolled the guy's bike up the ramp and laid it down in the bed, securing it with some rope so it wouldn't slide around.

When all that was done, I checked that the coast was clear one last time, and then got in my truck and drove back to the address the Directors told me to go to. A garage door opened, and I drove in onto a loading dock. There was no one around. The instructions said to shut off the truck and leave back through the door, so I did what they said. I didn't see anyone as I walked out the loading dock door. As they'd said, there was a taxicab waiting for me on the curb. It drove me home at no charge.

When I finally crawled into bed, my wife asked me what I'd been doing. I told her something for work and never mentioned it again.

Report ends.

Phase II. Preparation for Conditioning

The Subject has been successfully acquired.

Randy will be placed under prolonged sedation while we prepare him for the experiments to come. His clothes will be removed and destroyed. A studded leather collar will be secured permanently around his neck. His hands and feet will be covered with "mitts" that approximate a dog's front and rear paws. His ass will be filled with a plug that has a "tail" on the protruding end to simulate an actual dog's tail.

The Subject will have an electronic ring-like device installed around his genitals, through which we can remotely administer painful but undamaging electric shocks. The shocks will be used to discourage and punish inappropriate behavior.

During the preparation phase, Randy will be repeatedly injected with what we call "the K9 compound," a proprietary chemical mixture designed to make a person docile, submissive and eager to please. Randy will be the first human being the drug will be used upon.

When the preparations are complete, Subject will be moved to a conditioning room while still under sedation.

Phase III. Canine Conditioning

Observations of technician watching the conditioning room on a monitor.

The conditioning room has one door. A "bubble" in the ceiling hides the camera. In one corner of the room, there is a cage large enough for Subject to fit inside. The cage door is open, and inside the cage is a soft "doggy-bed." The walls of the room, the ceiling and the carpeted floor are neutral colors, beiges and grays. Several puppy chew-toys are scattered around the room. There is a small table with a single chair on one side of the room.

Randy is brought into the room through a concealed door, carried over the shoulder of one of the lab technicians. At this point, the canine compound has reached its optimum level in the Subject's bloodstream.

The technician places Subject on the floor of the room, then pulls a syringe from the pocket of his lab coat. The syringe contains a "wake-up" drug, designed to revive a person who's been in deep sedation. The technician injects Randy's neck with the syringe, empties the drug into him, then removes the syringe and leaves the room through the concealed door.

All our research, development and execution have been leading to this moment. Needless to say, we are excited.

Randy is waking up now. He starts to speak ("Where am ...") and we give him his first electric shock. He screams in pain and grabs for his cock and balls, but finds his hands bound into the mitts. He tries to remove the mitts but finds it impossible without the use of his fingers. He has equal difficulty removing the genital-ring and the tail-plug in his anus and soon gives up.

Now the Subject tries to stand up, and we administer his second shock. Randy falls back onto the floor and tries to protest ("What the hell?") and receives his third shock.

Even with the Subject's natural inclinations toward a dog-like persona and the injections of the K9 compound, we expect it to take some time before the Subject reaches the state of fully actualized submission we are hoping for.

We are patient.

Over the next hour, things proceed in a similar fashion – each time Randy speaks or tries to stand up, he is shocked. The Subject soon realizes that speaking and standing up on two legs result in pain. In a classic case of negative reinforcement, Randy understands that he must walk on all fours and must not talk.

Crawling, Randy explores the room. He approaches the cage and investigates the doggy-bed with his nose and mouth in a snout-like fashion. He seems pleased with it, although he does not enter the cage and lie down on the bed.

As we hoped, his affinity with dogs is beginning to merge with the effects of the K9 compound. In short, he is experiencing a shift from human self-identification to canine self-identification.

Over the next fifteen minutes the Subject explores the rest of the room. He shows mild interest in the chew-toys scattered around the room. Encouragingly, Randy seems to have given up the idea of using his hands to manipulate objects and now uses his "snout" exclusively. He is a fast learner.

We are pleased.

Phase IV. Sexual Training

This phase is arguably the most important. The Subject's Sexual Training will be conducted by one of our team members, in fact the same one who carried Randy into the room at the start of Phase III. His report follows.

I entered the room carrying two dog bowls, one filled with fresh water, the other with hot beef stew. [Note: Beef stew to be eventually replaced with commercially available dog food.] The Subject had not been fed since the previous day.

At my arrival, the Subject became agitated. Randy hopped up and down and shook his buttocks from side to side, making his "tail" wag in a very canine fashion. He crawled over to me rapidly, making tentative whimpering noises as we hoped he would. No shocks were given, and the Subject seemed to realize that non-linguistic vocalizations were permissible. He got braver and started whining, much like a hungry dog.

I walked into the room, Randy on my heels, and set the dog bowls on the table out of his reach. I closed and locked the door, then pulled the chair out from under the table, brought it to the center of the room and sat down on it. The Subject continued to whine and whimper, constantly looking back and forth between the bowls on the table and myself, as if to lead my attention back to the table, hoping he would receive an opportunity to eat and drink.

I slapped my knee with my hand to get the Subject's attention.

"Randy, come here," I said, and he obeyed, crawling in front of me, sitting on his haunches and facing me. I spread my legs and unbuttoned my pants. My penis was revealed, full and erect. "Come closer, Randy," I said and he did, his wide eyes on my cock. Now he was crouched between my legs. "You see this?" I asked, gripping my dick in one fist. The Subject nodded vigorously. "Lick it," I said.

Randy leaned forward with his tongue out and started licking my cock like it was a water fountain, and he was thirsty. He was so excited that he slobbered all over it and grunted and moaned in pleasure. After my dick was slick with his spit, I told him to suck it, and he did. He went down on me, slurping loudly. It wasn't the best blowjob I've ever received, but enthusiasm made up for lack of technique. I'm sure the Subject can be trained for better oral service.

Soon enough, I was ready to shoot my load, but didn't want the training session to end so soon. I grabbed Randy's face and forced him off my cock, to his great disappointment.

"Get up on your hind legs and bend at the waist, facing away from me," I instructed him. He gave a little groan of fear, undoubtedly remembering the shocks he'd received earlier when trying to stand like a human.

"It's okay," I said, "you can get on your hind legs for this one task, but not for anything else."

He smiled and wagged his butt, then followed my orders. When he was bent at the waist with his ass in the air in front of me I took my dick in my fist again. It was still very wet and got back up to full erection quickly.

"Back up," I told the Subject. He did what I said and his butt pressed against me. I removed the butt-pug "tail" and aimed my cock at his asshole, telling him to back up more. Inch by inch, Randy impaled himself on my stiff dick, moaning and growling the whole time. When I was all the way inside him, his asscheeks pressing against my pubic hair, I grabbed his hips.

"Now you're going to get fucked like the dog you are, Randy," I said, and started fucking him hard. He barked and panted as I screwed him, tightening his hole on my cock. I reached around and found his own dick stiff and dripping. I jerked him a few times to get him even more hot and bothered.

"I'm going to come, Randy," I said, "I'm going to shoot my load inside you!" He panted with excitement and tightened on me even harder. Gripping his hips, I shoved myself in as far as I could go.

"Oh yeah," I said, "take my load, dog!" My orgasm washed through me as I shot off inside him. "Good boy," I said, petting his head. "Good dog."

When I was done, I pulled out of him. The Subject dropped back down to all fours, seemingly exhausted by the fucking he'd received. I put my dick away and replaced the butt-plug tail in his ass, then stood up, closing my pants.

I walked over the table and picked up the bowls. Bringing them over to Randy, I set them down on the floor in front of him. The Subject barked with joy and licked my hands before tearing into his food and slurping up his water.

"You'll get fed only after you service your Master," I said to him, "Do you understand?" Randy nodded, and continued to consume the stew and water at record speed. When he was done he rolled over onto his back, apparently hoping to have his tummy rubbed. Before I could stop myself, I laughed at the sight.

Then I kneeled down next to the Subject and rubbed his stomach. He yipped with pleasure as I did. I considered something for a moment, then decided he deserved something special for performing as well as he did.

"And when you're a very good boy, Randy," I said, "you'll get a special reward." He looked up at me with interest and excitement, but this was nothing compared to the ecstasy that came over his face when I took his dick in my hand and started jerking it again. This time I didn't stop, and within seconds the Subject was yelping with joy and shooting a huge load of semen all over himself. He quivered and shuddered as his orgasm pulsed through him.

Although I hardly thought he needed it, I took a syringe full of the knockout drug out of the pocket of my lab coat and injected Randy with it. He went out like a light, and I picked him up and carried him over to his cage. I put him in his cage and closed the door. I signaled to the camera on the ceiling that I was done, and left the room through the door. As I closed the door behind me, the lights were turned off in the room, and I left the Subject to his slumber.

Report ends.

Conclusion

We are very pleased with the initial outcome of the K9 Project. Many more days of conditioning and training will follow for Randy, but these introductory phases point to a very positive future. When the Subject's training is complete, we will begin the process of finding a buyer for him.

We are considering a price of $1 million for Randy, and all subsequent K9s we create. Now that the K9 Project is successful, we will begin the process of acquiring more Subjects immediately.

STOLEN
Wade Johnson

I figured my apartment would probably get robbed sometime in my life, but I never thought it would be me that got stolen.

Work had been hard that day. I was really tired when I got home. Dropping my stuff, I took off my clothes and collapsed on my bed. I was asleep in seconds, unconscious to the world.

I don't know how long I slept, but when I woke up it was dark. Lying there staring at the ceiling, I tried to figure out what had woken me up. Usually, I was a heavy sleeper; it was very strange for me to wake up in the middle of the night like this. What could have caused it? I didn't remember any nightmares ... just then I heard it.

The noise came from my living room, not twenty feet away from me through my open bedroom door. The blood froze in my veins.

There was someone in my apartment.

I didn't know whether to be scared or furious. Knowing it was important to stay calm, I slowly turned my head, so I could look out my door into the other room. I opened my eyes enough to make out the large shape that was moving in my living room.

It was a man. He was dressed totally in black: black boots, black jeans, black jacket and shirt, black gloves on his hands and a black ski mask covering his face. He was holding a big black sack open with one hand while he put my stuff into it with the other.

A burglar! A thief in my home! I fought down the desire to jump out of bed and tackle the asshole, knowing that was a good way to get myself killed. Who knew if the guy had any weapons on him? I couldn't take any chances.

But I had to do something! I couldn't just sit there and let this happen! I glanced at the phone on my desk across the room. If I was real fast, I might be able to grab the phone and call 911 before he saw me. But then what? I didn't know, all I could think about was calling the police, letting someone know what was going on here.

I started moving very slowly, inching myself to the edge of my bed, trying to work up the courage I would need to jump across the room and grab the phone.

The burglar was walking back and forth in front of the door, taking my stuff and putting it in his sack. Maybe if I timed it just right, I could get over to my desk without him seeing me.

My feet were now hanging off the edge of the mattress. I knew it was now or never, I had to do this or I'd lose my nerve and never get it back. Glancing into the other room, I saw the man walk across the doorway into the kitchen. This was it!

Flinging the covers off, I jumped to my feet and headed for my desk. My eyes were on the phone, so I didn't know if the burglar had seen me or not. I grabbed it and dialed just as a gloved hand went over my mouth.

I screamed and dropped the phone. Trying to twist myself around to face the attacker, all I could do was struggle in place. He had grabbed my arm and wrenched it painfully behind my back. I tried to yell again, but his hand clamped down on my mouth even tighter.

I felt the tip of a knife in my back.

"Shut your fucking mouth or I'll kill you, I swear to God," the burglar said. His voice was low and masculine. I couldn't believe it, but my dick started to get hard at the sound of it.

"Do you understand me?" he said, pushing my arm even further up my back. I winced in pain, and nodded quickly.

"Good boy," he said. I felt him put my wrists together and wrap something around them. It got tighter and tighter, and suddenly I realized what he was doing. The burglar was tying me up! Before I could struggle, he had pulled the knots tight, and my hands were securely bound behind my back.

Suddenly, we both became aware of a noise below us. It was a voice, faint but insistent.

"Hello? Are you there? This is the 911 operator. Are you in trouble?"

The connection must have been made before I dropped the phone. I wanted to yell out, but I knew this guy could cut my throat if he wanted to. There was no sense in being stupid. I had to stay calm.

Silently, my attacker leaned over, picked up the phone and very gently set it back in its cradle.

"Shit." he said quietly.

I knew we were both thinking exactly the same thing. The 911 operator was tracing the call right now to this location. Policemen would be on their way soon.

"We gotta get out of here," he said. My blood froze again. We? What did he mean we?

He spun me around to face him. He was a big guy, and strong, too, by the look of those arms through his jacket. I could see his eyes through the holes in the ski mask.

Suddenly, the burglar hauled off and punched me in the stomach. It felt like an explosion inside my body. Moaning in pain, I stumbled onto my bed.

"Now you won't give me any trouble."

He knelt down next to me, and starting tying my ankles together. If I had been in less pain, I might have thought to kick the bastard in the face and run to a neighbor's apartment, but the pain in my stomach was so intense, I couldn't do anything but lie there groaning.

Seconds later my legs and feet were bound together. Then I heard him opening my dresser drawers. What was he looking for? A second later he came back into view, a jockstrap and a couple of my bandannas in his hand.

"This'll keep you quiet."

He stuffed the jockstrap in my mouth and tied it in place with one of the bandannas. The other one he used to blindfold me. Now I was really getting scared, although my dick was still hard from being dominated by this guy. Being tied up by him made me even hotter.

But I had to keep my cool. This guy was a criminal, probably a pro. What was he going to do with me? I heard him walk back into the other room. The pain had lessened a little bit, and I tried to move, but it was too late.

I was bound and gagged – the more I struggled, the tighter the ropes got. Loud noises suddenly came from the other room. What the hell was he doing now? It sounded like he was emptying his sack out on the floor. Why would he do that?

"Let's go, man, time to hit the road. You're coming with me." he said.

I felt his hands on me, trying to lift me up off the bed. Twisting violently, I forced myself away from his hands. Maybe if I could stall him long enough, the cops would get here before ...

"You're just determined to be a pain in the ass, aren't you?" he said, and started beating on me. My back, my stomach, my face, everywhere on me was fair game. He punched me in the gut, slapped my face, beat on my back. The blows rained down on me as I tried to get out of his way. But I was tied up, gagged and blindfolded. I didn't have a chance, and we both knew it.

I stopped fighting and tried to catch my breath.

That was the chance he'd been waiting for. He grabbed me by the shoulders and pulled me to my feet. Too tired and hurting to resist, I just let him do it.

"You're the most valuable thing in this apartment, man," he said as he picked me up and slung me over his shoulder. "I ain't leaving here without you." God, he was strong. Even after our little fight, he lifted me up like I weighed less than a hundred pounds. What was he going to do?

Then I felt it. He let me slide down off his shoulder into something. I realized he was putting me in his sack. *He meant what he said*, I thought. *He's stealing me!* My dick was now rock hard.

Once I was all the way in, he pulled the sack up over my head and pulled the drawstrings closed. The light disappeared, and the darkness closed over me as I slid into the big black bag.

Now, I was totally helpless. Bound and gagged and inside of a sack. I felt motion above me and guessed he was tying off the drawstrings, so I couldn't struggle my way out.

What was I going to do now? Nothing, I thought. There's nothing you can do. Just relax and don't panic. But what happened next surprised the hell out of me and made my cock start dripping.

The burglar hoisted his bag, with me in it, over his shoulder as easily as if it was a laundry sack. Either he's spinning on coke, I thought, or this guy lives at the gym when he's not breaking into apartments.

"Now we're ready," I heard him say. "And don't fight me, man, or I'll drop you off on the side of some back road somewhere. Or put you in a garbage dumpster. I don't want to do that, but I will. Don't give me any trouble, you got that?" he shook the sack, and I spoke through the gag.

"Yes, sir, yes, sir!" I said, my voice muffled.

"Good boy," he said. "Now shut the fuck up and keep still."

We were moving. He was carrying me through my apartment. I was getting stolen as if I was an expensive piece of merchandise. My kidnapper weaved back and forth as he walked. I figured he was avoiding the piles of my stuff he had dumped out.

Then we were out in the open air. I heard him very gently close my front door behind him. How had he broken in? I wondered. I'll have to get better security. I almost laughed out loud at myself then, for thinking I would get a chance to come back here. For all I knew, this guy was going to kill me. Maybe I was going to get sold to a maker of snuff movies, one of those psychos who film real people getting really killed, so they can sell the movies black market.

I had to stop thinking that way or I would really freak out. It was quiet outside. I knew if I made a loud noise my neighbors would hear it. But, would they be able to come out here and take the asshole before he could do something to me? I knew the pool was less than five feet away, he could toss me in there and I'd drown in seconds. Come to think of it, he could just drop me where I stood and my head would crack open on the cement of the courtyard.

No, I had to do what he said. I had to obey him. I had to keep quiet and not give him trouble. The more I cooperated, the longer I'd live.

We were moving again, traveling swiftly across the courtyard toward the back entrance where the cars were parked. My head was spinning. It was very disorienting to be carried backwards and upside-down. If I wasn't careful I'd throw up. That'd be pretty. Puking while gagged was a good recipe for choking to death, I figured.

The burglar carried me down the stairs to the parking area. His boots made loud scuffing sounds on the concrete. Then he stopped.

A key was being turned in a lock, and a door was being opened. Carefully, he leaned over and pulled me off his shoulder down onto some hard surface. Where was I? This didn't feel like the back seat of a car.

Then the door closed over me and I realized where I was. The fucker had put me in the trunk of a car. My one chance to get rescued was gone. I hadn't tried to alert my neighbors.

If the 911 operator had traced the call, the cops hadn't gotten here in time. That's it, I thought. I'm not paying any more city taxes if the cops can't even rescue me when I'm getting stolen out of my apartment! I laughed out loud this time, the noise sounding muffled and strangled through the gag. I was really thinking bizarre things now, I realized. Maybe I was crazy.

The thief got into the car and started it up, the noise deafeningly loud to me. He quickly backed up and turned around, heading out to the street.

I have to be crazy, I thought. This guy kidnapped me and might kill me, but my dick is hard as a rock and begging for attention. I knew I couldn't reach it with my hands tied up like they were, but maybe I could rub it.

My crotch started moving, as if by itself, back and forth against the surfaces it was pressed up against it. Mmmm, that felt good. It was rubbing against my boxers, which rubbed against my sweat pants, which rubbed against the canvas of the sack, which rubbed against the hard metal of the trunk's floor. Got some good friction going.

At least the night isn't a total loss, I thought as I rubbed and rubbed, loving the feeling on my dick. That's it, I am crazy.

The car got out onto the street and picked up speed. I struggled against my bondage, not really thinking I could get out of it, more to just feel the nylon of the rope rubbing against my wrists and ankles. Somehow that made the burning in my dick flame higher.

Now the thief was driving faster and faster. We must have been on a freeway. Where was I? Where was he taking me? My apartment building was next to a big freeway junction, so he could have gotten onto any highway heading any direction.

We could be going north, south, east or west. I had no sense of direction at all, so much so that my friends told me to my face that I was geographically impaired. Behind my back, I heard, they said I couldn't drive my way out of a paper bag.

Yeah, I thought, or get myself out of a burglar's sack.

I almost laughed again through the gag. What was happening to me? My dick felt so good as I rubbed it up and down, up and down. How could I be getting off on getting kidnapped?

How could I enjoy getting tied up, put into a bag, carried away and taken who knows where? What the fuck was going on with me?

I didn't know. All I did know was that I was more excited and scared than I'd ever been in my life. This was a real adventure. I felt really, truly, fully alive like I hadn't in months or maybe years. It was so intense, and I may not live through it, but what the hell, I was going to enjoy it!

The car drove on for a long time. I may have drifted in and out of sleep, because all of a sudden we were slowing down. I wondered what was going on, had we reached our destination?

The burglar stopped the car a minute later and got out. I heard a zipper get released and a loud trickling sound. He was pissing, right next to the car. I don't know why, but I started thinking about what it would be like to kneel in front of him and open my mouth wide, to be on the ground in front of this stud who had taken me out of my apartment like I was just another stereo to steal, to feel the flow of his piss as he re-directed it into my open mouth, to swallow down mouthful after mouthful of his juice, and then when he was done taking his whole thick organ into my mouth, caressing it with my tongue and slurping on it like it was a popsicle, hoping I could please him enough to get a load of his cum, hoping he would let me serve him a few minutes more before he stuffed me back in the sack and tossed me into the trunk ...

What the hell was I thinking? I had to calm down. I racked my brain, trying to figure out what his pissing so close to the car could mean.

He wouldn't have whipped out his meat like that if there were any people around, so we must have been somewhere isolated. Maybe a rest stop, or an empty parking lot. But I'd heard his boots crunching on gravel ...

Suddenly, the trickling sound stopped and he was zipping up his pants. He was walking over to the car and a second later the key was turning in the hole and the lid was being raised.

"You okay, man?" he said.

"Let me loose!" I shouted through the jockstrap shoved in my mouth. He laughed.

"Sorry, can't understand you."

"You can too understand me!" I yelled louder. "Let me loose you fucking asshole!"

Oh, that was smart, I thought, just before his fist connected with my gut again. My breath flew out of me as I wondered how he could tell where my stomach was through the material of the bag.

"You're not getting away, so stop hoping," he said. I doubled over in pain, trying to shield myself from more assaults. Damn, I thought. This fucker knows how to punch. He had me, I was helpless. Did he have to keep reminding me of that fact?

"Answer me by moving your head," he said. "I'm sick of hearing your voice."

I nodded my head vigorously, hoping he could see the motion.

"You got to take a piss?" he asked. The thought hadn't occurred to me with my dick being so hard and everything, but now I realized: I hadn't pissed since before I went to bed, hours and hours ago. I nodded again.

"Okay, let's get you out here," he said. "I don't want you pissing in there and stinking up my car."

Then his strong arms were around me, lifting the bag up and out of the trunk. He set me on the ground and I stumbled a little. I was still inside the sack, and had no way to judge my surroundings I was so disoriented. Now that I was standing up, I realized that my bladder was full and I had to go really badly.

"Don't try anything, man," the thief said. "Or I'll kill you I swear to God."

I shook my head to show I understood, and that I wouldn't. The noise of him untying the drawstrings was loud in my ears, then I felt the chill of the night air as he slid the canvas down over me, revealing me to the world.

I felt like a banana getting peeled. There must not be anyone around, because the strangeness of this sight would definitely have attracted the curious. The weirdness of what was happening to me, plus my bursting bladder, combined to make my erection disappear.

Waiting to be totally released from the sack, I was surprised when my kidnapper just let it pile up around my feet. Then his hands were grabbing my shorts, yanking them down. He did the same to my boxers, and then my dick felt the kiss of the air.

I felt his gloved hand roughly grab my flaccid meat and point it away from us.

"Let it go, man, I ain't gonna wait all night."

Willing my muscles to relax, I felt the first drops come and then it went all at once. It spurted out of me like a dam had been released. For what seemed like an hour, we stood there together, a bizarre pair, while I relieved myself.

I resisted the temptation to turn my body and give the burglar a golden shower. He probably wouldn't have appreciated it.

The last few spurts came out, and he started putting my equipment back inside. But with the piss gone, my cock was awakened by the incredible hotness of this man holding it. Oh no, I thought. Not now ...

But it was too late. My dick was hardening in the thief's hand, as if it had a will of its own. What was I going to do, what if the guy was a gay-hating fag-basher? He was likely to castrate me right then and there! I hoped fear would soften my organ, but it just made it hotter and more erect. My last chance would be for him to not notice, to just put it back in and be done with it.

But he didn't. He paused, my meat still in his gloved hand.

"What's this?" I heard him whisper to himself, and I froze in place, wanting so badly to wish myself out of there, to just be back in my bed ...

The burglar laughed softly.

"Looks like I got myself a horny little boy, didn't I?" he asked. Too mortified to answer, I made no movement or noise.

"Answer me!" he said angrily as he slapped the side of my head. I nodded quickly, hoping this was the end of it.

But it wasn't.

"Yeah, just what I thought," he said as he started rubbing my chest with the other hand. He kept my dick in his other hand, caressing it in his palm.

191

My back arched. I wanted to get away from him, but if I tried who knew what he would do. Not wanting to get punched again, I just stood there. It felt so fucking good! I knew I had to keep my cool, to stay rational, but the feeling was so intense ...

"Mmmm," I heard him whisper. "I got you going, man ..." His hands were all over my chest, stroking it up and down, pinching my nipples, slapping my abs.

"I'm gonna put you to good use, horny boy," the thief said suddenly, pushing my shoulders down and forcing me to my knees. "Go on," he said, shoving me forward.

I crawled blindly on my hands and knees, the hard gavel biting into my palms and knees. Out of the sack now, I found myself on softer ground. It was grass, thank God.

"Stop," the voice said, and I did so immediately. I heard my kidnapper kneel down next to me.

"Get down."

I dropped down to my stomach. Frightened by what I knew was coming, I started shivering. It would only get worse if I fought him, so I just lay there and waited for it.

Soon enough I heard that zipper being pulled down again, and this time the sound of him pushing his denim jeans down to his knees. It was so quiet around us, as if there were no animals or people anywhere nearby.

He lay down on top of me then his chest was pressing against my back. He hadn't even taken off his shirt. With one hand, he pushed my head down, forcing my face into the grass.

I could feel his hard cock pressing up between my naked butt-cheeks. Not knowing why I did it, I pushed up against it, arching my back so my ass rose to meet the dick that wanted inside me.

My kidnapper murmured in approval. I heard him work up some spit and lick his hand, then grease up his meat with it. Now it felt smooth and slippery against my cheeks, and my own penis was raging with desire.

"Please ..." I whispered.

"Please what, man?"

"Please ..." I said. He plunged his cock into me then, and I forced my ass back and up, trying to take as much of him inside me as I could.

This man had taken me against my will, he'd abducted me out of my apartment, put me in a sack, drove me away in his car, and now was using me for his pleasure in what must have been a deserted field in the middle of the night. As frightened as I was, it was also totally hot.

He moaned as he started pumping me, pulling his dick out and then pushing it in. It was the best fuck I'd ever had, just getting my ass raped by this stranger who'd taken me like I was a piece of merchandise that could be begged, borrowed and stolen. Here he was, screwing me, just plowing my ass like there was no tomorrow ...

I must have let out a little groan, because suddenly he clapped his hand over my mouth.

"Shut up!" he whispered fiercely. "Shut the fuck up. Just keep quiet. There's nothing you can do, so just take it like a man."

His hand over my mouth made me even hotter. It flashed me back to earlier when he had cornered me in my room, and I realized something that was more shocking and strange than anything that had happened yet.

The burglar scared me to death, yet I really wanted him to fuck me. I had wanted him to take me from the first moment I had seen him loading my stuff into his big black bag. And now it was happening, as incredible as it was. My dick ground itself into the grass, fertilizing it with globs of dripping precum.

"Yeah, that's it," he said into my ear as he started pumping me faster. "Take it, man, take it all, my horny boy, my horny little gay boy ... I bet you like taking it up the butt, don't you, gay boy? Bet you like being fucked by a real man, bet it's been too long since you got fucked nice and hard ..."

Then I felt his cock flex and shoot inside me, spurts of his cum splattering, filling me up.

"Yeah ..." he groaned. "Oh yeah ..."

He pulled out of me and grabbed me around the chest, lifting me up to my knees. I figured he was going to take me back to the car, but I was wrong.

I heard him hock some more spit into his palm, and then he grabbed hold of my dick and started working it! It was so fucking unbelievable I felt myself lifting up off my knees, as if the feeling could help me shatter the law of gravity.

"Come on, gay boy," my kidnapper said. "I figure this'll help keep you quiet, but I'm not waiting forever. If you're gonna do it, you better do it now!"

At the sound of his command, I felt the orgasm rocket through me like an explosion, tearing me apart from the inside out. I bucked and jerked in his arms, and he held me tight to prevent me from falling. I knew bursts of cum were shooting out of me, firing across the grass like rocks skipping on water. Moaning and panting, I tried to lie back down on the grass.

"Oh no you don't," I heard him say as he jerked me up to my feet. "We're getting out of here." He left me for a second, and even though I was still bound, gagged and blindfolded, I could've tried to get away or call for help.

But I didn't.

Instead I waited for him to come back and then cooperatively helped him get me back into his sack. He tied the drawstrings off again and hefted me up over his shoulder.

"That did it," he whispered to me. "You're going to be a good boy, now, aren't you?"

I didn't need to answer, we both knew I would.

He got me back in the trunk of his car, and we drove off. I didn't care anymore where we were going, or what he was going to do with me. I was so high on my orgasm that I just accepted that fate had dealt me a strange hand and there was nothing I could do except wait and see what happened.

In some strange way, I felt happy and content because before I knew it I was asleep, the droning sound of the highway passing beneath me as sweet as a lullaby.

The car stopped. I don't know how much later it was, but I sensed that it was still dark through my blindfold. It couldn't have been long. The trunk opened, and the thief picked me up again, lifting me out of his car and up over his shoulder again. This time he didn't speak to me, he just carried me a few feet, then up some stairs and into a building of some kind.

Beside some faint noise in the background, it was quiet. The burglar carried me down hallways, up stairs, deep into the depths of the place. The noises were so indistinct I couldn't tell what they were. It could have been a factory, an office building, a warehouse ... anything.

Then he finally stopped, and I heard a door close behind us.

"What the hell's this?" a voice said, and I started in the thief's arms. It had been so long since I'd heard anyone but him, it was startling to think there was someone else there, seeing me like this, the helpless victim of another man.

"This fucker called the police on me when I was doing his place," the burglar said. "So I took him instead of his stuff. What do you think he's worth?"

"Gotta see him first," the other voice said, and I found myself being lowered down off my kidnapper's shoulder. The sack was set down on a hard surface, probably a table or a countertop.

Someone pulled the drawstrings open, and I squirmed out from inside the sack like an animal being born. Through the blindfold bright light seeped in.

"Hmmm, he's a good one."

I felt hands on me, all over me, caressing and massaging my naked chest. It was probably the other man, assessing the value of the stolen property. He pinched my nipples and slapped my face lightly. My shorts were yanked down and my crotch exposed. The hand gripped my hard dick, bouncing it back and forth against my chest.

"You think I could get a good price for him?"

"He's nice all right, but I'd have to be able to tell the buyer about his performance value."

The thief laughed.

"I know all about his performance value! I did him in a field on the way here. He fucking loved it! This little faggot was born to be a slave!"

"Now you know how this works. I can't just take your word for it. I need proof."

"Do you want to use him yourself?" the burglar asked.

"I'd rather see you do him again, that way I can be an unbiased observer. Then I can tell how much we can get for him."

"Fine by me."

My arms were grabbed, and I was pulled roughly into a different position, with my head hanging upside down off the edge of the table.

I heard the burglar's zipper again, but this time there was more. Lots of sounds, of jeans being pulled down, of a shirt being pulled off ... he was completely undressing!

Then my gag was removed and my mouth was free. But before I could even yell for help, a big dick had been shoved into me.

"Take it, boy," the thief said. "Take it just like you did in the field..."

I started sucking his dick, caressing and working it with my lips and tongue. It felt so hot in my mouth, so full. I was totally being used by this man, used like a piece of property in front of someone else, someone that was watching to see how much I was worth ...

Suddenly I heard a loud noise.

"Freeze!" the other voice yelled.

"Oh shit!" my kidnapper said, and I could feel his dick get limp in my mouth. "You're a cop? A fucking cop?"

"You got it, man, now just back up nice and easy ..."

"I don't fucking believe this!" the thief said as he backed up out of my mouth. I was left alone, with no one touching me.

"We've been after you for a long time, scumbag," the cop said. "Now I've bagged you once and for all."

I heard the cocking of a gun. Then the sound of lots of voices. A bunch of men ran into the room – it must have been the cop's backup. Many voices assaulted my ears.

"We got him, boys!"

"It's about time."

"Hands behind your back, man!"

Clicking – they were handcuffing him.

"Get his clothes back on him."

Then there were hands on me, helping me to sit up, and yanking the blindfold off me. The light blinded me, and I couldn't see anything for a minute.

I opened them and saw my rescuer.

He was good-looking, blond, with a mustache, and great blue eyes. His hands were on my shoulders, and he was looking me straight in the eye.

"Are you all right, guy?" he asked.

"I … I think so," I said.

"Did that bastard hurt you?"

"No," I said. "I'm okay," And I glanced across the room, where a bunch of uniformed officers were swarming around a man that had to be the burglar.

He was hot.

About my age, late twenties, dark hair and eyes, clean-shaven. The police had gotten his pants back on him, but his big broad chest was still bare, and his muscled arms were cuffed behind his back. He saw me looking at him, and there was an electric look that passed between us.

For a split second, it was like we were alone.

He was the thief, and I was his catch.

And, somehow, that was the way it would always be.

Then, a second later, we were back in reality, and the cops were jostling him out of the room. Just before he was pulled out of my sight, the burglar cocked his head and gave me a sly lopsided smile.

Then he was gone.

I went down to the station with the officers and filled out a report like a good citizen. But I refused to testify. I didn't want to.

Every night after that, I found myself thinking about what had happened. In a strange way it was like I had never been rescued, like I was still bound and gagged inside that sack, a prisoner.

His prisoner.

And I jerked my hard cock off to the memory of our split second, the memory of his eyes and his lopsided smile and what it felt like to be slung over his shoulder.

But then it's like I wake up and the dream is over.

I don't know what happened to my thief. He may have been let off; he may have gotten a jail sentence. But either way, sooner or later, he's going to be back on the prowl again.

Maybe that's why I never did get better security at my apartment. And why I leave the door unlocked when I go to sleep at night. Someday, I hope, the midnight burglar will come for me again. And this time, I won't fight him.

CALVIN ROSE
John Caruso

Out of a forgetful haze, I awaken, leaving no wake of dreams, yet emerging so slowly I recall the warm place, semi-darkness, where my mind is housed, and I become aware of myself – first as something lost in the dark warmth, then something separate from it, something drawn by physics like a draft of cold air, and then finally, alarmed, intensely separate from both the cold and the warmth – until I'm thrust into consciousness as if reborn – blank as dawn.

My eyes pop open to a high water-stained ceiling in a dim, but day-lit, room of brown paneled walls. Only then do I feel my body. I'm first aware of an essential stiffness, an unnatural posture to my sleep. My arms are thrust above my head. They will not move, or I cannot move them. I focus on my hands and start to raise them. A painful stricture in my wrists halts their motion and a simultaneous metal clank follows the sound of their sudden arrest. I lift my eyes. My wrists are handcuffed around a vertical bar on an old iron-framed bed.

My waking haze evaporates in an instant, like drops of a sun shower on a blistering sidewalk. I yank on the iron bar, sear my wrists, as though this were not the first attempt to free myself. Clank, clank, clank, clank. I raise my head as far as it will go, look down the length of my body. I'm naked. My chest and stomach are mottled with crusty white spatters. Someone's prolific expenditure of sex on me. My ankles too are shackled to the iron grill at the foot of the bed.

"Jesus Chris–," I choke out my first words. My mouth and throat are so dry I can barely swallow let alone speak. Not only am I cuffed to a strange bed in a strange room, naked and semen-spattered, I don't even remember how I got here. At the moment, nothing of me comes to mind except my name. It was there all along like the consciousness of myself in sleep. Now I know, as in the remembrance of a dream, that my name was the warmth hovering there in the semi-darkness: Calvin Rose. Other things come back to me. I live in Cambridge. Another wave of panic hits. What day is it? Should I be at work or school? Then I think of my family. My parents live in Rye,

New Hampshire, by the sea. I have a sister at school in Minnesota, a brother in New York and another in Rye. How long have I been here? Long enough for my family to miss me and wonder where I am?

I break out into a sweat at the thought of it. I want to call for help, but I don't know where I am and who my rescuers would be, let alone what they would think, finding me naked, sexed and cuffed to a bed. I wait and breathe in and out as slowly as I can to stem the panic. If only I could remember how I got here. Bondage had never gotten the better of me before, and while I can't say I've never been so drunk I didn't pass out during a night of pleasure, I've never woken up like this – alone, compromised and seemingly abandoned god knows where, for all I know in another life.

My lower back aches from being too long supine. I scoot as far down as I can, extending my arms all the way, so I can bend my knees and take the pressure off my back. The movement causes a reflex clutch of my sphincter, which ordinarily I wouldn't notice except the sensation evokes the raw intensity of unnatural use. I close my eyes. I've either had a loose and violent evacuation or I've been sodomized. I'm no stranger to the feeling, nor is it so shocking I'd find myself on the receiving end of some random coupling, but I've never been taken by force. I just don't remember anything.

Behind me the click and turn of a key and the hushed intake of an opening door startles me. A cool breeze breaks the vacuum of the room and makes me shiver with cold. The door closes again, and heavy male steps enter the room. Footfall retreats to another room and the sound of grocery bags – the crumple of paper, packaged items bumping, cans clinking, thumping as they are set down – reaches me. It is as if this person is unaware of my presence, or is so casual about the naked man restrained on the bed as to require less urgency then perishables, something in no more need of attending to than a load of clothes waiting to be folded.

What I do at the return of my captor, a possibility I'd glanced but hadn't confronted directly, is not at all what I'd thought I'd do. I expected I would scream and curse and carry on, even plead for my release. I also considered faking it, pretending to awaken with a contented stretch and a casual hello, as if I always wake up handcuffed, and also as if I remember everything that led me here and the night of misspent passion. After all, having considered the dire possibility of ending up cooked and eaten by a psychotic cannibal killer, I also had to consider that my night's partner had playfully left me sleeping handcuffed while he went out to hunt up a more conventional breakfast. But I don't do either of those things. Instead, I close my eyes and pretend to sleep.

For a long time I wait, listening to the sound of groceries being put away, cupboards opening and closing, the white hum of the refrigerator when the door is opened. I notice a smell now. It hadn't hit me before, no doubt from my having been saturated so long in the room's atmosphere, but after the door opened and a fresh draft of air swept in, I recognized the difference as the room's smell settled in again. There is nothing here but the musky, pungent smell of male sex, the heaviness of which cannot be accounted for merely by my own diurnal sweats, or the bleachy funk of the deposits left upon my body, but something airborne, orgiastic and feral in its essence.

I wait and still nothing. Another more distant door closes and then there is silence. It stretches on for so long that even my anxiety cannot sustain its exhausting scenarios and, against all good sense, I drift off to sleep.

I awaken to the sensation of having to relieve myself. The pressure on my groin is palpable, even painful with intermittent cramps. I try to ride it out and hope it will subside. It does not. In fact one wave of cramps paralyzes my body, freezes my mouth in a rictus. I can't hold it much longer. I cry out. "Hey! Are you there? Help me. Please I have to go so bad. Hey, please."

I wait. The silence continues for maybe half a minute before a door opens and footsteps approach. As the steps enter the room – the clarity and immediacy of the sound is unmistakable, as is the slight tremor in the bed – I suddenly regret initiating this first confrontation with my captor.

He stands over the bed. I look him in the eye. He is not at all what I expect – some seedy and hideous lecher with cold malevolent eyes – but a casually hip fellow of about thirty, dressed in a brown T and jeans, average in height and only modestly solid in build – some mounding in his chest and shoulders adds drama and tension to the shapeless T. His hair is dark and uncombed, uneven bangs swept across his forehead, and a stylish rime of dark stubble darkens his face. A mild expression rules his large brown eyes, subtly handsome, increasingly so as a range of expressions register on his features, evincing not least genuine curiosity, intelligence and quite possibly pity.

I swallow and clear my throat to speak, but I don't know what to say. It seems odd to ask to use the bathroom without first demanding some explanation of the circumstance that predicates my urgent need, but I can't wait on introductions. "I need to pee so bad. Could you let me loose? Did you forget about me?"

The man just stands there, raises his eyebrows and folds his arms across his chest.

"Come on. I can't hold it any longer. Come on, please."

The man shifts his stance, unfolds his arms and puts his hands in his front pants pockets. I think he's reaching for a key, but he's actually feeling himself through his pockets.

"I told you, I can't hold it any longer. If you don't let me go I'm going to scream my head …"

As quickly as I utter the words, the man reaches into his back pocket for something and quickly plugs my mouth with it. A bitter latex taste dries my mouth. He's silenced me with a large tan dildo. My last words muffle in a hopeless groan. "Mmmfaah" is my best attempt at motherfucker.

Having silenced me, he undoes the button on his jeans and unzips his fly. He slides his pants down to his thighs and starts to stroke himself. It is all done unhurriedly and carefully, like a patient man peeling a banana

I stare back in disbelief. His cock is thicker and longer than his build intimates – slightly flattened but broad as a beer bottle, ten inches in length, olive toned, a shade darker than his face and arms, with a large vein standing out in relief and a massive mushroom head. It grows straight out with his stroking, the hardest kind of cock to take. I wonder if it already knows the way inside of me.

I groan as another paralyzing wave of cramps attacks my groin. I start to release, let go. I feel the stream coming up my shaft, just enough to relieve the cramp and then I hold it, but it's almost too late. The man is stroking faster now, his face deepening to the color of his cock. I press my knees together, clamping my own dick as a last resort to hold in my piss. I grit my teeth. I moan "please" one last time through the rubber cock and then it overwhelms me, the burning, rising, sweet hot tingle of relief in the head of my shaft. I close my eyes, let go and hot piss shoots up into my pubic hair and onto my stomach, running down again over my hips, some of it down past my balls between my legs, pooling warmly under my ass and in my crack.

A winded sound makes me open my eyes. The man is pumping his cock with fury, breathing hard, right over me. He doesn't cry out, but he lets out a long and satisfied exhalation when he shoots, a prodigious deposit on my humiliated balls and cock. The smell of his potent sex washes over me, the same feral smell that dominates the room.

He slaps his heavy meat against my hip to free the last drops of semen and wipes the eye on my stomach like a blade. Then, just as carefully as before but with more difficulty, he tucks his still swollen penis back into his pants, zips and buttons up. Then he reaches into the other back pocket and withdraws a syringe. He unsheathes the needle, holds it up and shoots out a little to make sure there's no air, leans over me, like a doctor with a sudden look of bedside concern and lowers the syringe to my exposed neck. I groan my protest in a long held out "Nooooh."

Then I feel the prick.

When I open my eyes again I'm staring at the floor. The bed to my left and I am midair, naked still, supported in some kind of sling. My arms are hanging down below, hands free, the sling supports my haunches and my legs are wide apart, my bottom spread, my cock and balls hanging free, so exposed I can feel the slightest movement of air on them. I tense my sphincter. It feels tight and normal, no raw feeling or soreness. I'm relieved.

I hear the man in the kitchen and smell cooking – something like onions and peppers, some kind of spice – and hear a faint tantalizing sizzle. I'm so hungry I almost feel sick to my stomach. Mingling with the smell of food is a manly smell of soap. My skin feels tight and astringent, and I realize the clean soap smell is me.

"Hey," I call out. "What's all this about? Huh? I'm sure we had a great time and all, but you have to let me go home sometime. Just let me down, and we can do whatever you want. Just name it. I'm game, but don't hold me like this. Come on."

No answer.

"You got a name? I don't know you. At least you don't look familiar."

Again silence.

"Just tell me how I got here. Where'd we meet? Why don't I remember?"

The man comes out carrying a folding table. He sets it down under me. He goes back to the kitchen and comes out with a plate and a tall plastic cup. There's a plastic spork on the plate, the kind they used to give you in the high school cafeteria. The plate is mounded with peppers, onions and mushrooms in some kind of egg frittata served with toast.

I don't waste any time eating. I drain the glass of water. He goes and fills it again. The food is good. As I eat, I'm thinking if this were a restaurant what you would call it. The Dungeon Gourmet. Chez Sade. The Prisoner's Palate. Masochist's Feast.

All of a sudden I feel a wet spray against my sphincter and before I know it, my mouth still full of food, I feel his massive mushroom head pushing on the slippery cusp of my anal ring. He's come around behind me while I've been dreaming up fanciful names for my predicament. I try to swallow and speak, but before I can, he's pushing himself into me with the slow and persistent force of someone pulling on a rubber glove that is three sizes too small. I feel my insides split, a sharp stab, a raw hard grinding, tearing me as he goes. I gasp in pain, drop my spork, spitting out my food and coughing, trying not to choke. "Uhohhhhh." The long slow syllables come out of my mouth like a verbalization of cock-in-ass pain, or pity for the male ass raped translated into the ecstatic rudiments of language. The man can't get all the way in, and so he withdraws and starts to pound his way into the tight just split cavity, bringing the pain sharper and faster, until he gives me every inch in every thrust. "Uho-uho-uho-uho-uho-uho…"

The problem is he doesn't have the decency to come like a fucking rapist into my pain and shame. No the sick fucker has to go on nailing me – with a cock as hard and contusing as a nylon dog bone – sometimes even removing himself completely just to sear my tender ring again – no, he just has to go on until the pain's been translated once more into some kind of pleasure, and I'm just helpless, breathing out now with the sound of a boy caught up in the wonder of something awesome, wanting more …

By the time he comes – answering my breathless awe with his own robust sigh of wonderment – I'm so filled with desire and hatred I don't know whether I'd embrace or kill him were I free.

He leaves me alone for the rest of the day. In fact, he leaves altogether not long after sodomizing me. This time he doesn't inject me with a sedative, but leaves me suspended, wide awake, his cum (there is always so much of it) oozing slowly out of me and seeping down my scrotum, as if my bottom was a kind of liquid hourglass. Then some time later, I understand why. My stomach starts to cramp and gurgle. All at once there is a rush and my bowels let go. Spread in a position conducive to elimination and so recently plied open, there's nothing I can do to stop the flow. It may be the after effects of his forceful plumbing, but I suspect he put laxative in my food and then left me here on purpose to defile the room. Somehow, I'm even more humiliated now than when he stood over me, getting off while I pissed myself. It's as if what's inside of me is so revolting he wouldn't even deign to stay let alone be aroused by it. How is it I feel rejected and wretched, left alone to endure the stench of my excrescence?

Something inside of me feels wronged, not the rape itself, but that when it was over I should feel it was nothing of the kind. Feel more cleansed than violated. It was harsh and yet somehow pure – for there was never any threat of harm or violence, as if coming to suspended like that, a creature born open, made his sudden transition from servant to master inevitable, almost arbitrary, not a question of choice but a matter of time. Just as it was inevitable that I would fill my mouth when he set down food.

Would I have felt more violated if my hands had been bound and he had picked up the spork and fed me, either as fussily as a mother feeds an infant, or whether he forced too much at once into my mouth? But, then who hasn't seen a hurried mother shovel strained peaches into a baby's mouth, when you can plainly see the kid has hardly swallowed, and the pabulum fairly oozes out from between its malleable, toothless gums? So then would it have been force had I been bound and hungry and desired the nourishment he offered? Would it have been a crime of any kind to forcibly feed a man's mouth, so long as he didn't asphyxiate in the process or die from an allergic reaction? Would it be called rape, or exploitation? There is no statute for that as far as I know. A crime to withhold, or starve, yes. Would I have considered it rape, or just an embarrassing fetish, if he had spooned egg scramble up my backside and filled my mouth up with his cock instead? And then for all of it, his cum, the savory frittata, to come out of that single orifice was every bit as inevitable also, whether hours hence in a slow and moderate evacuation, or by this precipitous laxative outpouring. Desire and violation, craving and satiation, both purged from my body in the end.

I can't help feeling he knows my desires and knows that when I'm hungry, bound or unbound, I will take any cock in any manner it is offered. He knows it is inevitable.

But now, unsedated and free to think for the first time since my captivity – neither deterred nor bullied by shame, my own foul stench – I also know something about my captor.

I'm troubled more now by how little I know of myself, apart from a certainty about my desires – that I have partaken in orgies and have surrendered what he forced upon me many times – how little detail I remember about the actual men I have coupled with, or even whether or not I have ever known the power of love, indeed whether he has abducted me from a lover. I recalled my family upon first awakening, my parents, the number and sex of my siblings and where they each reside, even the sense that I am somehow committed to some time-consuming occupation. Yet, having been since accosted and sedated in repeated rounds, I have no more searched the details of my past, as if those superficial facts were sufficient to embody my whole memory. Now, left awake for an entire day, suspended in my overwhelming essence, I cannot recall where it is I work, what my occupation is or the motions and mental processes of its special knowledge.

I know there are drugs that can affect the memory – date rape drugs, even excess of alcohol, that can cause blackouts, but these are short-term effects where only the events of a night, or a matter of hours are lost. The fact that my memory is somewhat variable, growing vaguer rather than clearer as my captivity endures, suggests it is directly related to the injections.

I latch onto the moment before penetration when I was eating – mind loosed in the unconscious – and a string of restaurant parodies came out of me, as though I'd slipped for a moment into a familiar mode of thought, found my sense of humor. Yet, that kind of self-discovery is all interior. It does not give me a life, an architecture of events to build a past on, a narrative of experiences or a connection to people. I wonder if I am a writer, or perhaps, I think it more likely, that I am in advertising. This is complete fancy, at best an impression. It is not memory. All I know for sure is that my name is Calvin Rose, and I have sex with men.

I am still awake, still thinking when he returns. He does not react to the smell and the mess I have left. He moves casually around his apartment. I hear the refrigerator open and close. Hear him pop a bottle top. He passes across the hall – at least I'm facing the hall and other rooms in my current suspension – and turns on a TV in another room. I strain to hear, hoping to catch something – the name of a show, the time of day, the name of a familiar broadcaster or actor, a line from a movie I have seen, anything at all to place myself in the world – but the volume is too low, and I can only make out undifferentiated voices. It is impossible to say whether they are lines of dialogue in a drama or conversations on a political talk show.

He passes again through the hall – T-shirt slung over his shoulder, still in his jeans – and goes into the bathroom. His bare torso is graceful and slim, just enough weight to his chest and shoulders to lend drama to his leanness. I hear the shower run. I have yet to see him naked, as if he hides himself from me, keeps himself covered and protected, while I am constantly exposed.

He comes out almost immediately still half dressed, unshowered, and enters the room, my room you could say, holding a stack of towels. These he spreads over the mess I've made on the floor. Then he withdraws handcuffs from his back pockets and stands before me. He looks at me appealingly, motioning for me to hold out my hands for cuffing. I comply. He's going to shower me. After I'm handcuffed, he lowers the sling by a pulley on the wall, releases the soiled supports under my haunches, and the cross support beneath my armpits until my feet touch down on the floor. Then he shackles my ankles and walks me into the bathroom.

I am still harnessed across my chest and around my waist. He guides me by the harness into a huge glassed-in shower stall. He gives me a push and I start to fall, but he has my harness and lowers me until I'm on my knees in the echoing stall under the drone of hot water. The water runs down my face and into my mouth. I crawl so that my head is out of the heavy stream and gasp for air. I kneel there for a moment, my back to him. I hear him behind me opening a door, followed by a thump of something on the floor. The next thing I know, a painful cold jet of water is rushing like a liquid plumber in my crack and up my sphincter.

"Ow, hey." I roll over on my back, hands slipping on the wet tile, and wind up flat on my back, legs splayed. The cold jet shocks my scrotum with surprising force.

"That's fucking cold you asshole ..."

The jet comes up into my mouth and stops me in a loud gurgle. I spit and choke and roll away, gasping facedown on the hard cold tile. I just lie there now, catching my breath and letting him hose me at will. He's cleaning all the shit and cum from my crack and scrotum, but he's overdoing it on purpose, pummeling my sack, tearing at my sphincter and the fragile line of flesh along my taint. Then the hose quits. I lay recovering, breathing hard from shocking cold, when I feel the sharp stab of a needle in my ass cheek.

When I awaken in the sling again, smell sausage, boiled eggs and coffee wafting from the kitchen, I know exactly what I'm going to do, because I know exactly what he wants to do to me. I start in as soon as he appears with the folding table.

"Hey, I've been thinking. You know what I really want to today?"

He hesitates on his way across the room, holding the table in front of him like a shield.

"It's kind of twisted, but what if you made me a really man-sized breakfast and fed it to my ass, you know stuff me full, pipe some hot coffee in, and cork me up good with a butt plug, then stop my mouth up with that cock of yours and give me a good pull on your cream, well I'd be happier than a fat man at an all-you-can-eat buffet."

His face suddenly freezes. His large and curious brown eyes turn cold and flinty. He just stands there for a minute looking at me with suspicion and contempt. Then he flings the folding table at the wall and storms off down the hall, muttering to himself.

He comes back now with what looks like a table tennis paddle, still muttering, goes behind me, swats my dangling sack without warning like he's going for a kill at the tennis table. "Aaaawwwgggg." I cry out once and then my breath is gone. First light shines behind my eyes and then darkness. I'm paralyzed with pain, wheezing air, and then he strikes again. My legs kick and gyrate.

"You see that coming, too?" he says his first words to me. I've broken his silence. He's broken my balls. "Or maybe this isn't quite what you wanted today? Not twisted enough for you." He strikes a third time. "Aaawwggg." Now I'm blind with pain, hovering on the sickening brink of rupture, no longer a man at all but a pair of roaring, battered testicles. He doses me again, not once but twice – a needle jabbed hard in my buttock and another in my inner thigh.

All the lights are on. I blink as I awaken to the overheads glaring in my eyes. I am in the sling, face up this time, legs pinned to my chest and straddled wide, bottom tilted up. I can see down the hall if I lift my head. There is no sign of my captor.

My sack is so sore its resting weight throbs like a toothache, the slightest shift in its position makes me wince. My sphincter hurts when I close it off. The change in my position worries me; I can only anticipate with dread what this might auger.

I recall everything that has happened since waking up a captive. I remember the rape and the shower. I know he's dosing me. I am still aware of him, although just now I cannot conjure up his face. There is something else. Surely there is more. I feel a history somehow, not only in the sensations of my body but in my strangled dreams, like the empty silhouette that remains after a shape has been cut out of dark background. If there is more, more than the shadow, the desire to make up what I'm lacking, I cannot fathom it, and if there is nothing why do I bother to resist or worry about what happens to me? This is who I am, and there is nothing to escape to. I am Calvin Rose, and I have sex with men.

As if in answer to my thought, the apartment door opens and a man walks in, but it is not my captor. He stands on the threshold for a moment. Above him on the wall to his right, there is a clock that wasn't there before. It is midnight.

He walks straight toward me without a word. He stares at me, the spread invitation of my suspended body, as if he's been charged with remembering it. In a moment, I see he's turning on to me, touching himself through his jeans. Then he unzips and lets his bulge out. He's six inches long and remarkably about half that in width. He pulls the leg straps of the sling to him, meets my eye with a modest nod of courtesy, as if asking me for a dance, or as if to say "excuse me," and then he simply fills me with the same slow unitary push as my captor, but with the utilitarian demeanor of a plumber joining male and female fittings. My bowel aches radically at the imposition despite his courtesy – that classic paralyzing anal pain, when the ring, as if subject to changes in the psyche (intramuscular withdrawals and virginal reversions) is unprepared for penetration. I grit my teeth and try not to cry out. If you plead for mercy in a sling, it is an invitation to receive cruelty. How do I know this if not by memory? The laws of a sling?

There is something modest and manly about his fucking, almost dutiful and pure like all true expressions of dominant masculinity. It is incumbent upon him to endure, it seems, rather than punish, and his cock is just a fact not a condemnation. He does endure, for a full half hour without a lapse of stoutness or vigor. When he comes, the exclamation is that of surprise, as if his virility and the pleasure that another man's ass affords him has never occurred to him before. But it is the pain of having to give up so much as a drop of his essence to me, even in the act of domination, that contorts his eyes and mouth with such loss and regret you'd think I'd tricked him into dying. And that is what makes him turn on me. Even as he pumps his cum in me, he knows I've seen him die, knows that he's been intimate with me despite himself. He pulls out and his eyes go cold. His mouth curls in a snarl and he cuffs my sack. "Awwwgggghh." He wipes the sudden sweat on his cheek with the back of his hand, buttons up and walks out of the room.

Another man enters. He is also dark, but tall and slender. He unzips and enters without so much as a glance of acknowledgment. He is slightly longer than his predecessor but not so stout.

He appears intent on getting off, but he does not pop off in five minutes as I suspect. He remains in me like the other man for precisely one half hour and then he comes with greater force and more obvious loss of self-control. This earns me a sadistic squeeze of my sack in his fist. I cry out, and it is the only time he looks me in the eye – to register my pain and helplessness. I know now, as I know all the other laws of the sling, that these men and all those that will follow do not have sex with men. I am their first.

When the third man walks in – dark-haired, slit-eyed with violent twisting lips – I know exactly what the night will bring. For his cock is seven inches long, I know by looking. It's going up in half hour increments. Six inches at twelve. Twelve inches by six. That is what will be. Perhaps my genius is into guessing cock size, like those people at carnivals who guess people's weight. My captor knew if I could see the clock that I would see the inverse pattern – he too knows my genius.

I will endure six hours of continuous pounding, friction, widening. It is one o'clock and I am ecstatically sore inside now. Both men have taken me to the point of auto-orgasm and left me hanging. My captor has built desire into this regimented rape, made me crave this sneering brute, who has only a stout seven inches with which to punish me. It is as if he knows his size is unequal to his capacity for cruelty and so he is intentionally rougher. He sees the lost expression on my face and is demonic in his efforts to make me come. If I do he will hurt me; if I don't he will hurt me more. I know this, too. It is as if I know each man's desire – by his look, by the size and shape of his cock, the order of his appearance, each an inversion of my mental and bodily state – even as my captor knows mine, knows that if I am forced to submit I can suffer my own desires without complicity. What will become of me once I climax? Once desire ebbs? He knows this, too. I will suffer as I only appear to suffer now.

Just before his climax, it finally flows out of me. He smiles at my sexual incontinence, having forced me to ejaculate against my will. Then he comes and the smile changes to a lurid mask of rage. I can see he wants to pull out, avoid the cataclysm of intimacy, master me with cum, but the heat and clutch of my bottom is too much, and he succumbs. Our desire ebbs together and his is replaced by fear and wrath.

He leans over me. Not only is he enraged at having lost his sex in another man's ass, but also because he's given me relief and pleasure despite his desire to be cruel. For this he knees me in the sac. I howl stupidly, absurdly like an animal, the pain is so spectacular. He absorbs it like nourishment and reaches into his pocket. Between his fingers is a silvery gleaming razor blade. My crotch is so inflamed I wonder if I will even feel the cuts he's about to make. He holds the blade delicately between his fingers like a surgeon, and makes a fine shallow incision up the center of my scrotum and up the back of my penis. I feel it. A vicious sting. Blood beads form and merge in a pure red line. Then the line wells and drops begin to roll down my scrotum. He leaves and the next man enters.

By 5:00 a.m. I am weeping, seeing the men through my tears, starry and blurred under the bright overhead lights. They are all the same. Dark-haired, masculine and cruel. Yet, I have broken the law of the sling and now I plead with each one. My canal is raw. The men have since found better utility in manly cruelty by coming on me.

Those early lubricious loads of semen have since absorbed. Though expanded, the ring stretched to an open portal now, my canal returns the necessary friction. For the cocks grow larger in their sequence, and my anus is rubbed harder as with massive rods of steel sealed in skins of emery. It is now unlined and each cock ejects red and pink with blood and mucus, like something born. "Please. You could just pretend, couldn't you? I can't take any more. I'm completely raw. Please don't ..."

But all I do is excite their mercenary cruelty.

The last man enters at 5:30. He is so large, engorged upon arrival – no doubt from hours of anticipation – he is wearing sweat pants to give with his erection. He is tall, dark-haired and handsome as the rest. He is a foot in length and every bit as stout as the man who entered me at midnight. His cock is harnessed and sheathed in mail of metal studs. His first thrust sears with unprecedented fire. All the studs feel like broken glass. He takes me stem to tip each time, lacerating me the full twelve inches. I cry out with every thrust, plead for him to stop and urge him on. It is inevitable. I am Calvin Rose, and I have sex with men.

Toward the end, I feel shredded inside, bruised around the mouth of my canal. My cries are ragged, too, echoing the laceration of my insides. The exact sensation reminds me of a burn. Not that I remember an event, but I recall the sensation of a deep burn on my arm, the crawling maddening unrelenting pain of nerves on fire. My insides have begun to crawl and burn and roar like that.

At last he delivers his load inside of me. He hesitates a moment, his hand in a fist. His face is red, ashamed. "Please don't hit me there. I'm going to rupture," I beg him. But he is not ashamed of what he is about to do, but ashamed of what he's done. I have given him the greatest pleasure a man can give another man, yet having taken pleasure he returns contempt. For, like all the men who've come in me tonight, he's lost his self-control, and having lost that it is beyond his power to regain. He strikes my sac with his fist, lingers to savor his revenge – to watch my mouth open, my eyes flutter, my muscles tense. Then he leaves.

I am drifting toward delirium. The hands of the clock blur and waver, settle vertically. Six o'clock. A moment later my captor enters. He approaches me like the others. His eyes are dark and dead, staring at my trembling body – my scrotum, swollen like a grapefruit, dark with hemotomas; my pitiful opening, a bloody cavern. It is as if all that remains is for my entrails and vital organs to come tumbling out. They, too, feel bruised, lacerated, dislodged from their tenuous connections and precise placements, like those people born with their organs on the opposite side. I am a man transformed – not merely naked, exposed and sodomized, balls bludgeoned to the point of rupture. For if I am damaged beyond repair, then my desire is desecrated, destroyed forever with it.

My captor does not undo his pants. He raises his hand, whispers something between closed lips, and then he makes a fist and plunges in.

In my sleep this time I dream. Who I am is not explicit. As in all dreams, identity is assumed, fluid. There is someone in the dream I never see, yet who remains next to me throughout. Not myself and not entirely another. A presence I depend on that keeps me strangely whole, like the embodiment of memory, something nearby but safely housed in an invisible body. There is nothing outstanding in the dream except that it is the most perfect summer day, and I feel good in a way I've only felt a handful of times in life. Most days are marred by at least some small distress: adverse news, an argument with a friend, the residue of bad dreams, the death of someone close, oversleeping, gloomy weather, financial worries. Not so today. There is not a cloud or a shadow in my dream.

I keep moving, sometimes traveling in a car, sometimes on foot. The road is open, the sky blue, perspective closing its aperture down the road in a distant V between the tops of trees. Then I am at a public street in a city by the sea. People I don't know speak to me as though everyone feels generous and free, unburdened by the blue open sky. Nothing happens, and there is no purpose to any of my movements, no destination to my intermittent travels. I belong here it seems, and everyone is happy to see me, looks at me with admiration. This is enough. I gradually become aware of the presence at my side. I don't see or speak to this presence. For it never rises quite to consciousness of itself. Yet, I understand then, that it is this invisible embodiment that fills me with elation and peace. At the height of the day, the joy and levity of the crowds, their generosity and freedom also, seems unbounded. Familiar faces that have passed before suddenly return with laughter and the joy swells to the point where I hear the word "love" inside his head. At that moment, a man with a seductive smile laughs at something witty I have said. He repeats it and then everybody laughs. The sun is very high and the day seems destined to defy all other days in its exceeding joy and permanence.

I awaken alone in the darkness. The dream dissolves, and in a moment, before I grasp the sweet, melting center of it, it vanishes beyond recall. The sedative has worn off too soon. I never awaken in the night, or at least I don't remember it.

My arms are thrust above my head. I cannot move them. I focus on my hands and start to raise them. A painful stricture in my wrists halts their motion and a simultaneous metal clank follows the sound of their sudden arrest. I have felt this before, but I can't remember it. I remember the sling. A dozen straight men in succession abusing my ass and sac, probably paid to absolve their curious lust but still ashamed. I remember my captor's fist. A sweat of panic breaks out on my forehead and in my armpits. I smell of manly soap, but in the background like a warning I smell sweat and semen, a lingering musk of masculine aggression. I must escape. I cannot endure one more cock or cruel fist. My sexual organs, inside and out, are like ruins, used up, broken cisterns, crumbling viaducts. They feel like the pulpy rinds of fruit trodden underfoot. The sweat breaks into rage. I have not forgotten my desire, but I swear I will kill the next man who whips out his cock or raises a hand to swat my sack.

I pull on the cuffs. Clank, clank, clank, clank. I stop. If my captor is home, he will come out. I imagine him stuffing a latex cock in my mouth to silence me. Yet, if I wait until the morning, there is no telling what I will be made to endure before I'm left alone again. I slide up as far as I can until I can grab the vertical bars on the headboard. They are not solid metal. Perhaps the bed itself is not that strong. I begin to rock. The headboard grill has give. If I can make it give it's going to be the head, because the grill at the foot is against a wall. I wait and listen. There is no sound from down the hall.

I rock again, harder. The bars themselves have begun to bend. I get another idea. I take hold with both hands on the bar around which I am cuffed and I begin to yank in earnest. I rest and listen. He either doesn't hear from behind his door or he is not home. I pull and pull, but I cannot see if I have made progress beyond the initial bending. Just when it seems I have reached an impasse, the weld around the base and top lets go. The bar begins to spin. I work it around and around. It bends more. It's loose at the top. All I need is for one end to come free.

I spin and spin and reverse the spin, and then it breaks and my hands are cuffed but free of the bed. I quickly scoot forward and put my manacled feet between the bars, drop them down to rest on the bottom of the grill. Then I begin the process again, but now with greater leverage. It is not long before my feet are free.

Still there is no sound from down the hall. I wonder what to do. Lie here as if still chained to the bed until he comes in and goes to sleep, or get up and wait behind the door, take the chance that I can take him from behind and overcome him before he flicks the light and sees that I am not in the bed. When my eyes adjust to the dark, I go down the hall as quietly as I can to see if he is already in bed. The door at the end of the hall is open. His bed is empty. I find a chair in his kitchen and carry it out to my room. Kneeling first and then sliding my feet under me as I hold the chair back I'm able to bring both shackled feet up on the chair. I stand up and remove the bulbs from the overhead light fixture.

I squat, back pressed to the wall and wait behind the door. I grow tired of standing and have to give my legs a rest, though the position recalls the sling and exerts gravity on my abused and beaten parts. The reminder keeps me alert and focused. I practice sliding up the wall silently in preparation for his return. I wait and listen.

Twice I hear footsteps outside the door, but they move on. The third time, the footsteps stop and the key turns. I slide up to a stand at the click and turn of the knob. He enters left hand on the doorknob, the right hand flicks the light switch. Nothing happens.

"Shit," he curses. He keeps the door partway open. In the slit of light, I see him in shadow, the back of his head. He starts for the light switch in the hall and I make my move, leaping out, cuffed hands raised, coming down over his head and jerking back suddenly on his neck. He gasps, staggers, pushing me back first into the door. It closes with a slam. I hold on. He lurches forward trying to throw me, hands going for the cuff chain at his throat. I pull with all my might. His wind grows thinner and he falls back into me. I crash again into the door, but this time I use the leverage to hold myself and master my stranglehold on him. My cock is pressed to the crack seam of his pants. It starts to stir and I know what I will do. I had no thought of anything but escape, yet a new desire has come to me. My cock pulses harder. My captor's wind is a high, thin wheeze about to quit like the last turn of a whistling water valve.

He goes silent and limp. I let his body fall to the floor, and then I go to work.

When he awakens, I have him naked in the sling and with the overhead lights on. The hard part was deciding whether I wanted him face up or down. On the one hand I wanted to see the look in his eyes, when I filled him up, see him react to the overmastering pain of a first cock thrust through him dry in a single stroke. On the other hand, face down he will feel even less in control, more mine, because he won't be able to anticipate it, and it will be enough to hear the pain and outrage in his voice. In the end, my choice to have him face down, unable even to guard his passage with his eyes, is aesthetic. For there is something about the inviolable tightness of the ass of a man who cannot conceive of his own penetration, not just the pristine, dime-sized, sun ray of a sphincter that has never taken more than a doctor's finger, but the very way he holds it. It has never provocatively pushed out or spread in his naked attitude, but held firm like a consolidation of his power. If it ever parts, it does so incidentally during some masculine endeavor like sports – the football huddle, the base runner's crouch – that invites the visual possibility of surrender in a context where it is impossible. My captive likes sex with men as well as I (he is too committed to my body for it to be otherwise,) but, now that I have seen his ass unguarded, I know he has never taken anything inside of him.

His body was far more elegant and beautiful than I imagined beneath the generic shapeless Ts and relaxed blue jeans. It is the kind of body I have always envisioned for Adam, elemental and uncomplicated. Not overly wrought and stiff with musculature. Not self-consciously masculine at all – his chest the modest well-formed mounds of an athletic teen, biceps attenuated, thighs long and articulate, the trapezius slope gently from his neck and then bunch and square at the deltoids. The points of his clavicle stand out like finials on the cupola of his shoulders. His beauty is in the clear articulation of the male form, uncluttered by the baroque striations and articulations of gym bodies. His mystery is in the rich straight dark hair that combs his arms, chest, and legs and again in a kind of dark ray rising from his pubis almost to his navel.

I sit facing him in a chair when he opens his eyes. It takes only a few seconds for him to see the situation, how it has reversed. I have a latex cock stuffed in his mouth and his hands are safely cuffed and hoisted on a guide above his head. He tries to speak to me, a wild urgency in his eyes, a protest as if against injustice.

"You think you haven't had this coming?" I tell him. "This is your fault. Look at me," I gesture at my swollen, blood-bruised balls. I stand up and turn, spread myself for him. "That's what's left of my desire, my body. So there must be new desires. I thought at first I could just leave here, escape, be free, but I cannot. You've not only damaged my body, but my mind as well. I cannot go anywhere without it. So I have to begin again, right now. And when I'm done with you, you're going to tell me everything."

I walk around behind him. He's trying to talk, vehemently now, but the words are all muffled by the rubber cock. I stand behind him, take hold of his narrow hips. I stare into the innocence of his virgin ass. He expects me to sodomize him roughly, and that is what I have planned, but suddenly I know that if a new desire is to be born in him, then he must come to love surrender, as he now loves control. After all, his worst fear is that my cock will give him pleasure (pain a mere artifact). And pleasure is what I intend to give him.

I go to the bathroom first and cut my nails very close. Then I get a bottle of oil from the kitchen cabinet above the stove. I keep the bottle behind my back until I'm around him. Then I uncap it and pour a generous stream down his crack and rub the oil over his tight cork. I push in a little and, even at that slight intrusion, he tries to tense his cheeks. The sling keeps him spread for me. It is hard not to be cruel, hard not to feel tender. I'm still torn by the aesthetics of revenge. Whether it will be best satisfied in his suffering cruelty or in my expressing tenderness. Those other men who had me would have preferred cruelty. For them, it would have been a punishment to endure, rather than an emotion to experience. This man knows emotion. I have seen it in his eyes in the care he took giving me a needle. I decide he must be punished and then tenderized.

I plunge my oily index finger in and pull it out. That is enough lubrication to let me through, but not enough to ease his pain. I plant the head of my cock against him. His ring is so tight and my head so swollen the disparity in size alone is going to pain him greatly. I take a hold of his hips. He knows what's coming. His body is tensed. I plunge hard, all the way. A cry stifles in his throat, comes out like a humiliated and astonished grrrrr. I pull out. I wait a minute. I sear the ring and plunge again. Grrrrrrr. Then I pound him, firmly and steadily until he opens for me. Each thrust is accompanied by a vocalization that reflects the changes in him. The first time any man takes a cock he cannot master the full feeling of having to evacuate. I hear the deep slow moan of discomfort and dread of incontinence. Penetration resonates with all the sensations he's ever had in his bowels – nerves, fear, vertigo, diarrhea, constipation, the expanding cramp that comes from holding it in too long – all contained in this constant filling and emptying of his canal. Yet it is none of those things because it is sex, a man having sex in his ass, plumbing its history without limit, and all those private sensations are now exposed like imminent possibilities to him. He reveals himself in every sound he makes.

A half-hour in I pull the dildo from his mouth to better hear the sounds. He is so lost in them now, the torrent of words he screamed at the outset are diminished chants to himself. Over and over his protests, "No," "Oh," "Please," seem no longer directed at me but constitute a prayer to end his suffering that eventually, through repetition, becomes a mantra of endurance despite itself.

Near the end of the hour, he is weeping, for he is being pushed nearer and nearer the point of incontinence, thinking he will wet himself for the first time since he last wet the bed as a boy, fearing he will climax at his own rape. I fuck him harder. He cries out, a long held "Oh, noooo…" and then his cum sails to the floor like white ropes tossed down from the sky a length at a time. I grab his cock before he spills it all and dispense the last wad of it in the palm of my hand. I coat my index finger and work it into his pliable hole, and then I force myself on him again and drive his cum back into him. Now, he must endure my climax even while his is on the ebb. With the thrill of pleasure past, the raw and violated feeling is all that's left. I pound harder yet. It is so long coming, I have a feeling I will never climax. Then the sting, ethereal high pleasure, rises up my shaft, like a red line of mercury climbing a thermometer. I come and shout, rock until the last ebb of orgasm has subsided. I stand behind him for a while contemplating the beauty of his violation. It feels insufficient to my suffering. The utter ruin and loss of myself.

I walk slowly round and sit down to face him. His eyes are still shut tight, in expectation of some further violation. I could do anything. I could go at him another hour with the unforgiving size and texture of that latex cock, six hours if I wished to match him in temporal cruelty. I could paddle his sac as he paddled mine. Yet, all of this would just be pain.

He opens his large brown eyes. They are still wet with tears. His lashes, matted with tears, are remarkably long and childlike, but his eyes are not the eyes of a child. They are not bewildered, but resentful.

"You promised, no matter what happened, that you would never do that to me," he says.

I sit up. "What? I don't know who you are. You are lucky I don't do worse. I want to know what you've done with my memory. What you've been giving me. How I got here and who I am. I remember all the men, all that night. I remember your fist. But there's so much more I sense and keep losing. All I seem to know is that my name is Calvin Rose and I like having sex with men."

"Calvin Rose?" He shakes his head. "I am Calvin Rose."

"You're lying, that's my name."

"No, I'm Calvin Rose. I can show you."

"Who am I then?"

"You are..." he hesitates. His eyes lose focus and grow distant, as though remembering the dead. "Paul LaPlante."

I sit in silence and focus on the sounds of the name. It means nothing to me.

"Why can't I remember my own name? Why have you taken my memory from me?"

"Please, let me down from here, and I will tell you everything. No tricks. It's over. There's something you need to see."

He sits me down on a couch in the little room along the hall where he has his TV. He puts in a DVD and sits on the other end the couch. He is about to turn on the player, when he remembers something. He leaves and comes back with a small handheld mirror. Only then does it occur to me that there are no mirrors in the apartment. At least not in any room I've been in. I chance a look at myself. I am very pale, a little older than Calvin, but my eyes betray the stress of my captivity, bloodshot, dark circles and fine lines under my lids. My hair is coming back after having been shaved, sandy brown with flecks of gray. It is a handsome face heading toward premature ruin.

He sits down on the other end of the couch. We are both still naked, sign of some uneasy but bearable truce between us. He presses the clicker once and the video begins.

The lines waver and straighten out. The first image to appear is my own. I am much younger, my hair is brown with a sunny copper tint. My younger self looks to the side then into the camera and begins to speak.

"It's me. Paul LaPlante. Being of sound mind and body," I say.

Off-camera somebody mutters disagreement.

Paul LaPlante giggles, briefly, and then a genuinely serious expression comes over his face as he begins to talk.

"According to my own wishes and by my own design, I give my body over to the keeping of Calvin Rose." Calvin comes into the picture now, his head appearing in the close-up beside Paul's.

"He will keep me in this place, administer the illegal designer drug, Lethex, known on the street as Lex, and after I have forgotten much about myself including my instructions to him, I will be his captive indefinitely and submit to my own desires, unmitigated by the desires of others, or by any criminal law or restraint of human decency for the first time in my life. He will also videotape the results to verify that he has carried out my wishes.

"I have written my instructions out in detail for him and the order and sequence in which they will be acted out ..."

I sit speechless, staring at the screen.

"I wanted this?"

Calvin nods at me. He fast-forwards the DVD.

The image fixes. I'm face-up in the sling. A blond man walks into the room, straddles my body and begins without ceremony to sodomize me. I cry out. Calvin stops the DVD. The image of the rape in profile remains frozen on the screen, slightly blurred.

I cannot look at Calvin. "All the men this time were dark haired. How many times has this happened?"

Calvin sits back, pulls his knees into a tuck and looks up at the ceiling. "Many times. Blonds. Black men. Latinos. Asians. Athletes. Convicted rapists. Young suburban fathers with wives and children. Older married men. Skinhead punks. Dark-haired straight Italians."

"How long have I been here?"

"Nine years."

"Nine?" I tip my head back to keep the tears in. "All these years."

Still looking at the ceiling, I ask. "What was I, what did I do before – this."

Calvin looks at me. His eyes have that dead dark look, like the moment before he fisted me. "You," he says, and his eyes warm up, as if at a specific memory. "You were a year from completing your masters in Environmental Science – your focus was on weather and climate change. It was your other passion – and then you quit."

"How old was I?"

"Twenty-four."

"Did I ever tell you why I quit?"

"You said the only way desire had any meaning for you was if it you could experience it every time as if it were your first. And to do that meant forgetting all the other times before. It was the only way desire had any meaning for you. It was odd."

Calvin looks at me now, addresses me, but not as if I am the Paul of whom he speaks. "You said all the things you wanted didn't excite you any more, because you could control what happened. And when desire failed you, you could always opt out and say no to it. That was how desire died, you told me. And you said you'd rather die first."

"I gave up everything. Including all my memories?" I am stunned. I feel like all the light has gone out of my seeing, all the space and buoyancy of my insides has collapsed. My insides weigh dark and heavy, like something sinking in a sunless lake, yet I am strangely empty.

"I was afraid this would happen. One day you would forget so much of yourself, that even the deepest internal wish or desire would seem alien to you, and I no longer would be the one to fulfill your desires; I would become your torturer. I ..." Calvin falters.

"But why did you? If I didn't remember anything, you could have changed the rules. Changed the instructions. Anything."

Calvin looks away and says nothing.

"You gave up everything, too," I say, suddenly illumined. For only desire could have committed him for so many years.

"He said if I didn't agree to it. He'd find somebody else."

There is a long silence. We both stare at the frozen image of two men united in desire by strangeness and the willingness to forget and abandon everything except desire itself.

"Were we lovers?" I finally ask him.

He stares on for a minute, then turns to look at me. "What do you think?"

"I don't remember," I say.

We sit in silence again. Another question comes to me, not essentially different than my penultimate question, but somehow essential in its precision – because in a sense he is all that remains of me.

"Did you love me?" I ask, chancing once more to look at him.

He stares straight ahead at the frozen image on the screen.

"I don't remember."

THE AUTHORS

Shane Allison's ("Taking Brian") stories have graced the pages of *Best Black Gay Erotica*, *Best Gay Erotica 2007* and *2008*, *Ultimate Gay Erotica 2006*, *2007* and *2008*, and over a dozen other anthologies. He is the editor of *Hot Cops: Gay Erotic Stories* and the soon to be published *Firemen: Gay Erotic Tales*.

Mark Apoapsis's ("Bloodless Coup") stories have appeared in three Starbooks Press anthologies (*Lovers Who Stay With You*, *Muscle Worshipers*, and *Men on the Edge*) and in VelvetMafia.com issue 13.

K. Appleby ("Hudson Woods") was born in Sydney but moved to a farm in regional Australia at an early age. To his parents' horror, he became a vegan while working and growing up on the farm. He now resides in a small country town between the coast and the bush.

Lew Bull ("Passport to Freedom") has been published in such anthologies as *Ultimate Gay Erotica 2007* and *2008*, *Travelrotica for Gay Men* and *Travelrotica* Vol. 2, *Fast Balls*, *Dorm Porn 2*, *Treasure Trail*, *My First Time* Vol. 5, *Secret Slaves* and *Ultimate Undies*. In 2008, he is being published in *Cruise Lines* (Alyson Books) and STARbooks' upcoming anthologies: *Don't Ask, Don't Tie Me Up – Military BDSM Fantasies* and *Boys Will Be Boys*. He lives in South Africa with his partner of 30 years and should you wish to make contact with him, send to: lewbull@hotmail.com.

John Caruso ("Calvin Rose") is a novelist, essayist and short story writer, who lives with his lover of thirteen years in Vermont. He was born and raised in Connecticut, where he came of age chasing butterflies, reading stories, worrying about the signs of the apocalypse and watching sports. All of these seemed to be relatively normal American obsessions, with the exception of the butterflies. His short story, "The Art of Finding," currently appears on *Amazonshorts*.

Hank Edwards ("The Diplomat's Son") is the author of the novel *Fluffers, Inc*. His stories have been published in *Honcho*, *Mandate*, *Men*, and *100% Beef* as well as various erotic anthologies. He lives in a suburb of Detroit with his partner of many years. Visit his website at www.hankedwardsbooks.com.

O.H. Fowler ("Intervention") writes "I currently live in Georgia (God have mercy on my soul) but am looking forward to moving to South Africa this Spring. I have previously had poems in a chapbook collection by Sign of the George Press. Most of them did not rhyme."

Wade Johnson ("Stolen") is a writer from Texas now living in Los Angeles. He was going to try to lose his southern accent until guys told him it was sexy.

Jeff Mann ("FOG") has published two volumes of poetry, *Bones Washed with Wine* and *On the Tongue*; a collection of memoir and poetry, *Loving Mountains, Loving Men*; and a volume of short fiction, *A History of Barbed Wire*, winner of a Lambda Literary Award. He teaches at Virginia Tech in Blacksburg, Virginia.

Richard J. Polney ("Shank's Lesson") is by all accounts a fine man. He is a graduate of the Clarion Science Fiction Writer's Workshop and has appeared in other STARbooks Press publications. He wants to have sex with all of you.

Milton Stern ("After-Workout") With over twenty years experience in the publishing industry, Milton Stern has written several short stories for the Eric Summers anthologies, including, *Unmasked - Erotic Tales of Gay Superheroes, Don't Ask, Don't Tie Me Up*, and *Ride Me Cowboy*, and several books, including *Harriet Lane, America's First Lady* (2005) and *On Tuesdays, They Played Mah Jongg* (2006). His latest novel, *Michael's Secrets*, will be released by STARbooks Press in 2009. Residing in Washington, D.C., he is also an active volunteer in his community and the newsletter editor for the Straight Eights, the gay antique car club. You can visit him at www.miltonstern.com.

Logan Zachary ("Frat-Napped", "The Colony") writes "I have a short story in the Mayhem in the Midlands anthology and in the *Who Died in Here?* anthology. I have ghost written a mystery novel for a best selling cozy mystery writer. I have three gay erotica short stories coming out under the name of Logan Zachary, one for Greg Herren in his *Rough Trade: Sex for Hire* book, Neil Plakcy's *Hard Hat* anthology, and "Studs in the Woods"? has just been accepted by Eric Summers for the *Ride Me Cowboy* anthology. I'm an occupational therapist living and working in Minneapolis. I'm currently trying to find an agent for my two mystery series."

THE EDITOR

Christopher Pierce is the author of the novel *ROGUE: SLAVE* and the editor of *MEN ON THE EDGE*, both published by STARbooks Press. His erotic fiction has been published in more than twenty anthologies, including *Ultimate Gay Erotica* 2005, 2006, 2007 and 2008. He co-edited the *Fetish Chest Trilogy* of anthologies with Rachel Kramer Bussel for Alyson Books.

A sequel to *ROGUE: SLAVE* is forthcoming. He lives in South Florida with his partner of fourteen years.

Visit Chris online at www.christopherpierceerotica.com/.

aring any underwear. "Excuse me," I said, having a hard time look

inded by that bulge in his crotch, "but don't I know you?" "Maybe

ind of toabout a

with RayGod, y

t loser?in?" h

id. "Liks stron

ce bodye on G

lly, he I eve

up to tany ide

stakingie sam

, I coulery lot

ood raciie swe

ing withe in st

we go behin

ill see in pu

ed?" he vent to

rivacy.grabb

hard. I

k, tracit, so f

ed it, ha

with mybing o

bbing, In cock

he sound of unzipping filled the small space. I don't know who's h

, but before I knew it, I had his rod in my hand, and mine was in hi

it to do?" he asked, his tone challenging. I knew exactly, and sank

www.ingramcontent.com/pod-product-compliance
Lightning Source LLC
Chambersburg PA
CBHW020835260626
47169CB00003B/994